EVERHARD
VOLUME 2

THE EVERHARD SERIES

EVER HARD

VOLUME 2

BY

GORDON YOUNG

INTRODUCTION BY
THOMAS KRABACHER

STEEGER BOOKS • 2025

Table of Contents

Gordon Ray Young: Forgotten Adventurer

O **VER THE COURSE** of his life, Gordon Ray Young (1886-1948) was a cowboy, marine, sailor, marksman, reporter, occasional poet, sport fisherman, bibliophile, and literary critic. More importantly he was a storyteller, the author of some of the finest adventure fiction to grace the pages of the American pulp magazines during the first half of the twentieth century. Appearing regularly in titles such as *Adventure, Blue Book, Argosy, Romance,* and *Short Stories,* his fiction spanned genres as diverse as westerns, crime stories, South Seas adventure, international intrigue, historical fiction, and he often brought to them characters and motivations of considerable psychological complexity. His stories also made the jump to the silver screen as Hollywood adapted three of his stories for the motion pictures during his lifetime and two more after his death.

Despite this, Gordon Ray Young remains virtually unknown today. Even within the pulp-collecting community, he is likely only to be familiar to those collectors who specialize in magazines like *Adventure* or *Short Stories,* to which Young was a frequent contributor. My article attempts to redress this lamentable situation by providing an overview of Young's life and writing career.

DETAILS ABOUT YOUNG'S family background and early life are sketchy. He offered few details about himself to his pulp-magazine readers and never published a personal account or memoir. The obituaries that appeared at the time of his death provided only the most basic details. As a result, what information there is—mostly derived from public records and historical society archives—is woefully incomplete. Nonetheless, here is what is known.

Gordon Ray Young, like his contemporary Hamlin Garland, was a "Son of the Middle Border." He was born in rural Ray County, in the heart of Missouri, on September 27, 1886, to Arias Howard and Hettie (neé Kincaid) Young. Both the Kincaids and the Youngs were prominent families in Ray County, their presence there dating back as early as 1814. Arias Howard—or just Howard—Young was born in North Carolina in 1854. Howard then proceeded to live an unsettled lifestyle with different professions, multiple marriages, and constant movement from state to state, not arriving in Missouri sometime after 1880. There, he married Hettie Kincaid, Gordon's mother, in the same year Gordon was born.

Details of Gordon's childhood are few. It is not known how long the Young family remained in Missouri, for the 1890 census records are unavailable (most were destroyed by fire in 1921) and the state did not require systematic record-keeping at that time. The fact that the Youngs do not appear in any of the Ray County historical accounts suggests, however, they did not remain there long. Nonetheless, in later years Gordon would recall numerous incidents from his Missouri childhood, including one in which, unsupervised, he decided to take an unbroken horse of his uncle's for a ride at the age of six.

Gordon Young

Howard Young continued to move regularly and he took his family with him. The 1900 census shows them living in Warsaw, Indiana and lists Howard as a physician. In 1910 he is shown to be living in Pueblo, Colorado, and in 1920 he's in Idaho. The individual census records for 1930 have not yet been released so information for that year is unavailable, but a history of the Young family by Richardson Young indicates Howard died in Los Angeles in 1941 while in his mid-eighties.

As for Gordon, he seems to have remained close to his father throughout his life and to have inherited Howard's taste for wandering. In 1901, at the age of 15, Gordon was working as a cowboy on Fred Harvey's (of Harvey House fame) XY Ranch in eastern Colorado. How long he remained there is unknown, but the time spent working on the ranch gave him a familiarity and affinity with rural working life in the American West—something that would serve him in good stead as a writer later on.

The next seven years, between 1901 and 1908, are a blank insofar as what we know about Gordon's life, but in late 1908 the U.S. Marine Corps would send Gordon even farther afield.

ON DECEMBER 10, 1908, at the age of 22, Gordon Young enlisted in the United States Marine Corps at the Illinois Recruiting Station in Chicago. The Marine Corps Muster Rolls provide the earliest detailed record of events in Gordon Young's life, showing as they do his month-to-month duty assignments during his enlistment.

No information is available as to why Gordon decided to join the Corps, although if his family was still living in northern Indiana at this time, the Chicago enlistment makes sense. The next four months were spent in basic training at the Washington, D.C. Marine Barracks and by April he was on his way to the western Pacific and the Philippines.

The United States gained possession of the Philippines in 1899 as a result of the Spanish-American War. Almost immediately after war's conclusion the Philippine insurrection under Emilio Aquinaldo began and it was not put down until 1902 or 1903, and only then after brutal fighting on both sides. For yet another decade, American forces would have to contend with the Moro Rebellion, an anti-colonial insurgency originally instigated against the Spanish that would persist until 1913. This is the world Gordon Young encountered when he arrived in Manila in July 1909.

Assigned to Company E of the Second Marine Regiment, Private Young was stationed at various times at the Marine barracks at either Cavite or Olongapo. Cavite was the site of a former Spanish fort and had become a major American naval shipyard; Olongapo, further to the north, supported the naval facilities at Subic Bay and, prior to World War II, the installations on Corregidor.

According to Marine Corps histories of the period, it is unlikely that Gordon saw much, if any, fighting in the Moro Rebellion, since counter-insurgency operations at the time were primarily the responsibility of the U.S. Army. His time in the Philippines, nonetheless, would have given Gordon the opportunity to observe first-hand the interplay between white and native societies in the Pacific realm. While the American colonial policy in the Philippines was generally a benign one (particularly when compared to those of other colonial powers at the time), for the most part it was still a classical colonial society with sharp social and class distinctions between the colonizers and the colonized. Moreover, in contrast to other, more experienced colonial powers whose attitudes were more flexible and nuanced in this regard, the Americans brought to the administration of the Philippines their own distinctive attitudes toward the intersection of race and sex. Like his earlier ranching experience, his tenure in the Philippines, too, would provide Gordon material when he began to write.

Young spent just seven months in the Philippines before being transferred stateside to Mare Island Navy Yard just north of San Francisco. A few months later, in July 1910, he was assigned sea duty aboard the armored cruiser USS *West Virginia*. This proved to be his longest continuous duty assignment in the Corps, lasting 13 months. According to the ship's history, her operational area was the Pacific and the waters around the Hawaiian Islands during this time. In July 1911, Young was assigned to the Puget Sound Navy Ship Yard at Bremerton, Washington. He was discharged from the Corps "by purchase" one month later in August

1911; the purchase price was $80. At the time of discharge his character was listed as "excellent" and his physical condition "good."

In subsequent years, with only two exceptions to my knowledge, Young would make no written mention of his military experience or his time in the Philippines. The first exception is an early short story, "U.S.A." (*Adventure*, May 18, 1918), a Talbot Mundy-like story of military comradeship set in Manila during the Spanish-American War; the second occurs years later in a letter to the son of a friend in which he offers the young man advice on the advent of his enlistment at the beginning of WWII. Beyond these, he appears to have been silent on the subject.

However, Young's military experience had an impact on his life in two respects. First, it gave him first-hand experience with the Pacific realm and shipboard life, which would serve him well in his future writing. (Thus, when some years later a correspondent, commenting on the verisimilitude of one of his South Seas stories, wrote to ask "have you ever been out there?" he could respond with a "Yes.") Second, by mustering out in Washington, Gordon Young now found himself on the west coast.

Following his discharge from the Marine Corps, Young turned to journalism.

His draft-registration form of June 5, 1917 lists him as a member of the editorial board of the *Los Angeles Times*, specifically as its literary editor, a post he would hold for more than a decade. He had come to the *Times* in late 1913 following two years working as the telegraph editor for the *Stockton Evening Mail*. At the *Times*, Young quickly developed a reputation as a critic, for by 1918 his name found its way into advertising copy. An advertisement for a non-fiction business book from that year, *The Way of Success* by William H. Hamby, includes a blurb citing "Gordon Ray Young, the caustic critic of the *Los Angeles Times*..."

All of this seems pretty straightforward, although questions remain about the years immediately following Young's military discharge. One involves his career. Both his obituary and *Who's Who* entry suggests he went into newspaper work, first in Chicago and then San Francisco, before coming to Los Angeles. The question is, if so, when?

A possible answer is that he had some connection with a Chicago paper while in his late teens or early twenties prior to his enlistment in the Marines, and that he worked in San Francisco sometime between being discharged in 1911 and coming to Los Angeles in 1913. There is some circumstantial evidence to support this: Gordon's family was living in northern Indiana, not far from Chicago, in the years before his enlistment, and he did eventually enlist at the Chicago recruiting station. He would have been familiar with San Francisco from his time at Mare Island in 1910 and could well have drifted back to the city after his discharge, before taking his position on the Stockton paper. All of this, however, is speculation.

What is known is that on August 26, 1911, the same month as his marine discharge, Gordon married Regina Rosenbaum in San Francisco. He was 25 years old and Regina, the daughter of immigrant parents from Austro-Hungary, was 22. Their daughter, Lyna Valerie Young, was born in early 1916.

The same registration form shows that in 1917, the Young family was living in a house on Vestal Avenue, where they had moved the year before. The site is located atop one of the Echo Park hills, north and east of downtown Los Angeles, and provides a spectacular view of the Los Angeles basin to the south and the Silverlake district to the north and east. The house itself was modest, but Young later added a separate outbuilding on the grounds; it served as a library and writing space. This property is where he would live the rest of his life. Both the house and library building remain standing to this day.

Los Angeles in the early decades of the 20th century was experiencing a cultural awakening, and a nascent literary community was starting to take shape. Membership was fluid, constantly changing, and frequently avant-garde. Much of it was centered in the city's Echo Park district, the same area where the Youngs now lived. Gordon and Regina soon became active members. Fellow members included long-time Los Angeles bookseller Jake Zeitlin; modernist painter Edward Middleton Manigault (who died while starving himself in an attempt to discover new, unearthly colors); Karl Haverlin, an early Los Angeles radio pioneer, Civil War historian, and associate of Carl Sandberg; and Paul Jordan-Smith. An author, art and literary critic, and ardent bibliophile, Smith occupied the post of *Los Angeles Times* literary editor from 1932 until 1957. If he is remembered at all today, it is for his scholarly work on Robert Burton's *The Anatomy of Melancholy* and for perpetrating one of the great art hoaxes of the 20th century. Most importantly for us, he became Gordon Young's closest and most intimate friend.

Witty, charming, and personable, Jordan-Smith came to Los Angeles in November 1916 after failing to be reappointed to a teaching position at Berkeley. Soon after, he and Gordon met and quickly became close friends, remaining so for the next 30 years. They were of the same age, shared the same rural backgrounds (in Jordan-Smith's case, West Virginia), and shared similar interests in writing, chess, hunting and fishing, books and book collecting. More importantly, they had the same temperament: surviving letters show both men to be intelligent, literate, skeptical, and highly irreverent. Correspondence between them is cheerfully sprinkled with jokes and vulgarisms. It is this voluminous correspondence, now preserved in the Paul Jordan-Smith papers at UCLA, that provides the most detailed look at the events of Gordon Young's life from 1930 on.

GORDON YOUNG HAD been interested in writing since childhood, but it wasn't until 1917 that his writing career began in earnest. In 1913 he published a 2400-word short story entitled "The Lady's Picture" in the March 22 issue of *The Cavalier*. The story is a sentimental tale of the old West in which a notorious highwayman, Hugh Richmond, helps a young easterner get the money necessary to marry the girl he loves. The story-ending, O. Henry-like punch line reveals that Richmond has helped the boy because the girl in question is the highwayman's own sister.

After that single story, however, Young published nothing of note—only a few small pieces, including poetry, in various newspapers—for four years. The demands of career and family, and the need to relocate as a result of his newspaper work, seem to have occupied his full attention. It was only in 1917, with the stability provided by a family, home, and secure job, that Young was able to turn his attention to writing in a serious way. This was marked by the appearance that year of his first three Everhard stories in the pages of *Adventure,* the magazine with which he would develop a close, long-standing relationship. (More about these stories below.)

At the same time, however, Young takes the opportunity to experiment in other ways, with different characters in a wide range of genres and story settings. These experiments include crime stories, spy stories, Westerns, sea stories, and military adventures set in locales as different as the Old West, the urban underworld, the California gold rush, the wartime Philippines, and the South Seas. Reading them, one begins to identify key themes that will surface in Young's fiction again and again in future years. Among them: a mistrust of women, the search for revenge, the need to protect young lovers, and the protagonist who is under suspicion as an outcast or an outsider.

During this time—on October 11, 1919 to be exact—the first issue of Ridgway's short-lived *Romance* hit the newsstands. Intended as a companion magazine to *Adventure,* it had an editorial slant that would appeal to women readers as well as men. Arthur Sullivant Hoffman added the editorial responsibilities for the new magazine to those he already shouldered for *Adventure.* To help fill the early issues, he drew upon stories by several writers from what he termed his *Adventure* "Writers' Brigade." Gordon Young was one of these. Although only 12 issues of *Romance* appeared in 1919–1920 before the magazine folded, Young managed to place yarns in three of them.

All but one were minor stories. "Blood of Covenanters" merits brief mention. A muddled story featuring the sickly nephew of an island missionary, the mixed-race daughter of a local trader, and a bunch of angry natives, it introduces the character of Dan McGuire, a lazy-eyed beachcomber and wastrel, who will appear in several later stories by Young. Perhaps of greater interest, "Blood of Covenanters" is also the earliest of his stories to be adapted to the movies, serving as the basis for D.W. Griffith's *The Idol Dancer* (1920). The movie starred Richard Barthelmess and Clarine Seymour, and was shot in Florida where the beaches and swamps around Fort Lauderdale stood in for South Seas. Film historians generally consider it among the weakest of Griffith's films.

IF THESE EARLY stories can be viewed as an apprentice period, a time of experimentation for Young, his coming of age as a writer occurs with three novel-length tales that appeared in *Adventure* in fairly quick succession. "Savages" (July 18–September 3, 1919), "Wild Blood" (March 18–May 3, 1920), and "Storm Rovers" (December 18, 1920) are the first three stories in the Hurricane Williams saga and reflect the work of a writer who has fully mastered his craft. Williams is one of Young's most vivid creations. Briefly introduced in the short story "The Unlisted Legion" (May 3, 1918), Williams is an outlaw, a renegade—some say pirate—captain of a pearling schooner in the South Pacific of the 1880s. He has turned his back on civilization and distrusts all white men for reasons that are revealed as the series progresses, choosing to live among the natives of the remote Solomon and Santa Cruz Islands. Two of these novels, "Savages" and "Storm Rovers," not only represent some of Young's finest work but also rank among the finest sea stories ever to come out of the pulps.

"Savages" tells the story of Gilbert Lang, a young American from a prosperous background, who comes to the Solomons seeking vengeance on the man and woman who destroyed his family. In pursuit of his quest he takes up with Williams. Before a sort of rough justice is achieved, much of Williams' own past is revealed. Action abounds, but ultimately it is the relationship between Lang and Williams that is the story's heart; by the end, Gilbert Lang has come of age in ways he could never have imagined. Young's storytelling mixes a strong sense of locale with an easy familiarity with shipboard routine and island life. He is careful to avoid or subvert the cliches (such as the romance that inevitably springs up between a white man and an island maiden) common to most South Seas fiction of the time.

"Storm Rovers," a violent tale of mutiny at sea, boasts lean and unsentimental prose. Once again, Young avoids the standard clichés. This is no romantic swashbuckling affair *à la* Rafael Sabatini; this mutiny is a savage and brutal one where innocents are not necessarily spared. Most impressively, although Williams is absent for fully 80 percent of the book, his presence seems to overshadow events throughout. When he finally steps on stage the effect is almost electrifying. In terms of authenticity, depth of characterization, and style, this novel compares favorably to some of the best writing of Jack London.

Throughout the 1920s Young appeared in *Adventure* on a regular basis. Although his production levels never again reached that of 1919, he nonetheless placed several stories with the magazine each year. In addition to sundry short fiction, these included at least one, and sometimes two, serials every year for most of the decade; many of them would later see publication in book form. These included "Sorcery and Everhard" (June 18–August 3, 1921), "Men of the Night" (crime, January 10–February 10, 1922), "Hurricane Williams' Vengeance" (fourth in the series, May 30–June 30, 1923), "Days of '49" (historical, August 10–September 30, 1925), "La Rue of the 88" (Western, December 30, 1925–February 10, 1926, and "Treasure" (South Seas adventure, October 23–December 31, 1926), among others.

Two longer stories, both from 1924 and set in the South Seas, "Pearl-Hunger" and "Seibert of the Island," merit particular mention because they are reflective of the sophistication Young was then bringing to his writing. "Pearl-Hunger," serialized in *Adventure* in five installments during the summer of 1924, is of interest because, while the story takes place in an exotic locale, it contains little of the action typically associated with adventure fiction. Will Heddon and two fellow sailors attempt to carry out the last wishes of Captain Bennings, late of the schooner *Gloria*. Bennings wants to see his daughter, Gloria, now practically a young woman, placed in safekeeping away from the unsettled life of a pearling schooner. Gloria, who only knows the sea, does not want to leave. When Will is unable to come up with a satisfactory plan to fulfill his charge, Gloria remains aboard the ship as a constant reminder and annoyance. Things become further complicated when Gloria's estranged sister ends up aboard the ship; there's also the rumor that hidden aboard is Gloria's inheritance, a fortune in raw pearls. "Pearl-Hunger" is rich in incident but lacks a strong, overarching storyline. The plot is mainly personality-driven, as Will deals with his pathological dislike of women as a result of a traumatic experience in the past. At the yarn's conclusion, what once seemed the possibility of a happy ending is dashed as events conspire to leave Will, even more emotionally damaged then before, drifting in a world that appears to have no meaning. (The "damaged man," an individual psychologically scarred by a traumatic past experience with a woman, can be found in many of Young's stories.)

Despite its lack of high adventure, "Pearl-Hunger" reads easily and holds the reader's attention. Again, Young's easy familiarity with ship-handling, and the air of authenticity he gives to his island settings, are in large part responsible for this. The story itself is a reflection of Young's efforts, particularly in the 1920s, to move beyond the usual strictures of conventional adventure fiction. Its appearance in *Adventure* also reflects editor Arthur Sullivant Hoffman's continued willingness to accept and advocate for more sophisticated fiction in the magazine.

(A side note: The story sparked no little controversy among *Adventure* readers over its use of the word "whore." Ordinarily it was *Adventure's* policy to replace swear words and certain pejoratives with a dash (——) and readers seemed to prefer it that way. Young's use of the word "whore," however, generated two and a half pages of comment in the January 10, 1925 Camp-Fire. Hoffman supported Young in his use of the term.)

"Seibert of the Island," also published in 1924, was one

of the few Young novels to see issuance in hard covers without prior magazine serialization. It, too, is set in the South Seas. Hurricane Williams appears in a supporting role, although he is not central to the narrative. Like "Pearl-Hunger," it is a story driven more by the personalities of the characters than external events. Briefly, the novel tells a Joseph Conrad/Somerset Maugham type story about the romantic rivalry between two sisters—the daughters of an island trader—for the affections of a recently arrived young American. Further complicating matters is the fact that one of the sisters is married to a strong-willed and somewhat crude German planter, the Seibert of the title, who is also one of the most powerful men on this island.

Young spent nine months working on this elaborate yarn in the hope that he could produce something more along the lines of a true novel rather than another magazine serial, and the results show. The writing is polished and the plotting, pacing, and characterization is a cut above Young's ordinary work. When it was completed, however, Young initially was unable to find a publisher, reportedly because of the story's bittersweet ending; the magazines weren't interested (Hoffman, the story goes, rejected "Seibert" because it was too focused on the female characters), and Young's usual publishing house, Bobbs-Merrill, wasn't interested. Only after British publishing house Allen & Unwin bought it in 1924 did Doran agree to bring out an American edition the following year. The experience made Young question whether trying to write for a more literary market was worth the time and effort it entailed.

Readers of *Adventure's* February 15, 1927 issue encountered something different from Young. "Boyhood" was not a work of fiction but an article about growing up as a young boy in northern Michigan in the late 19th century. As Gordon explained in the issue's Camp-Fire letter column, a visitor to the Young household fell to talking of his childhood experiences and "… he held my nine-year-old daughter, my wife, and myself fascinated for some two hours, and the two of us talked of little else yesterday or today other than Mr. ——'s boyhood." The richly evocative article contained no plot or moral as such, but merely recounted the joys of hunting, fishing, and trapping in a simpler time. As Young noted, it resonated with his own childhood memories. He went on to suggest that a regular series dealing with boyhoods in various parts of the country might make an interesting feature for the magazine.

The decade between 1917 and 1927 was the most productive period of Gordon Young's writing life. He was writing eight hours a day and, in his own mind, producing good stuff. Although he would continue to write and sell in the Thirties and Forties it would never again approach the quantity, and seldom the quality, of what he was producing now. Arthur Sullivant Hoffman appreciated this, for he saw that Young more than most of his writers illustrated his belief that entertaining adventure fiction and literary quality need not be mutually exclusive. He made this explicit in the May 1, 1927 Camp-Fire, including a 500-word commentary praising Gordon for these qualities and citing what he saw as a growing appreciation for Young's writing among critics, some of whom were tentatively comparing him to Conrad and Stevenson.

Based on the scattered evidence available, Young's

personal life during this period appears to have been a stimulating and comfortable one. For most of the decade he continued in his position as chief book reviewer for the *Los Angeles Times*, which kept him in close contact with the local literary community. He was a regular denizen of the numerous bookshops in downtown Los Angeles and was gradually building a collection of rare volumes of which he was quite proud. His holdings included a 1523 copy of *Erasmus* and a second edition copy of *Holinshead's Chronicles* that, he liked to pretend, "might have been the copy Shakespeare used."

Young's friendship with Paul Jordan-Smith remained strong and was important to him. The two men corresponded regularly and fished, played chess, talked, and exchanged books whenever possible. Since both came from rural backgrounds, their letters were frequently full of jocular exchanges in fake hillbilly slang. While Jordan-Smith was working on his bibliography of Burton's *Anatomy of Melancholy*, Gordon on several occasions proved able to supply information on obscure classical allusions Paul had been unable to track down.

Following publication of the final installment of "Wastrel," which appeared in the June 15, 1927 issue of *Adventure*, Young took a lengthy sabbatical. He wouldn't grace the magazine's pages for almost two years, until the summer of 1929. A year or two previously (the date is uncertain) he had resigned his *Times* position to write fiction full-time. Now, however, he took a respite, bringing his family to Europe, where they stayed for close to a year, touring France, Italy, England, Austria, and Hungary. They wintered in the most romantic of all places—Paris, the "city of lights." But Gordon didn't like the place; he found the city cold and damp.

PRESUMABLY REFRESHED, YOUNG returned to the pages of *Adventure* in the December 15, 1928 issue with a story entitled simply "Don Everhard." His next two stories, both of which also feature Everhard, were published after lengthy intervals: "The Doublecross" (August 15–September 15, 1929) and "Everhard Breaks Through" (June 1, 1930). The following year saw publication of the four-part serial and Hurricane Williams swan song, "If There Be Courage" (June 1–July 15). It wasn't until 1932 that Young appeared in the pages of *Adventure* on a regular basis.

As the 1930s progressed, the nature of Young's stories changed, largely in response to the demands of the changing pulp-magazine market. The changes are seen in various ways. For one thing, his stories of the 1930s tend to be less psychologically driven and more action-oriented than those of the 1920s. For another, plots are frequently simpler and more straightforward. Increasingly, characters are delineated just enough to carry the action forward. In this period Young places greater emphasis on series characters in his stories. Don Everhard continues to turn up regularly, and this decade sees the introduction of two additional series characters, Red Clark and Cap'n Bill Jones.

Red Clark first appeared as a secondary character in 1925's "La Rue of the 88." In 1931 he dropped his thick cowboy accent and struck out on his own in the serial "Fighting Blood" (*Short Stories*, November 10–December 25, 1931). Red is:

> ... the son of a famous sheriff [who] had almost from birth
> learned a lot of things about gunmen, gamblers, and rustlers;
> and he was recklessly unafraid of any and all dishonest men,
> just as his father the sheriff had been."

Young additionally describes him as:

> "... red-headed, gangling, and full of fun; and also one
> never to back away from a fight."

The Red Clark stories are pure adolescent fantasy, set in a mythic West that never existed. Gunfights are hourly occurrences; bullets fly and bodies drop with reckless abandon. There are few real-world consequences in a Red Clark story, yet moments of realism unexpectedly emerge. In "Fighting Blood," fully 20 pages of the novel's total of 180 (based on the book edition) are devoted to the breaking in of an untamed horse. It proves to be the most exciting and memorable sequence in the book and reveals Young's own familiarity with horses and ranch life, acquired decades earlier as a youth on the plains of eastern Colorado. In all, Red Clark will go on to become Young's most popular series character, starring in 14 novels in the years to come.

Cap'n Bill Jones, Young's second series character of the 1930s, makes his debut in a four-part serial, "Scalawag" (*Adventure,* December 1, 1932–January 15, 1933). He, too, will go on to appear in a half-dozen or so additional stories throughout the rest of the decade. Bill, captain of the schooner *Marigold,* is by profession "a trader, blackbirder, pearler, or whatever else was to seaward..." in the South Pacific of the 19th century.

"… [He] was brawny, deep-chested with a massive muscular body, tousled red hair and honey face; had clear blue eyes that, if unangered, were usually a-twinkle with good nature. But many minor magistrates throughout the island found him troublesome."

Twinkling blue eyes. A stark contrast to the "damaged men" like Will Haddon or Hurricane Williams that sailed the Pacific of Gordon Young's stories from a decade earlier.

The Cap'n Bill Jones stories, like those of Red Clark, are light-hearted fun and nothing more; the author seems to be saying one would be a fool to take them seriously. It's all a game where the stakes are never high and violence, when it occurs, is never shocking; in both series the commonly recommended way for dealing with some scoundrel is to give him "a poke in the nose." Young makes no pretense to writing serious fiction here; he has turned to genre writing and is resigned to playing by its rules.

The 1930s saw publication of two substantial historical novels by Young. "When the Bravest Trembled," a six-parter serialized in *Adventure* from December 1933 to May 1934, takes place during the early days of the Civil War. Its protagonist is Rand Banister, a Texan who has come north to fight against the Confederacy because of a promise made to his mother, a Northern woman who disliked the slave-holding South. His defection causes him to be viewed with suspicion by Northerners and with contempt by other members of his family. Intrigue swirls about the Texan since Rand's background makes him a potential pawn for both sides. Added to the mix is the mysterious Laura Lorraine, who claims to have fled the

South because of her racially mixed blood but may actually be a spy. The story reaches its climax at the battle of Bull Run.

"Huroc the Avenger" (*Adventure,* October 15, 1935– March 1936), on the other hand, is set during the late Middle Ages and recounts the struggles of Harrack (Huroc), an Englishman who, having escaped from the galleys of North Africa's Tripolitan Corsairs, seeks revenge against the ruthless Venetian trading family, the Piombos, who sold his sister into slavery years before. Both stories are fast-paced and rich with historical detail, not to mention heavy on action, intrigue, and romance.

Until the mid-Thirties Young published almost exclusively in *Adventure,* only rarely selling to other magazines. Starting in 1935, he began submitting stories to other markets, in particular *Argosy* and *Short Stories.* As time went on, both his Red Clark and Bill Jones yarns appeared in various titles. Young finally abandoned *Adventure* completely in 1938, following its publication of his Red Clark serial, "The Redhead from Tulluco" (December 1937–April 1938). After that his fiction, with a few key exceptions, appeared in the pages of *Short Stories.*

IN TERMS OF his personal life, the early Depression years were good ones for Young. He was writing and selling stories with regularity, if not as prolifically as before, and he was getting favorable reviews. Paul Jordan-Smith, having followed in Young's footsteps as literary editor of the *Times,* ensured that his friend's books received good notices on a regular basis. Although Gordon occasionally complained about the creative limitations of writing magazine fiction and worried that his writer's well might be running dry, the stories nonetheless continued to come.

Financially, the Youngs got a boost from the sale of "Cap'n Calamity" (*Adventure,* September 1, 1934), a Captain Bill Jones story, to the movies. It was the second of Gordon's stories to make the transition to the silver screen. The 1936 film adaptation starred erstwhile opera singer George Houston as Jones and, though quickly and cheaply made using an early two-tone color process, stayed reasonably close to Young's original story, even using some of its dialogue in the script.

Socially, Gordon and Regina were regular participants in the cultural and literary life of Los Angeles. They could be found frequently entertaining at home, or attending lectures, gallery openings, and other public events. In a 1977 oral history, long-time Los Angeles book dealer Jacob Zeitlin recalled evenings when the Zeitlins, Youngs, and Jordan-Smiths got together for spaghetti, wine, good talk, and—if the evening was lively enough—extemporaneous dancing. Young himself continued to derive satisfaction from numerous hobbies, including chess, book collecting, the imbibing (during Prohibition) of alcohol, and target shooting at both the Burbank and Glendale Rifle and Revolver Clubs. He took great pride when, in 1934, his teen-aged daughter Lyna beat him in target shooting— and even greater pride when she went off to Occidental College the following year.

Tragically, his wife Regina died in the fall of 1936. The exact cause and date of her death are unknown, although it was probably in October of that year. The emotional impact on Gordon was devastating. In the Young/Jordan-

Smith correspondence held in the UCLA library, there's a brief but solemn letter from Gordon to Paul from November 1936, explaining why he isn't receiving visitors and describing how he is coping with his loss. Accompanying the letter is a lengthy poem Young wrote, pouring out his grief. Even when read today, this verse impresses one as emotionally searing. On the back of the poem's third page is the following note handwritten in pencil:

> Dear Paul—
> Please never speak to me of this, for if you do you will have to say it is very fine, or some kind of thing and I do not want any compliments on how I have expressed my grief. It is my confession, and as such I want you to know.
> Gordon.

He mourned Regina for over a year but eventually got on with his life. In 1938 he traveled to New York and stayed several weeks, partly to conduct business and partly to visit friends. The following year, this time in the company of friend Carl Haverlin, he traveled first to Texas and then again to New York before driving south to visit Civil War historical sites.

In 1939 Young married a woman named Pearl, about whom little is known, although his correspondence indicates that his relationship with her was a close one. Within the next few years his daughter Lyna married and provided him with two grandchildren, Nancy Carol and Roger.

These were positive events in Gordon Young's life. At the same time, however, a shadow appeared in the form of a lawsuit, brought against him over the collapse of a retaining wall on his property during the Los Angeles floods of March 1938. The collapse indirectly but tragically resulted in the destruction of an adjacent house and loss of life. Judgments in the amount of $43,371 were eventually levied against him, but Young countersued, contesting the judgments on the grounds that inappropriate actions by a process-server deprived him of timely notice of a key court summons and robbed him of the opportunity to respond promptly. Court proceedings continued well into 1942 and proved a repeated source of distraction for Young.

By 1939 the situation in Europe—particularly the treatment of Jews expelled from Germany—was rapidly becoming intolerable to many Americans, among them Gordon Young. The indifference of such isolationist politicians as Senators Wheeler and Nye and the open anti-Semitism of such high-profile Americans as Charles Lindbergh appear to have angered him deeply. In response, he began work on what he referred to as his "dictator story." He wrote to Paul Jordan-Smith in June of that year, "I don't want to write propaganda, for anything detectable as propaganda defeats its own purpose; but in so far as I can, I want to stab the loathsome sons of bitches that are trying, and are succeeding, in infecting America with a 'Jewish problem.'" The story never appeared, but the anger persisted.

BY THE LATE 1930s Young was increasingly dissatisfied with writing only for the pulps. He recognized they were his bread and butter, but at the same time he worried about the future of the pulps and longed to break into the higher-paying slicks—in his own words, "to scramble up the slick incline of smooth papers where the big money grows on tall trees." He got his chance in the early 1940s.

Mr. Beamish, published by Coward-McCann in 1940, is, without a doubt, the most atypical Gordon Young novel ever to see print. Appearing under the pseudonym, Hugh Richmond (which was the name of the protagonist in Young's very first published story, "The Lady's Picture"), it tells the light-hearted story of a mild-mannered, middle-aged copy editor and bibliophile. The story follows Beamish as he moves through a world of books, pets, friends and acquaintances, unassumingly dispensing wisdom and guidance along the way. The novel is gentle, whimsical, and told with a complete lack of irony. In the end, it is a story about books, love, and, ultimately, happiness. This novel is a delight.

The following year, Young's "The Iron Rainbow" was serialized in *Blue Book* in fall of 1941. It made the transition to hard covers the following year. In the 1940s *Blue Book's* large "bedsheet" format, distinctive cover art by Herbert Morton Stoops, and frequent use of two-tone interior illustrations set it apart from the typical rough-paper magazines. While the magazine's motto was "Stories of adventure for MEN, by MEN," its fiction frequently featured strong female characters (often played up in the illustrations) in an effort to appeal to a broader market.

"The Iron Rainbow" centers on the construction of the Kansas railroad in the years immediately following the Civil War. Ruthless competition between rival companies competing for the railroad charter makes for violence and intrigue, all of which is further stoked by resentments lingering from the War. The iron rainbow of the title refers to the path westward represented by railroads in the nation's expansion. Young explained that the story was based in part on the tales he heard from old-timers when he worked as a ranch hand along the Colorado-Kansas border 40 years earlier.

Young finally made it into the high-paying, slick paper magazines in 1942 when *The Saturday Evening Post* serialized his Western novel "Tall in the Saddle" (March 7–April 25). The story follows Ken Rocklin, a cowboy who arrives in the town of Santa Inez to take a job as ranch foreman only to find his employer murdered. As Rocklin attempts to find out what happened he becomes involved in land fraud, range violence, and the rivalry between two ranching families. Like most of Young's protagonists he has been burned by his experience with women in the past, but that doesn't prevent him from getting involved with two of them, first as a protector and, then, romantically.

This novel easily ranks among Young's best. The prose is lean and terse, well suited to the setting and characters. The plot, while complicated, unfolds smoothly and never leaves the reader confused. And the characters—especially Rocklin and rancher's daughter Arly Harolday—are among Young's most memorable.

Although Young was unhappy with the way "Saddle" was treated by the magazine's editors, it went on to become his most popular and best-known story. This was due in part to its high-profile appearance in the *Post* and subsequent publication in hard covers by Doubleday, and even more so to the success of its film version, released by RKO in 1944. Starring John Wayne and directed by Edwin L. Marin, the movie rates among the best of Wayne's

Forties pictures. It sticks closely to Young, taking much of its dialogue from the novel. (Rocklin: "I never feel sorry for anything that happens to a woman."). Wayne and Ella Raines sparkle as they mix it up on screen as Rocklin and Arly Harolday. It's well worth watching, even today.

DURING THE WORLD War II years Young focused primarily on writing Westerns. The majority of these were novels in his popular Red Clark series, for which there seemed to be a ready market. Among them were *Trouble Rides Double* (1943), *Red Clark's Short Cut* (1944), *Red Clark in Paradise* (1945), and *Red Clark at the Showdown* (1944). Typically he submitted these novels to *Short Stories*—now his most reliable market—for serialization prior to book publications by Doubleday or one of its related imprints. With the appearance of pocket books, cheap paperback reprints followed as well.

By 1945, however, Young's age had caught up with him. In May of that year he was hospitalized for what doctors described as an "overstrained heart." He was released not long after, but doctors insisted he take it easy. Still, in a letter he boasted of having "finished a Red Clark before the doctors landed on me, therefore, I have written at least one novel this year."

Gordon continued to write, but the work was becoming increasingly difficult. "Knocking out two to three novels a year is the best I can hope for," he stated in one letter, "and just now, this day, the effort to begin another leaves me feeling as empty and inadequate as a staved-in rain barrel."

This dissatisfaction was accompanied by an increasingly dour view of the world taking shape in the post-

World War II years. Much of his cynicism derived from the emergence, once again, of the old pre-war politics; he was particularly critical of British and Dutch attempts to re-impose authority over their colonial possessions for what he saw as purely selfish purposes. In addition, there was the looming menace of the atom bomb and the new atomic age. Like many others at that time, he expected within a generation another conflict that would truly be "the war to end all wars." But as he acknowledged in a July 1946 letter, "growing old overshadows it all."

Still he continued to write. In the spring of 1947 his novel "Quarter Horse" appeared as a two-part serial in *Blue Book,* and in the fall of that year *Short Stories* serialized a slightly revised version of "Crooked Shadows," an early Everhard story that originally appeared in *Adventure* in June, 1922. *Short Stories* purchased another Western for serialization the following year.

The tone of letters Young wrote in late 1947 and the early weeks of 1948 suggests he knew the end was near. He had had yet another heart "incident" in recent months and admitted he was having difficulty reading. He discussed the disposition of his library when he was gone. He reminisced nostalgically about the days of his childhood in Missouri, when he would sneak out to the barn to read those precursors to the pulps, dime novels.

Shortly thereafter, on February 10, 1948, Gordon Ray Young died of heart failure at Monte Santo Hospital in Los Angeles. His final yarn, "Hard-Hunted," was serialized in *Short Stories* that summer, six months after his death, and saw publication in book form the following year under the title *Wanted—Dead or Alive!* Many of his westerns, including *Tall in the Saddle* and *Quarter Horse*, remained in print as paperback reprints well into the mid-Fifties. The latter, under the title *Hell on Hoofs*, appeared as half of one of the early Ace Double westerns (D-10). Most popular, however, were the Red Clark westerns, which remained in print from Popular Library, under various titles, as late as 1955.

Young's stories also served as the basis for two additional movies in the early 1950s. Paramount's *Hurricane Smith* (1952), loosely based on the Hurricane Williams stories, starred John Ireland in the title role with Yvonne De Carlo as the love interest, Luana, and Forrest Tucker as Dan McGuire. However, other than the use of character names (mainly from *Storm Rovers*), the movie had little to do with Young's originals. Despite a screenplay by fellow pulp writer Frank Gruber, the result was just another entry in the long list of run-of-the-mill Technicolor South Seas adventures Hollywood was turning out at the time. *Born to the Saddle* appeared the following year from the short-lived Elliott-Shelton Films, Inc. Directed by William Beaudine (who would later go on to direct for Disney and television), this film was a reasonably faithful adaptation of *Quarter Horse* but, given its low budget and lackluster cast, did not prove memorable.

By the late 1950s Young's stories had proven a thing of the past. To my knowledge, none of his works has seen print since then. And he has been neglected in many of the critical surveys of genre fiction that have appeared in recent decades. While Young receives a very brief reference in James Vinson's encyclopedic *Twentieth-Century Western Writers* (1982), he is overlooked in several others. Nor does he appear in any of Professor A. Grove Day's anthologies or reference works on Pacific Island literature, such as *Best South Seas Stories* (edited with Carl Stroven) or *Pacific Islands Literature: One Hundred Basic Books*, even though both include numerous examples of popular fiction. Even more notable is how little attention is paid to the place of the Don Everhard stories in the development of hard-boiled detective fiction.

It's unclear why this should be the case. It may simply be a matter of the management of Young's literary estate. It may also reflect the fact that Young's best writing generally was not to be found in his short stories, always more easily anthologized, but in his longer fiction. Or maybe the more measured, literate writing style that characterizes many of his best novels has simply gone out of vogue when it comes to adventure fiction.

In many ways, Young embodied what Arthur Sullivant Hoffman, legendary editor of *Adventure,* believed popular fiction could and should be: sophisticated and literately written, as well as entertaining to the average reader. His fiction deserves to be better known and it is satisfying to see that a few small-press publishers are beginning to take an interest in reprinting some of his works. For the moment, however, Gordon Ray Young remains—in the words of the title of one of his early stories—a member of that "unlisted legion" of writers who dutifully provided entertainment for the reading public during the pulp era. He produced some great stories and they're out there, waiting to be rediscovered. The stories contained here are just one example.

Adventure

Gaboreau
A Complete Novel
By Gordon Young

Gaboreau

1

THE ORIEL WAS a small café and nestled unobtrusively in the basement just around the corner from a street that had more or less traffic on it and a reputation that was not of the fairest. But the Oriel seated and served the people who came, and no questions were asked. There was nothing Bohemian nor boisterous about it, nor was there the air of quiet refinement which small and interesting cafés are often said to possess.

Two blocks south the district was notoriously disreputable; two blocks north respectability was unquestioned; so the Oriel took on something of the colors of each, and it was the sort of place where an observant one might expect to see curious people. A sort of a sanctuary, it was, in that No Man's Land between the stamping grounds of the sheep and the goats—to borrow a phrase from the pulpit.

To the north lay those good people who hadn't thrown away their chance of heaven; to the south were the unregenerate, and they mingled at the tables of the Oriel because the service and food was such as brings a man back again and again though he may have had some scruples about sitting across from a fellow with loose lips and shifty eyes. It was the sort of a place where one could entertain himself by guessing from which direction, north or south, the men and women around about him came.

There was a pleasant quality of uncertainty as to who

was who; and I found it none the less interesting because I did not care a whit from which district man or woman came when he or she sat beside me or across from me. And some one was always sitting close, for the Oriel was small and crowded, and no doubt preserved what traces of respectability were upon it by closing before midnight. It furnished food and a pale table wine—not entertainment.

I came so frequently that the waiters spoke to me as to a regular and valued patron, which I was far from being, though none for the life of them could have told my name. And being one who does not easily enter into conversation with strangers, and one who tells nothing when the strangers solicit the conversation, I was no better known in the place than though I had been a mute and visited it but once. The habit of talking is one in which I have discouraged myself with persistency; for I get myself dragged into so many curious, and sometimes sinister, affairs that even discreet and casual remarks have occasionally come back like carelessly thrown boomerangs.

I never came to the Oriel seeking trouble, or the synonym for it which is more euphoniously called "romance." I will go as far as any man should to avoid trouble. And as for romance—that means a woman is implicated—and I will travel fast and far to evade one of them; or at least all of them except one. But there is trouble enough in the world to lay almost any man by the heels even when he moves as cautiously and unobtrusively as I do; and I sometimes wonder what on earth could have happened to me that has failed to happen if I had gone about looking for trouble.

Take the Oriel café, for instance. The man that sat opposite me appeared uneasy and kept pulling out his watch. He ate rapidly, but at last, with his dinner unfinished, he left as though in haste to keep an appointment. I never saw him nor heard of him again. He was a complete stranger. But he was the direct and immediate cause of my getting into one of the worst affairs of my rather unquiet life.

I followed him casually with my eyes and saw him bump into the woman who was coming down the steps and through the door as hurriedly as he was going out.

I noticed at once that she was breathless and excited. There is not much that goes on around me that I do not see. I would have been gathered to the grave of my fathers at a very immature age if I had not been wary and observant from my youth. And I saw that the girl was breathless and excited from more than haste. She was frightened and badly frightened. For a moment she stood indecisively by the door like some hunted, cornered creature that did not know which way to turn.

Then she saw the vacant place opposite me and came rapidly to the table. It was the only unoccupied seat in sight.

"Please, please talk to me!" she said in a low voice as she dropped into the chair and began feverishly to unloosen her coat.

I noticed that she tore a bunch of violets from the coat and threw them under the table, stooping over and making sure that not one was left in sight on the floor.

"Talk to me, please! Please! Say something—anything— but swear I've been with you all the evening!"

She appeared to be unusually young for a woman who was in trouble in the section of the city around the Oriel. She seemed to be nothing more than a girl, scarcely more than a child; but I am never very positive when it comes to telling either the age of a woman or the experiences that have been hers. Perhaps most people would have called her pretty. She was not ugly. I could tell that much all right.

"You must talk to me. You must," she said, leaning forward and fixing her light-blue eyes on me.

I glanced past her to the door and stared in that direction for a moment.

"Oh, talk to me, please!"

"Very well," I said, slowly, taking my eyes from the door and looking into her face. "The tall man with a black Vandyke beard, rather closely trimmed, has just come in."

She made a repressed gesture of alarm, and the blue eyes were lit with a flash of fear.

I had guessed correctly, as any one might have done, when I associated her fright with the man who came in soon after her.

"He is looking around," I went on. "He has seen you. He is watching me. He hesitates—but—no—yes, he is coming this way."

"Oh, don't let him take me! Swear that you know me. If he recognizes me he will take me and—"

I leaned back in my chair and put my hand up to hide a yawn, for the man was not far away, and I could tell that he was scrutinizing my face. He was welcome to scrutinize all that he pleased. I ignored him and the fact that he was approaching. But there was consternation on the face of the girl, so I said loudly enough to be heard by any one who was listening a few feet away:

"There are many more interesting places than this in the city, but if you enjoy it—"

THE MAN WITH the black Vandyke was by the side of our table. There was no ignoring him longer. He had stopped.

I have often remarked the ability of women, even the young ones, to dissimulate. They turn pale at the sight of a caterpillar and climb chairs if a mouse squeaks; sometimes they faint at the sight of a gun, and they are invariably fluttered by signs of danger; but at the crucial instant they draw upon some mysterious reserve force and seem instinctively to take the rôle which is most difficult to simulate—that of calmness, of unconcern. Terror was in her eyes as she seemed to feel the man approach. Then she gripped herself with that reserve force, or ability to dissimulate, or whatever it is that women have so much more of than men; and she smiled and carelessly brushed back a stray from her bright, copper-colored hair.

"Pardon me, monsieur," said the man with the black Vandyke, "but I wish to speak to this woman."

I straightened up in my chair and looked at him inquiringly. Then I asked coldly as one had the right to do of an impudent intruder:

"And why do you wish to speak to Miss Deering?"

That surprised him. He did not blink, but I fancy he came near doing so, for he looked at me a moment in an abstract, blank way that people do when hearing something they haven't expected to hear and do not understand. Then he stared down at her, and I could see plainly enough that he was sure he had made no mistake. But she, as though unaware of his interest, was busily powdering her nose with the aid of a small mirror which she had taken from an initialed hand-bag. She held the mirror low—down by the edge of the table—as though modestly keeping it out of sight. All of which gave her an excellent pretense for bending over and keeping her face somewhat averted.

Then the man again looked at me, and speaking quietly, decisively, he said:

"Pardon me, monsieur. I do not wish to make trouble, but—"

"Trouble?" I asked softly with a rising inflection, at the same time pushing my chair back a little, but not taking my eyes from his face.

"But, monsieur," he protested, raising a hand as though to sooth me, "I must speak."

"I am not interested," I told him.

"But, monsieur—" and he raised his voice slightly, and a note of threat crept in—"this woman—"

"More respect, sir!" I said sharply.

"Ah, I beg pardon," he began humbly, and then his voice went in a distressed crescendo as he explained, "But, monsieur, this *lady* just came in here—"

Again I checked him with an interruption and asked:

"Just came in? How do you know?"

"I followed her. By accident we met. I knew it was—" and he stopped.

"Who?"

"I can not speak of it," he began, and his tone grew rapidly insolent. "This is very important. I do not know you. She must go with me."

"Must?" I asked, and paused to give him a second or two to think it over.

And while he was thinking I stared at him with narrowed eyes and slowly got up from the chair.

"You make a very reckless use of words, my strange man," I added. "And you have exceedingly strange manners as well. You bustle in here off the street, and peremptorily ask for my guest. Look there"—and I pointed down at the table—"she just came in, did she? And had a half-finished dinner awaiting her? Look at that salad—half gone. The fish—eaten. The wine—half drunk. One must wait to be served in this crowded place, yet you say she has just come in.

"I don't know why I take the trouble to point these things out to you when it would be as easy to complain to the proprietor. Perhaps to the police—especially, as you admit having followed some strange woman you meet by accident. Jeannette," I said, being careful to select names that conformed with the initials I had noticed on her hand-bag, "do you know this fellow? Have you ever seen him?"

She raised her head and gave him a cold stare. Her eyes met his and held them. She did not flinch. She might have been inspecting a servant of whom she did not in the least approve. For that matter there was no sign of approval or disapproval. The man seemed of no more interest to her than thin air.

I am very careful not to admire women, particularly strange ones. But I thought she did remarkably well, especially as she said nothing at all, but looked away indifferently, as though it was not worth while to make a denial. Most women would have been less artful and have taken the trouble to say that they never had laid eyes on him before. She conveyed the impression that she even resented the patience I was taking not to be rude to so preposterous a fellow.

"Have you any further remarks to make?" I asked cynically.

And the man with the black Vandyke seemed for a moment almost persuaded that he had made a mistake. He knew that he hadn't; and yet he looked at her coat as though seeking some distinctive mark that would reassure him. I presumed that he missed the bunch of violets. He stared at the dishes before her as though they were animate things that had in some way taken part in a conspiracy against him. He was baffled, but incredulous.

He was no dunce, that man. He had a keen face and a cat-like personality—one of those soft, male feline fellows with claws that disappear under suavity and shoot out again. I could tell that his scratch would be painful; and I could tell also that he was one who made at times a discriminating use of his head. He knew that he could not press me farther without having his fur rumpled; and he showed his wit as well as his wily duplicity in the way he made an about-face and said that evidently there was a mistake; that he was regretful, and that he thanked me for my courtesy, and would the lady accept his deepest apology.

But there was a sardonic quality in his voice and manner—so faint that one could not fasten upon it and show resentment, but strong enough to indicate how little he cared whether or not I believed that he had been duped.

The girl shrugged her shoulders and continued to stare across the room. She did not give him so much as a parting glance, and his eyes watched for it. No doubt he hoped that if he could catch her for a moment off guard he would break down her poise. But she was not to be caught off guard. She avoided his face, and rather overdid the part, in fact.

Then he again apologized to me, but between his words was the sardonic warning that he did not consider the incident closed; and the implication that if I knew who he was I would have some difficulty in feeling comfortable.

I listened and said nothing. I had played my hand and, figuratively speaking, had won the girl—whom I did not in the least want. I felt that when he forced himself into the game again it would be time enough for me to show him that he had probably made a mistake in thinking it was an easy matter to make me uncomfortable. Moreover, I might have told him that he talked too much to be impressive, but there seemed to be no reason why I should give him pointers on how to play his hand more effectively.

He left my table, but at the door I saw him stop and speak to the cashier, then point toward me. The cashier, with patrons in line before her, gave a hasty glance and shook her head. She might have looked carefully and cudgeled her memory for all the information it would have gained him, for she did not know my name. The precautionary non-communicativeness with which I hedge myself about had not been amiss. Perhaps if he had heard my name he would not have been surprised that he had been bluffed out.

But when the man with the black Vandyke started through the door and up the steps he stopped and looked back at me. Across his shoulder I caught and held the stare of his hard black eyes. It was plainly a threat he sent. Like many men who are more intent upon being impressive than upon winning whatever may be at stake, he had not only warned me with his tone, but over his shoulder he cast a menacing threat; whereas it would perhaps have been the better for him and what plans he had if he had disarmed my suspicions.

I would probably have been suspicious of him anyway. But I don't think he knew that, or realized it. Perhaps it is a wise provision of nature that makes the cutthroat sneer and so give warning when he is kicked away and means to sneak back some time and have revenge. He was not a typical cutthroat. He was far too well dressed and had better manners, though he did misuse them. And after he had stared as wickedly as he could and had not succeeded in beating down my eyes, he seemed to sneer in his beard at my presumption in not being intimidated, and went out.

THE GIRL SAT with her hands clenched and her face drawn. She had braced herself capably to meet the crisis, but the crisis was over and she was about ready to go to pieces. She seemed even more frightened than when she came in.

I was not inclined to be sympathetic. Being sympathetic with women is a hazardous procedure; and moreover, I really knew nothing about her. I didn't know whether she came from the north or the south, and was respectable or otherwise. Some men say they can look into a woman's face and always tell; but I have known some of them to make mistakes—sometimes getting a slap in the face and sometimes getting a purse lifted.

"He has gone," I said. "Now I would like to hear something about it. What, may I ask, is the occasion for this—these amateur theatricals?"

She looked at me as though I had hurt her, which is always an easy thing for a woman to do; and indicated by the expression on her lips and in her eyes that she thought it ungallant of me to refer so lightly to her predicament. But at least she did not break down, as she was near to doing. Her pride was touched painfully, so she pulled herself together and said with an attempt at sarcasm:

"I suppose you think this has been just an—an interesting adventure for you!"

"Hardly an adventure—yet."

She looked at me intently for some time, as though trying to read on my face the meaning of my words. No doubt my manner was something new and disappointing to her. She expected, and as a young and pretty girl had the right to expect, something different.

I do not know much about women, though many of them have got me into trouble. That has not been due to any alert gallantry on my part, for I mistrust any woman who is pretty, and no one ever heard of an ugly one making any real trouble for a man unless he was shortsighted enough to marry her. But willy-nilly, I have often been mixed in their affairs—just as in this instance.

And being in, I have always played my hand as well as I could; and about all that experience has taught me is that he is a wiser man than I who can tell the first thing about what any woman will do under any given circumstance. There is only one woman in the world who is intimately known to me; but she does as she pleases and has a way of seeing that I do too. But Vivian is not like any other woman that I have ever met, except in so far as she is a bewildering perplexity.

The girl with the red hair assumed the manner of one who has a surprise to make. She asked in low portentous tones:

"Do you know who that man was?"

I shook my head slightly.

"Antoine Gaboreau!" she said, and watched closely to see what I would do.

I did nothing more than continue to tap the edge of the table noiselessly with my fingers and watch her face.

But I knew Gaboreau by reputation for a daring and mysterious rascal. There were many stories told about him; strange stories which one heard and overheard. For my part, I had given little attention to him. He operated, I knew, though I had never seen the man, a princely gambling establishment, but as the mechanical games were featured, I was never sufficiently interested to make any effort to locate his establishment—which was changed from time to time. I play cards, not roulette.

It was said that the police had long looked askance at Gaboreau for more than gambling; but it is one thing to know that a man is a crook and quite another thing to prove it. I recalled rather indistinctly something about Gaboreau having been arrested at one time, and then the police had been astounded to discover that the Gaboreau they had picked up wasn't in the least the Gaboreau they wanted. He was said to have a brother that resembled him as one twin resembles another. Some people said he had two brothers. I had heard that he had as many as three. Quite a remarkable family, it would seem.

I had also heard him spoken of as "charming," as a very handsome and piquant scoundrel. Women were said to love him at sight; but that means nothing, for the world is overrun with women who will love at sight any man with black beard and eyes. But from what I had heard of him, he was not the manner of fellow who would follow a woman accidentally met on the street. He did not need to. Yet the man with the black Vandyke did resemble the man Gaboreau as I had heard him described.

"Gaboreau?" I questioned indifferently.

"Yes," she whispered tensely.

"And what," I asked, "is the reason for his interest in you?"

"He wants to get hold of me! I have been warned against him!"

She was not unthrilled by the idea, though considerably disturbed. That is, she was not blind to the fact that it put her in a dramatic situation; and, perhaps naturally, she expected me to be impressed.

"So?" I asked, not caring to appear too much as though I believed her.

As a matter of fact I did not know whether or not to believe her. Women like to think that they are in danger of having some man forcibly get hold of them. Perhaps it is a fond racial memory of the stone age, when men are said to have wooed them with a club. I usually believe only those women who tell me something that agrees with what I already know.

"Don't you believe me?" she asked.

"Well, so far I have no particularly good reason for thinking you have staged this little theatrical for my personal benefit."

"You must think I am an adventuress!" she retorted with some heat.

"No, not at all. On the other hand, it is quite obvious that you are not used to adventures. They rather upset you—make you nervous."

It is never well to show tender solicitude for a strange woman, particularly to the young ones, who seem to demand it as a right. Youthful romantic men are very susceptible to beauty in distress, and beauty in distress knows it. I am not romantic. Behind all romance, as behind every comedy on the stage, there is dull prosaic work of shifting scenes, stitching bangles on fluffy skirts, the jealousies and quarrels, and now and then the gleam of a knife. All the romance that I have known has been from behind the scenes.

I have met the men in anger, the women in a rage. It is romance or tragedy, according to whether you happen to be the man who gets the girl or the man who gets shot. I have sometimes assisted both ways, and I know the ugly seams with which the garments of romance are patched together. I never care to wear any of them. So young women with innocent blue eyes and pitiful tales are likely to find me unresponsive.

She did not know just what to say. But if I had known she was wholly alone and a stranger in the city, and without money too, I would have been a little more considerate—though perhaps as wary. It is no fault of mine that I am cautious. If the recording angel has attended faithfully to his work he has notations to show that women themselves are largely responsible for that.

"I am a stranger," she said simply, and a bit pathetically.

"But you knew Gaboreau?"

"I had never seen him before."

"No?"

"No. I had not. Why are you so suspicious of me? You act as though you do not believe a word I say!"

"Perhaps I don't," I said and did not smile.

"But if I were to tell you the truth you wouldn't believe me. Nobody would."

I neither denied nor affirmed, nor encouraged her to go on. She waited for me to say something, but I had nothing to say.

"I don't know how he came to recognize me," she went on. "I haven't been here much over two hours—in the city, I mean. Frank told—that is, I was warned to look out for Gaboreau. But I never thought I would meet him. I never dreamed of it. I heard a long, long time ago that he was a tall man with a black beard, and I have never forgotten. I noticed him when he passed me—I was noticing everybody. Then he stopped and spoke to me. He mentioned the violets—I had been told to wear them. But I recognized him at once. He was tall and had a black, closely trimmed beard. I ran from him. He followed me. I ran faster and turned the corner. Then I saw this café and darted down the steps.

"I didn't know what I was going to do. Then I saw this vacant seat at your table, and I thought if I hid the violets and you would only talk to me that he wouldn't notice. I thought he would look for some one who was alone. I was sure he didn't have time to see me closely. That's why I rushed up to you. And you—I thank you. It was—was fine of you."

"Go on," I said.

"Go on?"

"Yes. If you didn't intend to tell me everything, you had no business to tell so much."

"There is nothing more that—that I can tell you."

"And who," I asked, "is Frank?"

"Frank?" She was trying to pretend that she had not mentioned his name. It was poor pretense. As an actress she was coming down in my estimation.

"Oh, Frank. Oh, you see—his name isn't really Frank."

"No?"

"No. It is Franklin."

"I see. And who is he?"

"I was to meet some one who would take me to him. He couldn't come himself. That's why I wore the violets and came down the left side of the street. The man who was to meet me did not know me. And I didn't know him. And I was late, dreadfully late. I lost my purse on the train, and I had only some change in my bag. I had to take a street car and I got all twisted."

"And who is Franklin?" I repeated.

"A friend of mine," she answered evasively and with stubborn finality.

"Why couldn't he come?"

Again there was apparent in her light-blue eyes the assurance that I would be surprised, perhaps startled, at what she had to tell me. She leaned forward and whispered tensely—

"His life is in danger!"

THUS HER MELODRAMA was being compounded.

It was not much of a plausible tale to be unfolding to my ears, for though I have known stranger things to happen than she spoke of, I have found that it is only on the stage or on the screen that melodrama pays attention to such details as she was suggesting. There was something suspicious about her story. Whether she was holding back something from me or had herself been duped, was not for me to decide then. I was far from being sure of her, though she looked innocent enough, unsophisticated in fact. But unsophistication is a part of the worldly maiden repertoire.

I drummed lightly on the table and looked away. I was not exactly pretending that I was giving no attention to what she had said, but I was in fact giving more attention to the little foreign-appearing man who had scarcely more than slits for eyes and who was using them as soon as he passed the door to pick out something more than a seat for his dinner.

I saw him look about the room, and I saw that his eyes rested upon the woman with me. More than that, I noticed that he expressed dissatisfaction when the waiter tried to lead him to a table some distance from us. He stood pretending to be looking for a table that suited him, but again and again his eyes returned to the woman and occasionally he gave me a studious stare. But I did not let him see that I was watching.

"So his life is in danger?" I asked abstractedly.

"It is," she said emphatically. "And so is mine!"

"You are fortunate to know it," I assured her.

That nearly took her breath.

"Fortunate?" she asked, in amazement.

"Yes. One seldom need be alarmed when he knows there

is danger. The time to be badly scared is when the waters are unruffled and no breeze blows."

"I don't understand," she said, with unmistakable sincerity. "My life *is* in danger. Really in danger!"

I looked at her and perhaps showed the trace of a smile, for she asked me of what I was thinking.

I did not tell her that I was thinking that she acted as though conscious that a camera was catching every expression and a dictagraph was taking down every word, all later to be reproduced in some theater where she would probably be herself a spectator and anxious to approve of the leading lady's work. In other words, that she was theatric. But then, most people are in the midst of their first adventure.

"You have no place to go?" I asked.

"I don't know the first thing about the city. I only know one person in it, and I don't know where he is."

"You have no money?"

"If I could get a check cashed."

"Hardly, if you are a stranger, and have nothing to identify you."

"Well, I must go some place, I suppose," she said, rather helplessly.

"And being a stranger and in danger, you will be very foolish to wander around alone."

"Are you offering to take care of me?" she asked with a chilling, challenging intonation. She did not think much of me.

"No," I said, still keeping an eye on the little foreign-appearing fellow who fidgeted by the door, "I am not offering to 'take care' of you. But I can take you to either of two places where I am sure you will not be molested. One of them is the police station."

She gasped a little at that, and was too surprised to answer at once; and she watched me with puzzlement and showed a faint trace of alarm.

"Police station?" she asked, as though to make sure she had heard aright.

"Yes."

I said nothing more just then. I was not intentionally tantalizing her, but I was busily watching something else.

The man and woman at the table next to ours had arisen and were reaching for their wraps, while the waiter hovered helpfully around them, and solicitously looking out for his tip.

"But why?" the girl asked. "Why the police station?"

"Because it is a safe place," I answered, without looking at her.

"I won't go there. Of course not."

She pronounced it with finality. She was a little indignant. I had been absurd, preposterous.

I leaned toward her and said in a low voice:

"Listen closely. In a few minutes, seconds maybe, I shall make some remark about leaving. Please don't argue or hesitate about it, but get right up and come with me. I shall explain outside. No, there's no mystery about it. Only I can't say anything more now."

I spoke to her with a directness that conveyed what I wished to convey; that is, that I meant what I said. She saw that I was in earnest. I never shout or frown and seldom threaten because, fortunately, I have never needed to do those things to be convincing.

I had scarcely finished and leaned back in my chair when the little foreign fellow, at last discovering a table that pleased him, hurried forward and took one of the vacant places almost at my elbow.

She did not notice him. She was looking at me closely and wondering what I was about.

"There is really no need for being so solemn," I assured her.

"I am not so sure."

"But I am positive."

"But why the police station?" she insisted.

What I told her was not exactly the truth—or at least what I made her think was not the truth, though what I told her may have been; but I was speaking for the benefit of the keen ears that had come near us to listen. The little fellow sat fumbling with the menu scarcely an arm's reach away. I could have reached over and placed a wad of cotton in each ear had I wished to close them. But I did not wish. It was more interesting to know that he was listening. I answered with that air of conscious modesty which some men always use when being impressive, and said the police station was a place where I had some influence—and none of it was political.

"Oh," she said, and understood that I was a policeman or a detective.

What the little man by us understood, I do not know, but he tried to catch another glimpse of me by turning his face around and not moving his body. He almost choked himself.

Since he had come close to hear, I had no wish to disappoint him by keeping silent. Besides, I thought I could make a remark or two that would keep him attentive, particularly when I heard him ask the waiter for pickled peppers and spaghetti.

"Do you find the Oriel as interesting as you expected you would?" I asked her.

She laughed in a surprised, nervous way, and said that she thought she had probably found it a little more interesting than most people do.

"Such curious types," I went on. "Look about you."

She turned her head this way and that, but didn't in the least understand.

"They run strongly to ears. Have you noticed what prominent, large, flappy ears they have. Look at any one of the people close by."

She thought I was jesting strangely.

And perhaps I was. But the little foreigner with his back to us fidgeted in his chair and fumbled with menu and ice water and cutlery, and whatever else was in reach; but he couldn't resist the temptation, and at last raised a hand and gently felt of his ear—first one and then the other—touching it appraisingly.

"And," I went on, "there is still another reason why the police are given to watching this place."

I let whoever heard think, if they cared to, that the police watched people with large ears.

"Do they watch this place?" she asked, a little apprehensively, and I could not tell whether it was because she regretted having fallen into dubious company, or whether she did not care to be under the surveillance of the police.

"Indeed. The police have found that the criminal class

comes here a good deal. The food is highly seasoned, you know. Perhaps that attracts them."

I was libeling the Oriel outrageously, but the order for pickled peppers from the table by the side of us could not go unnoticed. And the little fellow still seemed worried about his ears, and touched them from time to time tenderly.

"I don't understand," she said.

"Highly seasoned food, you know. You have heard of the criminal appetite, haven't you? Well, it is the kind that craves pickled peppers, chilli, spaghetti heavy with peppery sauces. If you make a careful study of it, as the police have done, you will find that men with large, spreading ears—the sort of ears that catch every word spoken at the table next to them—usually order pickled peppers or some such thing."

"Really?" she asked, with the interest of one who has forgotten her unpleasant situation.

"Oh, yes, it is very well known to the police. But, of course, the information is not given out to reporters, you know. If the crooks heard about the discovery that science had made, then these large-eared gentlemen would eat their pickled peppers in private, and some of the most valuable clues of the police would be lost."

"I see," she said, a little bewildered, for I had spoken without trace of smile or jest.

I glanced at my watch.

"I believe it is about time for us to be going."

She looked at me indecisively for a moment, then said all right, and stood up. But she was not at her ease.

I caught my waiter passing, and got the check. He had

forgotten that the dishes before Jeannette, or whatever her name was, had not been served to her, and made no remarks.

The little fellow at the next table had also forgotten about his ears and his peppers, and was fidgeting more than ever in his chair. I surmised that he had been instructed to follow as well as to listen to us.

I WAS SLOW and deliberate about leaving. I enjoyed watching him fidget, and took all the time possible so he would be the longer on pins and needles. I fumbled about the napkin as though looking for something that had been laid on the table and could not be found. I talked with the waiter about trivial things, and in one way and another I lingered for some time and out of the corner of my eye watched the little fellow squirm and twist, jiggle his knife, tap his glass, and turn his head from side to side, as though to give each ear an equal portion of service.

The girl was beginning to be more than uneasy. She was downright suspicious, and could not understand the first thing of what I was up to. No more had I understood about her, so we were even. But all my life it has been that the more nervous the other party became the more reason I have felt for not being nervous myself. She watched me with evasive eyes, as though trying to find out something when I did not think she was looking.

"Are you ready, Jeannette?" I asked.

She said that she was.

"Are you quite sure you haven't forgotten anything?" and I glanced significantly toward the floor under the table, where lay her scattered bunch of violets.

"I have everything, everything. Thank you."

"Very well, then, we must be on our way. We shall have to hurry."

I suggested that we would have to hurry because I didn't want the little fellow to think he had plenty of time in which to follow us; because if he dogged along far enough behind he might succeed as a shadower.

But as I received my change from the cashier I saw that he was not intending to wait for his pickled peppers. He had no intention of letting us get out of his sight.

As I passed through the door and started up the steps, I saw him rise and hurry forward.

The Oriel was on a quiet street. There were few people in sight, and not a taxi anywhere. The modest Oriel was not a profitable loitering place for cabs. I wanted one, but I did not intend to go about looking for it. I counted upon having an engagement very soon in the darkened doorway of the wholesale Italian grocery that was just above the Oriel. I saw a young fellow passing who appeared as though he would not be offended at the offer of an easy dollar, so I gave him one and asked him to bring a taxi. I stood to one side of the stairway leading down to the Oriel and right by the grocery doorway.

The little foreigner came bounding up the stairway and hastily looked about.

I had pushed him into the darkened doorway before he knew what had happened.

"Listen," I said quietly, putting my coat pocket against him so that he could feel the muzzle, "you go back down there and finish your dinner. Tell the waiter that you have changed your mind again and that you are hungry and that you are not in a hurry. And if Gaboreau wants to know who has interfered with you, tell him to call on Captain Harrison at Headquarters, any morning between 10 and 12, and any afternoon between 2 and 4. And by the way, haven't I seen you some place before? Your face looks familiar. And those ears—one could never forget them. Maybe it is just your picture that I remember. We have quite a collection of pictures at Headquarters. All right, get along now. And take your time with dinner."

The little fellow's eyes were no longer slits. They had opened wide. He seemed trying to sink into himself, and started to speak; but I told him not to say one word, not one, because I did not like to be informed that I was mistaken; that if he wasn't intending to follow me, so much the better for him, because I had a decided prejudice against being followed, particularly by strangers; but that I was sure he needed the dinner any way, and for him to go back and get it.

He went. But he gave me a lingering look, as much as to say that he was inclined to think that I was bluffing but that he was in no position to find out. I haven't a doubt but that, too, he dreaded having to think up some suitable excuse to explain to Gaboreau why he had failed. But his worries were not mine. I could have figured out ten suitable excuses for Gaboreau while I teased my head for one idea as to what I should do with the girl.

But I am never long without a plan, no matter what the exigency. I would have known very quickly what to do with her if I had known what sort of a girl she was; but I didn't. I am not one of those discerning young men who can read a woman's soul in her eyes. Not much. And I am of the opinion that many of them often mistake belladonna for the light of innocence.

When the little fellow went below to finish his dinner the girl came closer to me with something of reassurance in her face.

"I heard what you said," she told me.

"Yes?"

"Yes. I think it fine the way you got rid of him. How did you know he was trying to follow us?"

That is the way with many people; they depend on their ears only for what they find out. That was the trouble with the little fellow I had sent back to finish his pickled peppers. If he had been content to sit across the room from us and use his eyes, and had taken the first available seat when he came in, I would probably not have noticed him. I might have, though. It does not take much to make me suspicious. And I was suspicious of her air of reassurance.

I told her that I knew he was following us because he got up and came after us; and she said something about the police training making one observant. I admitted that that was what it was supposed to do.

I had begun to think that the messenger had made off with my dollar without troubling himself to earn it; but as I had kept the appointment which I had in mind when I dispatched him, I felt free to go look for one myself. But presently a taxi came up, and he climbed off the seat where he had ridden to point the way.

I helped the girl inside, then told the chauffeur to drive on and I would give him the address later.

"Why did you say that you would give the address later?" she asked me as I got in and sat down across from her.

"Because as yet you haven't decided where you want to go."

"I really don't care, now," she said, lightly, as though wholly reassured.

"No?" I asked a bit dubiously.

"But why do you want to take me to the station, Captain Harrison?"

She was not afraid when chaperoned by the police captain.

"My name isn't Harrison. I am not a captain. I am not connected with the police."

"But you told that man—"

"Yes," I interrupted, "that Captain Harrison could be seen between the hours of 10 and 12, and 2 and 4. And so he can. But I have never had the pleasure of meeting him."

"But you told me—"

"That I have some influence with the Police Department, and that it is not political. And so I have. A certain commissioner and I are very well acquainted. In fact, we meet frequently over a quiet little game of cards, and I have influence enough to see that he contributes a goodly share of his graft to charity—to my pet charities."

"Oh," she said in a mystified way that showed she did not know whether to be reassured or to be alarmed.

Then, after a pause, during which she had evidently reached conclusions that brought her a little alarm, though she was trying not to show it, she asked—

"Where are you taking me?"

"I haven't decided yet."

"I think you had better let me out." She tried to speak firmly.

"You have no money. You are a stranger. Gaboreau hasn't gone to bed or isn't sulking in a corner."

"But where are you taking me!"

"As I told you, I haven't decided. You can have your choice. I shall take you either to the police station or to my apartment."

I watched her very closely, and she saw that I was watching her closely, but no doubt she thought it was for another reason than the one I had. She simply sat and looked at me. She looked at me hard, and did not say anything at all for some time. No. She did not say: "Sir, you insult me," nor "You have made a mistake, for I am not that kind of a girl"; nor any of the other cant phrases with which women of the kind guise a ready complaisance. I noticed all that very carefully, and wondered if I were not a dunce for my caution. But it is better to be a cautious than a trusting dunce; for we both sat in silence and stared at each other.

Her eyes were indignant and her lips quivered a little as she said, doing her best to control her voice—

"Take me to the station!"

"Yes. I have heard that is a good safe place for lonely young girls in a strange city," I said.

Then I spoke to the driver and gave him the address of my apartment.

"You did not tell him the police station," she said.

"This isn't a village, you know," I replied. "We have many police stations. And our streets are numbered. I don't believe I heard you say what town you came from."

She did not answer. I was unfit to be talked to. No doubt I was one of those sly, crafty fellows that girls read about. Perhaps before now I had given stubborn maidens the key to my apartment and told them to drop in when they grew tired of buffeting the world. The fair daughters of Oshkosh and Kalamazoo can not be too wary when alone in Gomorrah.

She would have a fine story to tell when she arrived at the station. I had insulted her, impersonated Captain Harrison, got her into the taxi under false pretenses, and no doubt I had a bottle of chloroform in my pocket. I must be watched very closely, and she must be ready to scream if I made a move. But then I must have a few remnants of decency in me if I did take her to the station. I could not be wholly bad.

NEITHER OF US spoke for some time. Then I asked—

"By the way, what *is* your name?"

She said nothing; and I repeated the question.

"The one you have given me does very well," she replied coldly, drawing herself more into the corner, as though to be farther from me.

I looked out of the window, so she could not notice that I smiled. After a time she asked—

"Aren't we nearly there?"

"Nearly," I said.

Then—and I knew she had studied a long time before saying it, and that she had some difficulty in nerving herself to do it—she said:

"I am glad to see that you—that you—that you are a— gentleman—after all."

"Yes," I admitted, "people are surprised every little while to find that out."

"Oh."

"This is your first trip to the city, isn't it?" I asked, hopeful that she might again talk with me, since she had concluded that I was after all something of a gentleman. I had reached the point where I really wanted to reassure her.

She hesitated and then admitted that it was.

"And you are about nineteen?" I hazarded, never able to be sure with women's age; but she was obviously young, very young.

"I am older than that."

"Some weeks, or maybe months. And you think you know something of men, particularly of gentlemen. I am sorry to disillusion you about myself, but I really think you should be shown how little fitted you are to wander around alone in this city. You were content to go with me as long as you thought I was taking you to the police station. Any one else might hoodwink you as easily as myself. We are now within a block of my apartment.

"Sh-h-h. Don't scream. Sit still and keep quiet. You will hurt yourself if you try to jump through that window, and then it will be the hospital. Take out your hatpin if it will make you feel more comfortable. But don't make a noise."

"You—you—you—"

"Wretch!" I supplied.

"How dare you! Let me out. Let me out, I say."

"Remove your hatpin. It is good as a dagger."

She did take out her hatpin, and then she glared at me. The hatpin was gripped firmly and held poised, ready to strike at the first movement I made toward her. If Gaboreau had known what a tartar he was trying to pick up, he might not have been so angry with me for keeping his hide from getting pricked. Her body was rigid and she was determined to fight. A badly frightened girl she was, and no doubt felt that she had tumbled into a worse affair than the one from which I extricated her.

In some way or other I always have ill success with women. I cast about in my head for something that would reassure her, and naturally I assumed that if I gave her to understand that I was not infatuated with beauty, or anything of the sort, that she would then know I was not the kind of a man she took me for. She was no doubt aware of every point of beauty that she had. Most women are. And when I told her that I did not think she was pretty— which was, in a degree, the truth—she appeared more angry than ever.

When I hastened on to remark that if I had thought she was pretty, I would not have brought her to my apartment, she became silently furious. Those blue eyes became like the deadly orbs of the basilisk, and I began to reflect that possibly I had made a bungle of my rôle as a Samaritan.

Men who know more about them than I pretend to, say that women the world over like to be coddled and coaxed. "The colonel's lady and Judy O'Grady are sisters under the skin," as the one poet I can understand has put it. But the dilemma is that I know nothing about Judy O'Grady and have no acquaintance with the colonel's lady.

The girl did not understand my attitude in the least. There was, perhaps, no chance for her to. No doubt she had been brought up with men at her feet and scalps at her belt. I was not quite old enough to pretend that my interest in her was purely fatherly; and I was not quite young enough to make a good brother. I was not, and did not care to be, anything faintly resembling a lover.

To me she was just a young girl, and helpless, for some unexplained reason, alone in the city, which contained many astute rascals, and one in particular who seemed eager to get his hands on her. I had not questioned her intently about her affairs, since so far it was none of my business. I was inclined to think, however, that her affairs would be my business before long. I was interested. No one could well help being. But I could not very well get to my knees and ask her to command me.

I had been intensely skeptical about her. But when I had, with deliberate forethought, suggested bringing her to my apartment and she had expressed a preference for the police station, I knew enough to satisfy myself that she was really deserving of a little protective attention. If she had offered, no matter with what air of reluctance, to come to my apartment, I should have taken her straight to the police station and allowed her to tell her troubles to the matron. A man can not be too cautious in dealing with a woman—even with a young one. Some of these women seem to come out of their cradles with more knowledge of the world than many a graybeard carries with him to the grave.

I did not tell her anything of the kind. But I set myself to be convincing, and it is not too much for me to say that I usually am convincing when I really mean to be, and I told her that I knew of no place where she could be so safe and so comfortable as with a woman—"a friend," I said—in the same apartment house.

I did not mention that in addition to this "friend" there was my very close companion, one Yang Li, as watchful a Chinaman as ever kept a secret. Yang could not very well get rid of his secrets, being a mute. I told her that if she would come into the reception-room of the apartment house and meet this "friend" I would not ask anything more; and that if she then wished to go some place else I would see that she was taken wherever she wished to go.

"But you have deceived me so many times," she said, plausibly enough.

"Not at all. I have taken only the precaution to make sure that you did not deceive me."

"I deceive you!" she exclaimed. "How could I do that?"

"This is no place to talk it over," I said. "Here is the apartment. Put your head out of the window and look the street over. It is quiet and has an air of comfortable respectability. If it were morning, instead of evening, you might see many nursemaids solicitously trundling their charges toward the park just around the corner. This is one of the few dignified apartments where babies as well as dogs are tolerated."

She studied the apartment-house carefully through the taxi window. It looked, as I said, entirely respectable, and perhaps a little imposing. The entire block seemed respectable. All were apartment-houses, many windows were lighted, and a few people were passing along the street and in and out of the entrances. They were well dressed and mannerly folk, and would no doubt have been amused to know with what suspicions a pair of light-blue eyes in an innocent, girlish face was scrutinizing them.

With evident reluctance she persuaded herself to get out of the taxi. At the door she hesitated again, and peered within. I permitted her to take all the time she wished for she was like some timid animal being coaxed into shelter;

and not in the least like the girl who had brazenly outfaced the quite capable Gaboreau.

But she ventured in. I said to the boy on watch at the desk—

"Please get Mrs. Everhard on the phone for me."

Then I showed the girl into the waiting-room, and used the telephone there, so she might hear what I said and know that I was not surreptitiously plotting to have her drugged and carried off.

"Listen, Vivian," I said. "Can you come right down? I have a young lady with me. Yes. A young lady. Very young. She is a stranger. Doesn't know a soul. How's that? Had her purse stolen or something. I am *not* always finding young ladies who have had their purses stolen. Of course, she can hear me. No—*she* is suspicious of *me*. I can't tell you more than that. No. No. No."—Vivian was wanting to know if she was pretty—"Not in the least. I can't tell you what she looks like, except that she's half frightened to death. I couldn't ask her to come up until she has met you. All right. Come on down."

Presently Vivian came down.

No woman whom I have ever known meets all situations with an easier manner and a more kind heart than Vivian. She has a great deal of what is called temperament, but she has too much humor ever to lose her temper—except occasionally with me. I had known Vivian for many, many years, and we had caused a great deal of trouble for each other; but as it all came out very well in the end, we got along splendidly.

Vivian is slender and dark, with black hair, and eyes that I call purple; and enough vitality for ten women. She has perception and courage. Indeed, she is brave and wilful, and possesses an extremely accurate faculty for sizing up people the moment she sees them. Also she speaks her mind freely, and there is little ambiguity about what she has to say when in earnest.

Vivian stood for a moment in the doorway. She glanced at me and looked at the girl.

"Miss Deering," I said, taking the name I had used and not wishing to hesitate over the introduction, "this is Mrs. Everhard, my wife."

That was the little surprise I had saved for her, and the girl was astonished. Whatever she may have expected, it was not that.

And no one could for an instant doubt Vivian's impulsive and generous manner. Her tongue is nearly as quick as her brain, and she sees things in flashes. An expression, a mere word, and Vivian understands.

The girl stood up. Her lips trembled and her eyes filled with tears. Her hands went out to Vivian, and the next minute Vivian's arms were around her. The ordeal was over for the girl, but I was in for it.

"There, don't cry. Don't cry, Whatever else you do, you must not cry!"

But the girl began to sob. The reaction was too much for her. Suspicion had drawn her nerves tight to resist the worst, and she had found Vivian's solicitous arms about her.

Then, turning on me, Vivian snapped—

"Don, in some way you've been a brute to this child!"

I made a deprecating gesture, silently disavowing the charge, but did not attempt to explain. Why explain to one who can talk twice as fast as yourself and put a barb to every word?

I went out to dismiss the taxi. I knew it would not be wanted again that night by Miss Deering.

WHEN I CAME in I found they had already gone up to the apartment. Ours is anything but a diminutive apartment. It is, in fact, two apartments. Vivian insisted upon having "room to turn around in"; which meant room to trip in, dance in, whirl about in, throw slippers and pillows at me, and dodge in. She was a little, cheerful, tormenting tornado.

Also she insisted upon having room enough in which to keep Yang Li out of sight. She did not like my Chinaman, though in all her life she has never had the slightest reason for her distrust.

The two women were closeted together for an hour or more.

Yang was in my room when I came in, but I said nothing was wanted, and he silently disappeared.

I sat with my feet on the table and shuffled a deck of cards in my hands, and tried to think of all that I had ever heard concerning Antoine Gaboreau.

I remembered distinctly that he was said to run continuously—though not always at the same place—a veritable mansion, as a gambling house and to have an exclusive clientele, including women well known in society. A murder, suicide or something on the premises a year or two back had caused one place to be closed and had got him a great deal of notoriety.

I could not imagine why a man reputed to have such

interests would be concerning himself with a pretty girl on the streets. It seemed to me that he would turn such work over to some one else—if he had really been Gaboreau. He was supposed to have a double, or be a double, or something mysterious of the kind. I had not given much attention to reports about him, and I had had no curiosity about the places that he ran.

For one thing, I was not playing cards as much as I once did, although I kept my skill by constant practise, and now and then went to Johnny Blix's rooms for a game, or spent a few hours at the club, where my friend the police commissioner enjoyed a sport that he was ostensibly suppressing.

But Vivian disapproved more strongly than ever of my gambling, particularly as I no longer needed to do it, as though needing money has much to do with the reason that men play poker. She said that she did not object to my getting into trouble as long as I took her with me; and she came very nearly meaning it, too.

I reflected that men of Gaboreau's type are more kinds of scoundrel than one as a usual thing. Clever, unscrupulous fellows turn their hands to any affair that has profit in it; and brainy crooks can no more work alone than a field marshal. A petty larcenist may go by himself, but even he doesn't go far—except on a trip to the penitentiary—unless there is a man higher up who tells him what to do and how to do it.

Occasionally a super-crook, like my friend Jerry Kelly, goes it alone, because he knows he is capable and that few people in the world are to be given confidence. But even he had to trust a pawn-broker or two, and one of them gave him the double-cross. But Gaboreau was a man of different caliber than Kelly. Gaboreau must need plenty of trusted men, even if he did nothing more than run a gambling layout. Nobody has so many hungry grafters at his heels as the gambling proprietor in a "closed town"; and each gambling proprietor knows something of the other.

So I telephoned to Johnny Blix and asked what he could tell me of Gaboreau. He let go with a string of adjectives, not profane either, and replied that he could tell more than would be advisable to pass over the telephone. He said Gaboreau would be guilty of anything but coarse work.

"Is he the sort of a man," I asked, "who would follow a girl along the street, into a café and try to take her away from the man with whom she was sitting?"

"Not much," Johnny retorted. "He *would* take her!"

"But she was with me," I said.

"That's different," he admitted. "But are you sure it was Gaboreau?"

"A tall man with a black Vandyke, rather handsome—and catlike."

"He has a dozen tall, black-bearded fellows on his staff, Mr. Everhard. There's a lot of mystery about that chap. Cool customer. Slick. The time that woman killed herself in his gambling place off Grant Park, the police nabbed the man they thought was Gaboreau. A tall man with a black Vandyke, handsome too, and catlike. Was simply one of the 'doubles' Gaboreau uses. Nobody knows how many he's got or where he got 'em. Say, I'm slipping this to you in a whisper, but I have it on the quiet that Gaboreau is suspected of the last big killing in this town—the very biggest. Get me?"

I thought a minute, and said that I did.

"Well, if you are mixed up with him, Mr. Everhard, you're in for more trouble than you've had for some time. You know I'd do anything for you—and you know why—and I'm giving you this as a straight tip. Better get out of Gaboreau's game. He's one of the fellows that don't have to buy off the police. He outguesses 'em. I know you, and I know you play a hard game, but I know Gaboreau, too. His 'rep,' I mean. Something of him, too."

"Do you think he is a procurer?" I asked.

"He's anything. But he don't go about picking up women off the street—drugging strange girls—if that's what you mean. He has a lot of wires. What 'd this girl say about him?"

"Somebody warned her about him. That's about all I know."

"Well, I'm warning you, too, Mr. Everhard. But maybe she's just taking you in."

"It may be," I admitted, for there was no use in arguing with Johnny.

"I'd drop her. She's nothing to you, is she?"

"Not a thing, except that Mrs. Everhard has taken a fancy to her."

"That's just like women. They always find the dangerous things to meddle with. You'd better take a trip, Mr. Everhard. Go exploring—any place."

"I'll tell you, Johnny. Get in touch with your friend the inspector, will you, and see what you can find out about Gaboreau."

"I've already been in touch with him—ever since that thing I told you about—you know—the last big killing.

I'm on the inside there. That's why I'm saying you oughtn't
to sit in."

"Well, Johnny," I said, "it looks as if I had unintentionally called for cards in Gaboreau's game, and I think maybe
I'll stick around for the showdown."

"You'll need a royal flush up your sleeve," was Johnny's
pessimistic comment.

But he promised to tell me what he knew and to find out
what he could about Gaboreau, and meet me the next day.

WHEN VIVIAN CAME in I knew that I was due to
be flayed.

"Don, take your feet off the table," she said.

And when I obeyed with alacrity she climbed on my lap
and clinched a small fist in my hair.

"Why didn't you tell that poor child that you were
married? Why did you frighten the life out of her? Tell me!"

"But, my dear, she wouldn't have believed me."

Vivian gave my hair a pull and went on:

"You know what she thought. You made her think it.
Deliberately made her think the worst possible about you!
She's nothing but a child. A poor, foolish child who has
no parents, nothing but a pious aunt and a lot of money
and a man she loves. Oh, why do women love men! The
brutes—you, for instance. And she came here to meet the
man she loves and left the man she doesn't love away back
in Los Angeles."

"What's Gaboreau to do with all that?" I asked.

"Who is he, anyway?"

"I don't know. He's a gambling man, and quite naturally
a rascal—"

"Of course," she agreed, giving my hair another pull.

"I don't know anything about this case at all. I don't know anything about women. I wouldn't have brought her to the apartment if she had not preferred the police station—"

"Indeed, you don't know much about women!" Vivian retorted scornfully. "Just look at that girl and you ought to have known that she would die rather than go to a man's apartment."

"I did look at her, and I didn't know anything of the kind until I had made sure. And if she had been one of the other sort, and I had brought her in here for you to mother— well, now you would have both your hands in my hair!"

"Oh, why don't you use your eyes!" she exclaimed; and with her free hand gave my nose a pull. "And now the girl is ashamed of having suspected you. I told her she ought to have used that hatpin. She wanted to come in and apologize to *you!* I told her never to apologize to any man. It's their business to apologize to us—always. And the first thing in the morning, you do it, and do it handsomely. Say you have a weird sense of humor and wanted to tease her. Say anything. But don't you dare let her suspect what you were driving at when you made her choose between your rooms and the police station. You ought to be ashamed. Good and ashamed. Aren't you?"

And, of course, I said that I was.

2

THE GIRL SAID that her name was Jessie Dutton, but that she thought Jeannette Deering a much prettier name; and the one she had had been taken from an aunt—the aunt whom she disliked very much. She asked us to call her Jeannette, but I would not agree to anything of the kind. I thought her dislike of her own name was merely a preference for one more stagey. But of course Vivian told me it was nothing of the kind, that the poor girl wanted to forget her aunt and all about her. But as near as I could tell from what Jessie said, the aunt was an inoffensive soul who had given more attention to religion than to her niece.

But Vivian told me that I did not understand women in the least, which was all the more strange because I could look at a man and almost tell of what he was thinking, what he had done in the past and hoped to do in the future—all of which was not in the least true.

I know two things only about men: they are honest or they are dishonest; which means that the honest men have not been sufficiently tempted. Of women I know less. That is because they are likely as not to remain honest when somebody offers them the world on a silver platter; and again they will poke their heads through a noose to steal a bite of sugar.

Jessie and I talked together for an hour or more the

next morning; and she told me more than she intended to, which is something that most people do if they are not interrupted. Vivian was entirely sympathetic. Vivian is always sympathetic. She would tumble laws and justice and the established order of things into the ocean and set up a world of emotions in which everybody would do what they *felt* was right without any regard for what they *thought* was right.

There is a big difference. A man may think it is right to take stiff interest from a widow who mortgages furniture to buy coal, but I do not believe that even the usurers feel particularly comfortable in doing so. And Vivian felt that Jessie had done exactly right in leaving her aunt and friends and rushing across country to the man she loved. But Vivian says that no one ever does anything wrong if it is done for love. Perhaps not; but a lot of foolish things may be done. And it seemed to me that Jessie had done her share.

To repeat all that she said, or to show in what manner the information she did not intend to give was disclosed, would be to make my recital as tedious as her own. She was extremely conscious of being the center of a romance, and did not neglect to put on little poses of mystery—feeling very much, as I afterward suggested to Vivian and got a sarcastic jab for my comment, as she thought the heroine ought to feel.

She was young, and like all girls was much interested in herself; and enjoyed to the hilt the attentive encouragement which our ears gave while she talked of several men, particularly two, of her aunt, of some girl friends, of a few dinners and dances, all of which were supposed to be pertinent to our interest because they concerned her. It would be wronging the girl if I neglected to insist that she was fine and sweet; but then she was a girl, a "flapper" as the English call their immature females, and she seemed to think this was a mighty small world since she and her affairs filled such a large part of it.

Franklin De Mey was her "true love" and, to borrow an expressive colloquialism from the rural community, "she was his'n." No wonder she loved him. He was handsome. He was brave. He was gallant. He had done wonderful things. He could say the most charming things. He had poise and passion and surprising muscles. He had once whipped a half-dozen men in a single fist fight and they were all larger than himself. She knew it was so for he had told her; and who could know more about it than the man who had done it?

So am I to be blamed for asking if this peerless gentleman was a movie actor?

I asked it quietly, almost with an air of humbleness as one does when merely seeking for the explicit answer to confirm what seems already to have been affirmed by indirection. But it appeared that I had dealt the paragon a mortal insult. Vivian kicked me on the leg, which is her favorite method of secret punishment; and Jessie became several inches taller as she replied with dramatic hauteur:

"Of course not! How absurd!"

No. Franklin was a gentleman. But he had very real dangers which caused him to be cautious. He was not a detective or anything so common, in the sense of plebeian, as that; but he had defied and offended the terrible Antoine Gaboreau so that all of Gaboreau's henchmen were out to do murder and their eyes were fastened upon Frank's heart. So of course, even the bravest man in the world would have to go into hiding in a case like that. Frank had told her so.

I gathered that it came about in this way. Franklin, or Frank as she called him, was such a bold and gallant fellow that Gaboreau had tried to entice him into ways of profitable wickedness. But of course Frank had spurned Gaboreau's solicitations. I gathered that Franklin wore his honor before her as conspicuously and spotlessly as he wore the bosom of his shirt when dressed for dinner; but I could not understand how Gaboreau would be such a blazing fool as to have offered Franklin the profits of dubious enterprises unless Franklin had in some way indicated that he would be open to such an offer. Men above suspicion do not receive propositions from crooks. At least that was my idea of the situation.

Gaboreau, she said, undoubtedly knew that Frank loved her and that she loved him. How he had found all this out was not quite clear; but according to Frank, Antoine Gaboreau had hundreds—if not thousands—of spies in all parts of the country; and no doubt some of them had succeeded in overhearing her and Frank's mutual affirmations of adoration.

I was inclined to believe that among Frank's other qualities was that of a large imagination.

Frank had appeared in Los Angeles, been taken up in Pasadena, welcomed at Montecito. Every one liked him. He had been immensely popular. No doors, to hear her tell it, were closed to him.

But Frank had suddenly been called from Los Angeles about two months before; and he had urged her then to leave with him. Since then he had repeatedly written and telegraphed for her to come to him; and at last she had dared to slip quietly away from her friends and aunt and hasten to the arms that had failed to welcome her. It appeared that even the courageous Frank could be even more courageous and resolute if she were by his side. And where the heart is, the will would also be, she said. Vivian nodded approval.

But Frank had not failed to repeat warnings against the sinister Gaboreau, who was so terrible that Frank himself did not dare come into the evening lights to meet her. It was arranged that as she walked along the left side of Water Street, in the block between Olive and Fenton— the Oriel café was on Fenton—she should wear a bunch of violets. And she would be met by a man who would recognize her by the red hair and violets, and this man would speak to her and take her to Frank. Thus were the myrmidons of Gaboreau to be circumvented.

However, the dreaded Gaboreau himself had discovered her, and she was forced to fly into the Oriel and drop at my table. Frank would certainly be grateful to me for my protection, but she did not know how to get in touch with him.

"To where did you address your letters to him?" I asked.

"Oh," she said, taking an attitude of loyal obstinacy, "he warned me to tell no one that!"

"Did he?" I said. "A wise precaution no doubt. But the circumstances have changed. To where did you address your letters?"

"To the Tremaine Hotel," she said, looking at me with

something like alarm in her eyes for she understood that I was not to be put off.

I had grown weary of her words and attitudinizing.

"Then perhaps we can have this little mystery over with in no time," I replied and went to the telephone.

I called the Tremaine and asked for Mr. Franklin De Mey, but was assured that no one was stopping there or had been stopping there by that name.

I asked who, then, had received the mail and telegrams addressed to De Mey which had been sent to him at the Tremaine.

I was informed that the hotel regretted that people often took the liberty of having mail sent there and got it from there though they were never guests. It was the sort of an imposition which the hotel regretted but could not very well prevent.

I asked if any one remembered the individual who had called for De Mey's mail; but it seemed that the Tremaine was too busy a hotel for Mr. De Mey's personality to have impressed itself on any one of the clerks.

There was nothing more to be gained, so I put up the receiver.

"It is well for society," I remarked cynically, "that Gaboreau did not succeed in making a crook out of your friend. He covers his tracks so well."

Jessie did not seem to recognize that I had paid a dubious compliment to her Franklin, for she assured me that there was not a possibility on earth of Frank's ever doing anything wrong. I don't know whether or not Shakespeare said "What fools these lovers be!" but he overlooked a bet if he didn't.

Then I asked, and again with directness that startled her—

"Did Franklin describe Gaboreau to you?"

"Why yes—that is, no I don't think he ever did. I remembered that when he first told me about his danger, Franklin called him a 'black-beard.' I asked if he had a long black beard. He said, 'No. A short one. A tall man with a short black beard.' But I never forgot. He warned me over and over in his letters about Gaboreau. He said he was afraid that if I did not leave Los Angeles Gaboreau would get me; and I became terribly frightened. A picture of Gaboreau was always in my mind, so when that black-bearded fellow spoke to me, the first thing I thought was—Gaboreau! And I ran."

"Gaboreau seemed to have been looking for you."

"It might have been an accident," Vivian suggested.

But I have no faith in coincidences. Such things are, it is true. But they are too readily accepted as explanations for what is often design and foresight; and I knew altogether too much about the laws of chance to feel it was conceivable that Gaboreau should have met this girl, in the midst of hundreds of thousands of women, at the only place in the city where there was any certainty that she would be. It seemed, too, preposterous to suppose that he would have recognized her unless he was looking for her. Red-haired girls are not rare; but red-haired girls with violets are conspicuous enough to be recognized if one is expecting such a girl at a certain corner; so to my mind it was obvious that Gaboreau knew what he was about.

"But I told no one," she protested. "I destroyed the letters Frank wrote me, so Gaboreau couldn't have found out even if it was one of his spies who stole my purse. I may have lost it, but one can never tell. And I am sure Frank never breathed a word. He was so careful to warn me against Gaboreau."

"He did not describe the friend that was to meet you?" I asked.

"No. He said that this friend—the very best he has on earth—would meet me. That he would recognize me and speak to me."

I said nothing for a while, but reflected that that was just what Gaboreau had done. Then I asked:

"He did not describe Gaboreau to you in detail?"

She shook her head and said—

"Nothing more than I told you."

"When he first mentioned his deadly enemy some time ago—said he was black-bearded and tall? He might have forgotten that he told you—don't you think?"

"I never thought of it. I don't know what you are driving at. Frank needed me and I came. I love him!"

Vivian, as I have said, was sympathetic. The situation really appealed to her. She was capable of doing just such crazy things herself.

For my part, I thought that probably Jessie's devotion to Frank was exceedingly out of proportion to his desserts. Any man who would call a girl some three thousand miles into a strange city and not meet her himself, had something radically wrong with him. That was so obvious that it exasperated me to think that she did not see it. I did not point it out to her, of course. Vivian however saw it; but she was more charitable to Frank than I.

"Now, Don," she said when we were alone, "you know

that you have been in places where you couldn't have met me if I had come."

"Perhaps," I said, "but I never had you come."

"I know, but—but of course, Frank isn't like you!"

So I was flattered into admitting that it was barely possible—just barely—that Frank might have a decent explanation; but I could not begin to imagine what it would be. I could not imagine what his plan or plot was one way or the other. It might be that Gaboreau was outwitting him at every turn, and had found out all there was to know of the girl's coming and arrival. It might be that Franklin, for reasons unimaginable, had himself conveyed the information to Gaboreau. Until I had the opportunity to meet Mr. De Mey, and look into his face, I had to content myself with wondering whether he was a crook or merely a coward. Of course, as Vivian suggested, it might possibly be that he had a reasonable explanation.

JESSIE TOLD ME much more about herself.

There was another man, an old man she called him. He was at least thirty-five. Very old indeed! He was prosaic; and a practical, unromantic sort of fellow; a real estate agent! Of all things, could anything be more unattractive, she asked. Oh, she had known him for years and years. He had wanted to get married and had pestered the life out of her. She liked him, but not that way. He was all right for a friend, except that he was too old and too dull.

And he hated Frank. That showed how unendurable he was. He had said awful things about Frank to her. Why, if she had told Frank some of the things that Walter Guernsey said about him, Frank would have done something dreadful to Mr. Guernsey. Frank was very touchy about his honor; and my! how he could fight. He did not give an inch to anybody.

"Except Gaboreau," I remarked, softly as I could.

But both she and Vivian heard me, and again I was out of grace.

She had not told Mr. Guernsey or anybody where she was going when she left Los Angeles. She had simply run away—to be near Frank, who, of course, was to marry her at once. Then they were to leave for Europe.

But there was no way to find Frank—so she wept.

Vivian comforted her and said that I could find him, that I could do it easily; that there was nothing I could not do when I made up my mind.

But Vivian had no delusions about me or my resourcefulness. She wanted to cheer Jessie. However, she told me to begin trying to locate Frank, just as though she were asking me to get a name out of the telephone book; and all I knew of him was that his name was, or was supposed to be, Franklin De Mey, and that he was supposed to be in the city along with some millions of other people.

I asked for a little time to think it over.

I moved to the search in a way that probably would not have met with approval from Vivian and Jessie had they known of it. I sent four telegrams before I dropped in on Johnny Blix.

All four went to Los Angeles. One to the chief of police; one to the Chamber of Commerce; one to the First National Bank; and one to *The Times*.

The first asked for information on one Franklin De Mey.

The others inquired about Walter Guernsey.

Then I went to see Johnny Blix.

Johnny runs a quiet little gambling house in a quiet district, and though he pays high for the privilege he is content with modest profits. He is as nearly on the "square" as any gambler can be and not go into bankruptcy, and has very desirable patronage; mostly middle-aged gentlemen of means who seek amusement and the opportunity to make what is called a "cleaning." The men who come, and some of them are young bloods bent on plunging, know they have a reasonable chance to win and they never complain if they lose.

It must be said to Johnny's credit that he had no idea of my real dexterity with cards, but I fancy he would let me play in his house anyway. Johnny is all gratitude. If one ever does him a favor, that one may become a pensioner on Johnny for life and will probably be remembered in his will.

It must also be said for my credit that I have never cheated anybody in Johnny's place that did not deserve it. I mean that they were either fellows who were trying to put over something a bit shady themselves, exchanging signals usually, or they were becoming too cocky because they happened to be winning everything in sight. Perhaps I must also say to my credit that at such times I never left the table without losing, usually to the heaviest losers, the chips taken in by my "questionable" methods.

But I do not deserve so very much credit for that, after all. The time has passed when I am badly in need of money. I can now afford to be honest. But I seldom question dishonesty that extends merely to money matters. Money getting is a shrewd game, full of kinks and tricks and legal rules which are in no sense honest since they leave the inexperienced rustic completely at the mercy of the perfectly legal financier.

But there are other forms of dishonesty—sheer stealing, for instance—which break the legal rules; and while I may have no particular sympathy with these forms—but let ministers explain why empty sacks can not long stand upright, then I shall be better able to tell why needy men when strongly tempted can not long remain honest. I am not defending thievery. Not at all. But I have defended and have helped many thieves, and I have not thrown in a dissertation on ethics with my help.

Johnny is a gambler and pays graft. But I like and trust him. He is a dapper little fellow with a square chin, and he talks as fast as marbles rattling down stair steps. He took me into his private office, which is about the size of a pigeonhole, and began to talk even before he shut the door.

"I hinted last night that Gaboreau had killed Kingston—which means he had him killed. Gaboreau's got three or four fellows, maybe more, who look like him. Tall, black-bearded, Frenchy fellows. The inspector's crazy because he can't touch Gaboreau. He's pretty sure he knows which is Gaboreau because only one goes into the house he's been having watched. He says he's absolutely got a line on three separate men that all look alike and pretend to be Gaboreau, and he's sure one of them is."

"But what about the Kingston murder?" I asked.

Kingston's death was a matter of intense interest at that time. Kingston was one of those men of immense wealth and notorious piety. He had been shot down through the window of his library and the police were desperately impoverished for clues.

"I'll tell you," said Johnny, "if you give me time. Gaboreau's got a new palace. Had it about six months. Clever. Private home—swell people live in it. See their name in the society paper every day. Inspector wouldn't tell me their name, but he told me that they rent the house from Kingston—or did. Gaboreau uses them for a blind. See the circle? Inspector says he knows Kingston heard about the gambling layout and had a fit and said he'd expose those swell tenants of his. Soon after that he was killed. Gaboreau didn't want to lose his swell new quarters or get his swell friends in bad. Either that or bump Kingston off, see? You know how long he'd hesitate.

"No, I don't know where that joint is. I've asked all around, quiet like, but it's well covered. Inspector says it's so exclusive only people with Dutch names are admitted.

"Further proof? Isn't any. That's enough, if you know Gaboreau. The inspector says right out that the police are afraid to take a chance and raid the joint. Says these tenants are big bugs with a pull right down the line. All the swells in town—the real swells—go there. Biggest thing ever put over. Leave it to Gaboreau!

"But I tell you, Mr. Everhard, if you've stepped on Gaboreau's foot you'd better take another trip to South Africa. I know you're used to trouble, and I haven't forgot what you did for me when that fellow swore out a lying affidavit about Mrs. Blix. But breaking in lone-handed to the district attorney's house, trussing him into a closet, stealing the affidavit and then kidnaping the —— liar that swore it out just to get at me, won't be nothing compared—"

"I didn't break in lone-handed, Johnny; or anything like lone-handed. And I very nearly stole everything in the place so that the district attorney wouldn't suspect what I was after. And you will remember that the police 'recovered' everything—everything—except some papers which the thieves had presumably lost. And as for kidnaping that fellow—remember, Johnny, I merely aided the sheriff from that little town down in Oklahoma who didn't care to monkey around with extradition proceedings. He knew the fellow was wanted for murder. That sheriff was a fine officer."

"You don't need to explain to me, Mr. Everhard. I know what you did for me. And I've never done anything for you."

"You will notice, Johnny, that I never hurt anybody much—not if I can help it. I usually tie them up so they will keep quiet until the game is over. That way they can't get in and steal the pot. Putting a gag into a man's mouth and sticking him into a closet, or setting Yang Li to watch him is just as effective as putting him into a coffin. And I can always let him go again, and he is usually so glad to be alive that he forgets all about the inconvenience."

"I know. I know. I know. You just play with rattlesnakes for the fun of it. But Gaboreau—he's one of those big snakes. What you call 'em? Boa something. The inspector's awfully close with his information. He come at me to find out what I knew about Gaboreau and dropped some information himself. I'll get more out of him, though—give me time. I know the inspector. He'll get disgusted one of these days and tell me all he thinks."

Then I spoke something of the little incident at the Oriel café. And Johnny wondered what on earth could have caused Gaboreau—or any one of his impersonators—to have tried to get hold of the girl. It wasn't like Gaboreau to fool around with a stray girl.

"This Franklin De Mey," I asked, "ever hear of him?"

"Never," Johnny answered promptly. "But if he's stepped on Gaboreau's foot I can see where he's wise to keep out of sight."

"Did it occur to you," I asked, for Johnny has a keen mind and has had lots of experience, "that Gaboreau would not have done anything so clumsy as to follow and intrude upon that girl unless—well, unless he expected that she would go with him without protest? Not even all three or four or forty Gaboreaus would try to seize and carry off a girl on a street like that."

"Don't be too sure," Johnny suggested in tone of dubiousness as to what Gaboreau would do.

"Anyway, if Gaboreau knew who she was, and knew that through her he could have located this fellow De Mey— why wouldn't he have kept out of sight and followed her, or have had some one else follow her, just as he tried to do after he left me in the Oriel?"

Johnny said that he couldn't understand that either.

THANKS TO THE difference between Atlantic and Pacific time, all my telegrams were answered by midnight. The chief of police answered last, and said that he had no record of one Franklin De Mey.

The bank reported that Walter Guernsey's rating was high.

From the Chamber of Commerce I learned that Walter Guernsey was the junior in the Guernsey & Son Realty Investment Company, with big holdings throughout southern California. Guernsey, Sr., had practically retired from active work in the firm, and the son was the actual head.

The Times News Service answered that Guernsey had never been implicated in any kind of a scandal, but that he had figured in the papers as a racer up until a few years before. He had been one of the most daring and successful auto drivers among the amateurs of the State.

So with my telegrams at hand, I meditated. Any one knows very well that a young man who is rated high by a bank, who is actively engaged in big business, too—which is something more than being rated by a bank because his father may give him a generous allowance—and who has distinguished himself in sport, is a man of good quality.

At least that is not the sort of a fellow who would send for a girl and then have some one else go for her because he was afraid to come out on the street after dark to meet a woman he loved or claimed to love.

I looked at the telegrams from many angles; and then a little after midnight I sent a telegram to Walter Guernsey himself. It was short and vague; yet explicit enough. It merely stated in so many words: "Jessie Dutton is here."

I designedly left it for Mr. Guernsey to take the initiative. I presented the information and waited to see what he would do with it. I was guessing from what Jessie had said that Mr. Guernsey would be much agitated by her absence. I thought I could tell much about the man, much more than I had learned from the bank, chamber of commerce, or newspaper, by the way he answered my message.

The answer came the next morning. I smiled for a long time after reading it. It was a model telegram; and I knew as soon as I glanced at it that Mr. Guernsey and I would not have any very serious disagreements. He had simply wired back: "I arrive Thursday."

That meant of course that he had looked up his train schedules, prepared to arrange for his absence from business, and also had made his decision with promptness. Thursday was less than a week away.

I have a weakness for men who are decisive and prompt. They often make mistakes, but they are the kind of people who never let such mistakes interfere with the main plan. There is a difference between haste and promptness. Haste shuts its eyes and leaps into the water. Promptness leaps as readily, but has its eyes on the life-buoy.

That afternoon I sent a personal to three newspapers. It was three fish-hooks that I was casting into the sea; and I hoped to get a nibble, even if I did not succeed in landing one Franklin De Mey.

They were blind personals, and the answers had to be made by mail. Also they were vague. Each said: "Jessie Dutton is alone. Friends please communicate."

I also moved through channels best known to myself to find out something about De Mey.

In one way or another several men have got themselves in debt to me, I do not mean in money matters. Money belongs to the higher reaches of the social state. Gratitude and loyalty among those who are friends to me is founded on something else. It is true that I have helped several people at one time and another with money, but the money was the least part of it. And I have found that there is no gratitude from any class of people that is so permanent, so selfless, so dependable, as that of crooks, who wish to turn to something more honorable—or safer, just as you please.

Among my friends was a huge burglar, or ex-burglar. Jerry Kelly had long been a crook and a bad one, from a certain point of view, and good one from another point of view. He tumbled into love with a girl who thought she saw possibilities in him and he turned to the ways of the righteous and became a drayman. Two weeks later he was pinched on suspicion and twenty years stared him in the face. That hurt Jerry very much. He was innocent. In the language of the day it got his goat.

Few people other than myself had known what it cost him in pride and money to become a drayman. He had taken his burglary as an art, a fine art; and though he had put over a number of little jobs without being arrested, still to be nabbed for one with which he had nothing to do made him disgusted with the world and its ways.

But Jerry had a good head and a great heart. He used the former at all times and the girl got to the latter. Jerry had used his fists on my behalf once upon a time when he did not suspect that my hands were in my pockets because two excellent automatics—cocked—were also there. A feather duster would have been a superfluous weapon when Jerry had finished with the three gentlemen who had thought it was my turn to seek an undertaker. Nevertheless, I felt obligated to Jerry. And when he was pinched he sent for me.

Perhaps what I did was not ethical, but Jerry was innocent. Details may be omitted; it is sufficient to remark that it was from my friend the police commissioner sitting in a private little game at the club that I extracted enough money to satisfy the particular inspector who could decide that after all the evidence wasn't sufficient to hold Jerry Kelly.

After that I had a hard time convincing Jerry that the strait and narrow path, taken from a drayman's perch, was really the better road. He suspected something of how I had got him out, for he was wise in the ways of justice and injustice; and the fact that I had, as he said, gone down the line for him, had much more effect in keeping him on the drayman's perch than my remarks to him on the utilitarian benefits of keeping straight.

Of course, he had lost his job in the meantime, and had to look about for another at a season when jobs were scarce. So, because I believe in poetic justice, when the police commissioner came at me again to win back what he had already lost, I collected enough more to tide Jerry over for about six weeks until he was able to find another dray. Jerry was appreciative.

I went to him and asked if he ever had heard of a Franklin De Mey.

He replied that he was not in touch with crooks much any more, for, as he said, the word had been passed that he was straight for keeps; but that he would inquire around.

"And any time I can ever do anything for you, Mr. Everhard—well, anything at anytime. That's me."

"Your turn will come, Jerry," I told him.

"Can't come any too quick to suit me. The little lady is telling me every day or so that we must do something to pay Mr. Everhard back. No, she don't mean money, either. Money ain't everything—"

"Just find out for me who this Franklin De Mey is and we shall call everything square."

"I'll find out if it's findable, but we won't do no such thing!" he said.

THAT EVENING VIVIAN told me something of what Jessie had said through the day, and I gathered that she was wealthy, but that De Mey was immensely rich; or at least he had made Jessie think that he was.

She talked a great deal of the free way in which he had spent money. He had lived at the best hotels; he had driven the best car; he sent the best candy in the largest packages; and he had traveled and told of it entertainingly.

"He never," I asked of Jessie, "complained that through a misunderstanding at the bank he was temporarily short of funds and took a few dollars from you to help him over for a day or two?"

"Certainly not!" she flared at me.

And I saw I had missed my guess, or she had not hesitated to shield De Mey from my suspicion.

Also Jessie was worrying herself into a state of prostration over Franklin's possible dangers. She insisted that she must go to him—though she had not the faintest notion of which way to start to reach him.

"You don't think," I suggested to Vivian, "that this fellow De Mey is merely a bit of her imagination, do you? She is romantic, you know. She is as bad as the average at the age."

I was slapped for my aspersion on maidens of nineteen, and was scolded for my question; I was told that I was the meanest, most suspicious man that ever lived. Then I was kissed very daintily and quickly and my hands grabbed futilely at flying skirts as Vivian ran out of the room.

Yang Li brought me a new deck of cards, so I sat and practised, which I find is as good a way to mull over ideas as to sit with idle hands and look solemn.

I wished to know who it was that had leased the Kingston house and gone into partnership with Gaboreau.

So I telephoned an attorney with whom I had done some business in a purely formal way—that is, he was one of the people who knew me as a thoroughly respectable citizen—and asked him to do what he could to find out what houses the Kingston estate owned in the fashionable district, and to whom they had been leased.

I was sure there would not be many such houses, and it would be comparatively easy to sift the list and arrive pretty closely at the party I wanted.

The attorney, of course, did not know what I wanted the information for, but he said that he thought it could be easily secured. I told him, however, that I was in something of a hurry.

3

I **RECEIVED MANY ANSWERS** from the personals that I had put into the papers.

All of the answers were from men—all excepting one. A number of them wrote that they were sorry to see that Jessie Dutton was alone; and some offered to show her a good time. A few wanted to be a "father" to her. Every one seemed to think that she had put in the personal herself, which was exactly what I wanted De Mey to think if he read it.

But excepting one from the secretary of an organization designed to assist lonely girls, every answer was of such a nature as to show that the man writing it was sadly in need of somebody to punch his nose. However, I prefer to use my head rather than my hands. Besides it was a little too much to undertake such wholesale punitive measures against the noses of so many; so I contented myself with hiring a public stenographer to answer each letter and to make an appointment in the name of Jessie Dutton in the same block at the same time with each of the mashers. Each was to wear a red necktie and a carnation in his buttonhole so she could recognize him. They were to meet her between six-thirty and seven and to wait in case she was a little late.

I thought it as good a plan as any to teach "suckers" not

to nibble at the bait I had thrown to catch a shark. At least I had an idea that De Mey was a shark. I don't know how the assignation turned out. I only know that subsequent letters were written by some who had kept the appointment; some were stupid enough, as mashers usually are, to think that a mistake had unintentionally been made since Miss Dutton did not appear.

But the letter that I wanted did not appear. No one answered giving the faintest inkling that he knew who Miss Dutton was. No one referred to Franklin De Mey. It seemed that Gaboreau had abandoned the girl, or else taken other means of locating her. And De Mey himself either did not read the papers or was afraid to write.

I had furnished postage so that all the letters might be mailed to me by the newspapers, and I would not have to send around for them. I had done this to hide trace of myself for any watcher who might loiter about to see who called for them. I did not care to have any one find out that I had Miss Dutton under my wing.

But on the fourth day I received a letter addressed to Mr. Donald Everhard direct. It was unsigned. The party writing it may, or may not, have got my address from some clerk in the newspapers' business offices. It was the most feasible way of getting it, however. It said:

> We know who you are and it will go hard with you if you don't do as we say herein. Let Jessie Dutton carry a pair of red gloves and be at the entrance of the Oriel café at eight o'clock. Friday night. You will get yours if this is not done.

It was signed with a black dagger drawn through a bleeding heart.

I am afraid that I smiled when I saw the would-be sinister signature. Daggers and bleeding hearts on paper never disturbed me much.

The letter was short but sufficient. The writer could not possibly have worded it more effectively to keep me from following instructions. I would not have turned Jessie over to a man who was the kind of a fellow to write such a letter. Had the note been gentlemanly, I might have done what seemed necessary to keep the appointment.

I had a suspicion that the writer was one of the mashers who had thought to get some information by writing her without letting it appear that that was what he was up to; and no doubt he had been one of many to keep the appointment I made, and had been greatly peeved when he saw the others who came with red ties and red carnations. I surmised this largely because of the instruction that she should wear red gloves. "Red" was no doubt on his mind; for red gloves are something rarely seen outside of a comic opera.

I had no way of telling whether the letter came from Gaboreau or De Mey. I was sure that it came from one or the other; and was inclined to believe that the latter was responsible. Gaboreau's threats, I reasoned, would be more impressive. Gaboreau might use the black dagger and bleeding heart as a signature, for many people are terrified by such things; but he would hardly write as a threat: "You will get yours if this is not done."

I gave the letter to Yang Li; he looked at it, grinned and filed it in a scrap-book with our other threatening letters.

Vivian calls Yang Li my bird of ill omen, which is a misnomer. Yang is a mute Chinaman. I have known him for years and he remains as mysterious as ever. He has told me nothing about himself, yet he can read and write English after a fashion. He is a peculiar fellow with a strange sense of alertness. I have never seen him sleep. He has the dog's faculty for watchfulness. Enter his room as quietly as you please at any hour of the night, and Yang's eyes will be open.

After all, he is perhaps just a common, inscrutable Chinaman, but worth his weight in diamonds. He does exactly what he is told to do, asks no questions and gives no explanations.

We first met in San Francisco after a tong war. Yang's friends had got much the worst of it. Some time before that somebody had cut out his tongue as though Yang had a secret they wished to have guarded forever. I suspected that Yang had once been in the service of a ceremonious dignitary, a viceroy, or maybe in some Peking palace. He punctiliously went through a lot of rigmarole like bowing and saluting and standing immobile when being spoken to.

He came to me as a servant and we got along fine. But Vivian had not liked having him around; she said that his noiselessness made her nervous. You might be sitting in a room with your eyes open, yet the first thing you knew Yang would be standing within a few feet of your face.

But after trying to do without him, I had persuaded Vivian into letting Yang come back. I liked to have him around, and his particular job was to watch over Vivian. It would take a regiment of hussars to look after her properly. Yang, with the long knife of his that he wears up the left capacious sleeve, does very well. When I am away from the house I know no one will get in.

AS IT WAS Thursday I saw that I would have a busy day. So I went shopping and bought a pair of red gloves and visiting a hair-dresser's succeeded in getting a wig that suited me; bought some theater tickets, and laid the preparations for receiving Mr. Guernsey between seven and eight. A subsequent telegram from him had told me that he would arrive about seven-fifteen.

I knew that a man who had raced across the country at a moment's notice would not linger long before reaching the address at which he hoped to find the girl.

I sent Jessie and Vivian to the theater. I sent Yang Li along, without their knowledge, to see that they were not molested. Yang hated street clothes, he looked and felt awkward in them, but nevertheless he could make himself inconspicuous and watchful. I felt there was no risk in letting them go, even alone; though I was less inclined to be easy about letting them return alone. I promised to meet them after the show and have a bite of supper with them.

Try as I did, I could not hurry them off to the theater. I was anxious that they should be out of the house before Mr. Guernsey arrived. At last they got away, and I took out my red gloves and wig and contemplated the things with a mixture of amusement and apprehension.

Then the telephone rang, and my attorney called up to say that he had found that Kingston's estate owned three houses which might be said to lie in the fashionable district; but there was really only one that was on the avenue. It was not generally known that Kingston owned the house at all. In fact the De Meyervelts were supposed to be the owners of that home as well as of other property.

"De Meyervelts?" I said, thinking quickly of some one else.

I elicited from him the information that the De Meyervelts were prominent socially. They were not intimate with the so-called "best" people—so-called for what reason I know not—but they succeeded in getting themselves invited occasionally to quite exclusive affairs, and were always making a splurge on the society pages. They passed, however, among the people who were not posted on social heraldry as members of the Four Hundred. They were not, according to my legal authority. They were on the outskirts. The second generation of the De Meyervelts would probably be, if they married well, at the hub of the social wheel; but at present the family was just about inside the rim.

I thanked him for his information and promptness.

"De Meyervelt?" I said to myself. "De Meyervelt—De Mey—Franklin De Mey-er-velt."

I sent one of the boys in the apartmenthouse office out to a drug store to look up the De Meyervelt family in the directory. And I was surprised to have him report that no such name as Frank or Franklin was given.

I called up the society editor of the *Herald* and found that the directory, though she knew nothing of Franklin, had omitted the names of several members of the De Meyervelt family. But I could not get a trace of Franklin.

It seemed to me something more than a coincidence, in which, as I have said, I have little faith, that De Mey, who feared—or said that he did—Gaboreau, should very nearly have the same name as the family which had presumably profited by a murder credited to Gaboreau.

Further inquiries that night were abruptly ended by the arrival of Mr. Guernsey.

"My name is Guernsey," he said with a touch of aggressive directness.

I looked him over carefully. Mr. Guernsey was not a particularly handsome man, but the marks of the solid, aggressive fellow were there on his face. He was not old, either. I liked his appearance though his nose had at some time been broken and not as skilfully set as the one who owned a broken nose might wish. He was not tall but rather chunky; he had a heavy jaw and dark hair and gray eyes.

"My name is Everhard," I replied, putting out my hand.

He took it, but rather dubiously. I asked him to sit down but he looked about instead and asked brusquely—

"Where is Miss Dutton?"

I told him that she was not in at present.

"Where is she?"

I said nothing but looked at him. He was suspicious, and inclined to be unmannerly. Then I asked him again to sit down.

"I came to see Miss Dutton," he said, lifting his voice challengingly.

I looked at him a bit harder, and I think he understood that it was not the time or place to grow noisy. Again I asked him to sit down. And he sat.

"Is she all right?" he asked impatiently.

"No," I said maliciously, "she is not."

Instantly he was back on his feet, demanding in a loud

voice that carried some menace and some of the distracted lover's anguish to know what was the matter.

"Very much the matter," I said.

He caught his breath and listened intently, expecting me to go on. I hesitated.

"Tell me, man, tell me. What is the matter?"

"She is in love with a fellow called Franklin De Mey. Who is he?"

I sent the last three words at him suddenly.

"Has he got her? Where is she? I'll break his —— neck! Has she married him? Did he bring her here. Tell me—tell me—can't you see that I am half crazy?"

I told him that I could.

That quieted him down somewhat. He was not by nature an emotional fellow; or what is usually called emotional by those who think Frenchmen are emotional because they so readily make a fuss. I have usually found that there is as much fire in a quiet man as in a noisy one; and Mr. Guernsey was not inclined by nature to be noisy. I could see that plainly enough; but he was sadly wrought up by his love for a slip of a red-haired girl who I found was tedious to be with. I can understand the madness that Vivian had inspired in more than one person—but red-haired maidens, never! I did not intend to hold a controversy in aesthetics with him; so I asked again—

"Who is Franklin De Mey?"

"I don't know. He's a bounder that popped up in Los Angeles last Summer. I tried to look him up but couldn't find a thing."

"Is he handsome?" I asked a bit maliciously.

"No!" and Mr. Guernsey replied with the emphasis of disgust.

"Is he brave?"

Mr. Guernsey seemed to perceive that I was asking as much to torment him as to find out about De Mey. He said:

"Oh, De Mey might beat up a cripple—a little one. That's the way I sized him up, anyway. But where is Miss Dutton?"

"That was not the name I met her under," I said testing the gentleman's nerves a little further.

"Has she married that whelp?" he shouted at me.

"No. Not yet."

Then I told him of how I had met her at the Oriel café when she dropped into a vacant chair at my table, and of the black-bearded man that came up and spoke to her.

"I'd like to have been there. I'd have punched his head for him!"

And I was convinced that he meant it.

"Did you ever hear of Gaboreau, of Antoine Gaboreau?"

"Never. What do you make of it, Mr. Everhard?"

We talked for some time, and I told him practically everything. I showed him the threatening letter with the black dagger for a signature; and spoke of how all effort to locate De Mey had failed, and in conclusion I said:

"I make of it simply this, which isn't a very profound deduction I will admit. De Mey is either with or against Gaboreau. But in neither case can I understand why Gaboreau should have displayed the interest he has in just the way he has. I fancy that De Mey's love is largely centered around the girl's pocketbook. She is wealthy, is she not?"

"Not so very," Mr. Guernsey said with some satisfaction.

"She appears to think that she is."

"Her father was, but he didn't leave much. And that has been badly managed. She has enough to live on and all that—but wealthy, no."

"And De Mey—he showed symptoms of wealth, I understand."

"He did spend a lot of money—but a lot of people do that for a Summer. It's no sign they can do it next Summer. He splashed, yes. I don't call any man wealthy who rents a car. He did. Always had the same make—but a different car frequently. I know. I know cars. But I want to see Jessie."

I told him that I did not think he had better see her; and he became rather excited again. He vowed he would see her; that there was going to be trouble if he did not see her; that he was going to talk some of that nonsense out of her head and take her right back with him. He looked at me suspiciously and he hinted—hinted vaguely but pointedly enough that I had an ax to grind, and intimated that I in asking my question regarding the state of her finances had not been totally disinterested.

I have much more patience than I have been credited with; so I listened without making a gesture of protest until he had finished. Then I asked him to sit down again. He resumed the chair and sat rather stiffly, waiting to see what I would say.

"If I haven't misunderstood," I remarked, "you are in love."

He made no reply, but looked as though he could bite my head off and would enjoy doing so.

"Do you want to win her or kidnap her?"

"I don't care. I want to get her out of trouble," he snapped.

"A laudable and gallant ambition, Mr. Guernsey. But she chances to be sufficiently old to be supposed to know her own mind. She ran away from you, I suspect, as much as she ran to this fellow De Mey."

"I don't understand."

"Perhaps you will if I am permitted to continue. She has frequently and repeatedly told me that she wished to avoid you. That you continually talk of marrying her. And all her waking hours have been given over to expressing worry about and love for a man other than yourself—a mysterious man, who we are agreed in thinking is probably a scoundrel. But if she sees you now or soon, and knows what you want, she will be more obstinate than ever.

"I don't know much about women, but I know you can not *make* them do anything. If you show them the error of their way, you must do it indirectly. If you convince them of anything, you must let them think that they arrived at their conclusions by their own intuition. They are very proud of that vague quality called 'intuition.'

"And Mr. Guernsey, if you were to carry her back home now she would always regard you as her enemy, as one who had spoiled the romance of her life, and she would enjoy a lot of sentimental sorrow such as most women nurse all through their lives if they fail to get the man they want. But if we can possibly locate this Franklin De Mey and uncover his mystery, I believe he will not then look so attractive to her.

"You know and I know that there is pretty sure to be something shady about him. It is barely possible that he has offended Gaboreau and has taken to a dark cellar for the good of his health. I expect to look Monsieur Gaboreau up within a few days and shall make a few direct inquiries of him. But for the present, you must keep out of sight."

Did he believe me? Scarcely a word. He thought that I was trying to trick him in some way. He showed about as much sense as men usually do when in love; but he did agree that if all the facts I had reported were true, it would be best for him to remain out of sight. The "fact" to which he took exception, however, was in my statement that Jessie would not want to see him.

I let him express himself as freely as he pleased, then told him that he would pay dearly for his foolishness.

He insisted upon coming to the theater with me to meet Vivian and Jessie, though he promised to keep out of sight on the way home. We arranged that he should then enter my room and play eavesdropper so that he could hear what was being said in the next room; though I warned him that he would hear much that was unpleasant to his ears. But he insisted, and I did not waste breath in trying to dissuade him.

WE WENT TO the theater together, and when Mr. Guernsey was hurrying out of the foyer as the crowd started to come through the door, he bumped into a little, slim man, whose clothes did not seem to fit him and whose almond eyes showed not a flicker of annoyance. Yang Li drew aside also for he knew that Vivian would be angry if she knew that he was watching over her. But he slipped a card into my pocket and when I looked at it, I saw the figure "2."

That meant that Yang Li had spotted two people who seemed to have been following Vivian and Jessie. But I knew that nothing would come of it that night; though it was well to be assured that there was some risk if either of the young women ventured out alone.

I met them, and we went to supper.

I smiled as I thought of the estimable Mr. Guernsey, highly rated by the banks of his city, adapting himself to the exigencies of a "shadower."

His patience, however, was equal to the occasion; and he no doubt had plenty of opportunity to assure himself that Jessie was not unhappy in the company of Vivian and myself.

When we returned to the apartment, I succeeded in smuggling him into my room. He told me nervously that some one else had been following us, too. He said there were two fellows; but from the way he looked at Yang Li, who slipped by us and disappeared into his own cubbyhole of a room, I knew that Mr. Guernsey had not detected the third man that had also followed. I believe Yang could evade observation if he were to be set down on a vacant lot.

But Mr. Guernsey was still desirous of playing the eavesdropper. No doubt he wished to hear Jessie's sweet voice. I gave him the opportunity.

Vivian was sleepy and Jessie was too. But Jessie could easily be persuaded to talk about herself and the beloved Franklin. She seemed to forget him now and then and be rather contented; but once his name was mentioned, she worried and chattered in the way that young women are supposed to fret and talk about an imperiled lover.

However, I kept my questions more or less around the name of Mr. Guernsey and really had an absorbing half-hour. She repeated that Mr. Guernsey was old, dull and prosaic, that he bored her to death though no doubt he really tried to make himself agreeable. But in no way was he comparable to Frank.

"This Mr. Guernsey must be a pretty good sort of a fellow, though," I said.

"Oh, he's all right, but *so* dull."

"Didn't you ever like him?"

"Yes," she said slowly, "but that was before I met Franklin—" and she had to tell more about the paragon.

"Don't you still like Mr. Guernsey?" I asked; and Vivian, somewhat mystified, looked at me.

She could not understand why I was asking such pointless questions, and repeating them.

"As a friend, of course. He's all right, only Frank—" and away she went again.

"Don," Vivian said suddenly, "I believe there's somebody in your room!"

I laughed at her, though I was sorry that she had been startled by the muffled expression of disgust which had come through the keyhole.

"I am sure I heard something," she insisted.

"I'll look," I said, "but nobody could get in there with Yang in the house."

I opened the door and pretended to look about. Mr. Guernsey was grinding his teeth. He could not speak for he knew that he would be heard; but his eyes were eloquent.

No, he was not an emotional man—he was simply much wrought up. And he indicated that he now knew it would not be best for the girl to catch sight of him. I reported to Vivian that she must have an overdeveloped imagination.

Fortunately Vivian is not easily alarmed, so she did not insist that she had heard anything suspicious. But Jessie, who had been so busy talking that she had heard nothing but her own words, was much perturbed by the possibility of any one being in the apartment, and even showed excitement after I had convinced her that all was safe and secure.

I resumed my questions and Jessie resumed her speeches about Mr. Guernsey and Mr. Franklin De Mey.

A few minutes later Vivian started up exclaiming:

"Don—there was somebody, too! I just heard the door close!"

Mr. Guernsey would not have made a good burglar. He lacked technical skill. In sneaking out he had closed the door with a click loud enough to be heard in a boiler factory.

I jumped up and rushed into the next room.

Jessie caught hold of Vivian and began saying little hysterical things while they both followed me.

I ran through my room and out into the hall as though in pursuit of some one. I wanted to tell Guernsey to hurry and get away in case he still lingered. But he had disappeared. So I was able to be truthful in reporting that I saw no one; and, after looking over the room, in saying that nothing had been disturbed.

"I must have had a bad case of nerves," Vivian said dubiously. "I could have sworn that I heard some one."

I smiled and lightly dismissed the click of the door, or

tried to. But Jessie declared that she also had heard the door close. I tried to explain that the show must have been too melodramatic and have put them into a highly agitated condition.

Vivian told me that it was precious little I knew about either nerves or melodrama, for the show to which I had bought tickets for them had been a musical comedy. She was not satisfied that no one had been in the room, and in looking about discovered the red gloves and wig which I had left on my desk.

Vivian pounced upon them at once.

"Aha! There was somebody, too! She left her gloves. Horrors, what taste! Don, explain yourself. Who put these ghastly things on your desk? I could pull every hair out of her head—see, I can even think I have done it"—and she brandished the red wig.

Jessie saw mystery compounded with mystery for she believed that some one had actually left the gloves and wig.

"My dear," I said to Vivian, "that is a little present I bought for you. Tomorrow evening between the hours of seven and eight you will wear them for a block or so—"

"Never!"

"Oh yes. Red gloves and a beautiful red wig—"

"Horrible! Such a combination!"

"And you will borrow the suit and coat Jessie has."

"Don, are you serious?" she asked quickly beginning to see method in my madness.

"Entirely my dear. You must keep the appointment alone. I will follow as close as I can in a taxi."

Then I told her something of what had happened, omitting however the threat contained in the letter for that sort of thing never failed to make Vivian uneasy—which was about the only thing I know of that would. "But red hair and those awful gloves!" she protested as she stood on her tiptoes and raised her lips to my face.

4

THE NEXT MORNING an early telephone call came from the pained and humble Mr. Guernsey. He apologized for his suspicion of me, and with a sense of humor that I had hardly credited him with remarked that I had fixed him "good and proper." He said that he now saw that the best thing he could do was to stay out of sight.

"De Mey must have her hypnotized," he suggested.

Hypnotism has taken the place among us that magic had among the ancients. In the olden days it was said that a man bewitched a maid when she seemed to prefer a worthless suitor for one of stalwart merit; but now we say that the scoundrel has her hypnotized; and we find in the term great consolation, for it presupposes that the girl has through no fault of her own lost control of her will. Perhaps not one person in a thousand is truly serious in suggesting hypnotism as an explanation; but as a usual thing such a person gets all the consolation out of the term without having faith in it.

Guernsey was determined to find De Mey. Since he knew something of how much Jessie cared for him, Guernsey was more positive than ever that the fellow must be a scoundrel. I have often wondered why it is a woman never seems able to inspire love in two decent, honorable men at the same time. All stories testify that one of the wooers must be a rascal; and every wooer believes the other fellow to be the rascal. In this case, however, I entirely agreed with Guernsey's opinion of De Mey.

"I want to offer a reward for that fellow," he said. "Put it in the papers. I'm going after him right."

"Yes, and scare him to death. Make him retreat further into his hole," I suggested sarcastically.

"Well, go to the police then. They ought to know something."

"They ought to, yes. But the police have a habit of pretending ignorance when they are wise; and of pretending to hold evidence when they are wholly up in the air. If you tell them the story they will probably say that they can't see any cause for their interference."

"What the devil are we to do?" he asked.

"Do you ever gamble?"

"Gamble? Sure. I'm in the real estate business. I don't mind taking a chance, if that's what you mean."

"Partly. Do you play poker, roulette—anything?"

"Never won anything, but I know one card from another. But I'm game."

"Well, you are no good as a burglar. Both my wife and the girl heard you close the door last night. Yang Li could have run through the house and slammed every door and nobody would have heard him. There are men like that. Jerry Kelly for instance, whom you may meet later on if this affair grows complicated. But you are not one of the kind. But I thought you might try your hand as a gambler. Are you willing to lose a little to pose as a sport?"

"Is it for her?" he asked, puzzled.

"Yes. All a part of the game."

"I'm on. I don't see the point, but I think I'll take your word for it after this. You certainly rubbed it into me last night. I came near biting that door-knob off!"

"All right, we shall work as sleuths then. I think you will be better as a detective than as a burglar. It doesn't mean so much if you fail as a sleuth. I would do it myself, but though I am not well known in this city by any means, still there are probably a few people with whom I have no speaking acquaintance that know me, and they might be suspicious. But you are a stranger. During the day I am going to find means of introducing you to our most exclusive gambling club. I'll meet you late this afternoon and give you the details."

I went into the cubbyhole that Yang Li used for a room and found him as usual squatted on the floor with a package of cigarets by his side. In his eyes was the far-away stare of one who dreams of things that may not be spoken. He possesses the true Oriental patience. Hours mean nothing to him; the clock is merely a contrivance which keeps people from forgetting themselves, and he seems never to notice what goes on around its face.

When in the house he wears the blouse and trousers of his country, and the soft felt slippers. And sometimes when he raises his hand to his lips to place or remove a cigaret, one may catch the glint of what appears to be a polished piece of wood in the sleeve of his left arm. That is the handle of a long knife, scarcely thicker in its blade than a razor, but two and a half times as long and tapering to the needle's point.

Men who have had experience with both weapons have told me that they stood more in fear of a knife than of a gun. Of course, that depends on who has the gun. It is true that awkward hands use the knife more effectively than the gun. I would rather have five hands coming at me with knives than have one man standing away and holding a gun if he could use it as well as myself; but I am inclined to think that I would rather have five ordinary men with guns trying to put an end to my usefulness than have Yang similarly inspired with that long, sinister, glittering blade of his. Every man knows how eagerly a razor bites into his flesh, as though the thing were actually animated with desire to get to blood: Yang's blade is the apotheosis of the bloodthirsting razor.

As I came into the little room, Yang rose to his feet. He got up simply by straightening his legs beneath him and lifting his body; not by climbing first to his hands and pushing up his back, as people of the Occident do when they have squatted. He stood attentively while I said one or two short sentences, then raised both hands, palm outward to his forehead and bowed. It seemed to me a rather ridiculous courtesy, but I took it seriously as I always did. If I should have to put my life into somebody's hands other than my own, I would choose those frail yellow hands of Yang's.

I had told him not to let either of the women out of his sight; and I hoped that it would not be difficult for him to obey, as I had asked Vivian, and practically ordered Jessie, to stay at home. If I had wanted Vivian to go out on to the street and wander about, I could have got her to do so by simply ordering her not to go outside her room.

I HAD A double, perhaps a triple mission, with Johnny

Blix. I talked over matters rather freely with him; and he had tried to locate the elusive Franklin De Mey, feeling much as I did that the name bore too close a resemblance to De Meyervelt to be an accident.

He had also taken the trouble to find out that De Meyervelt's was the home where Gaboreau had established his gambling layout; and when Johnny had quietly let the inspector become aware that the De Meyervelt house and its secret were known to him, the inspector had loosened up with more information about Gaboreau.

But before I let Johnny get started to talking I told him what I wanted to do with Guernsey. I told Johnny that he must scout around until some one was found who had entrance to the De Meyervelt house and would be willing to take a young friend of mine recently from Los Angeles.

Johnny usually had two or three gay youngsters in debt to him, though the real "swells" were not his steady patrons; and he said that he thought that by wiping the slate clean he could persuade somebody either to take Guernsey or to introduce him to some one who would.

"It's not easy, Mr. Everhard. That De Meyervelt joint is watched like a pawnbroker's safe. They're particular. Players are received as guests of the De Meyervelts, you know. The gambling layout is supposed to be for the amusement of the guests. Clever. Takes brains to operate like that and get away with it."

"I've told Mr. Guernsey that he will be expected to lose," I said.

"Wise-O. It'd look bad if he was to win. See that, don't you? Strangers never ought to win. Makes people suspicious. Attracts attention. You don't want no more attention attracted from Gaboreau than you can help, Mr. Everhard. He's a bad one. *The* bad one. I've found out some more about him."

"One of the things I particularly want, Johnny, is to know how and where I can get in touch with Gaboreau without breaking in upon any of his secret haunts."

"Easy. I was just going to tell you what the inspector loosened up with when I sprung on him the De Meyervelts. Could have knocked him over. That's the way with the cops. They think nobody knows anything about anything they've had a hard time learning.

"Inspector much as told me—did tell in fact—that he don't think he'll be able to hang anything on Gaboreau about Kingston's murder. First place there's too many Gaboreaus. Inspector says that he knows of three, and he thinks there's another one or two. Can't get the goods on any of them. Beats the devil. I wish you'd drop that Gaboreau stuff, Mr. Everhard. That fellow don't buy off the police. He just bluffs 'em out.

"Inspector thinks the real headquarters is 22 Stillwater Place. He's been having it watched day and night for two weeks. Just called off the dicks yesterday. Says there's nothing more to learn by watching an old man and two women that are stone deaf. Cook and a maid and an old servant the inspector says.

"But here's the point. One black-beard comes out every morning. Sometimes at four, sometimes at six. Always shows up about the time the game is over at the De Meyervelts. Of course, the inspector can't get anybody into the De Meyervelt house. He's tried it. But anybody can spot a plain-clothes man as far as he can see him. You know. They all look alike. But he's had men out in front of the house watching, and about an hour after the party busts up, then a black-beard shows up at Stillwater Place. See? But nobody ever sees Mr. Black-beard leave the De Meyervelt house. Sees him come all right. Usually comes from the Tremaine—"

"The Tremaine Hotel?" I interrupted.

"Sure. That's the funny part. Inspector says his men have seen as many as three black-beards go into the Tremaine before one came out. Get me? But never sees any two together.

"And that fellow that goes into the Stillwater place at five or six in the morning usually leaves about eight or nine and goes to the Tremaine. Then from the time he arrives till about midnight there is Mr. Black-beard hanging around the lobby. When does he sleep? That's the point. See? There's three or four of these black-beards, all of 'em look alike and they switch around on schedule so that nobody ever sees two of them at the same place, or can locate any two of them at the same time."

"What did the inspector find out at Stillwater Place?"

"Nothing, I've been telling you. The servants are deaf and won't talk. The old man—butler or something, the inspector says, never leaves the house."

"The detectives didn't manage to get in and look around?"

"Who ever heard of a detective getting any place without breaking down the door?" Johnny answered scornfully.

"And if I want to see Gaboreau I am to go to the Tremaine?"

"That's the ticket. He loafs around there from eight or nine in the morning until midnight."

"The Tremaine," I said, "is where De Mey had his letters sent. Remember?"

"That's what you said. I remember now. Humph—funny."

"And the Tremaine clerk said he never heard of Franklin De Mey. Johnny, do you think it possible that Gaboreau is impersonating this fellow De Mey? There was such a fellow out at Los Angeles—but maybe he has been done for—bumped off and Gaboreau is playing his part."

"Might be. Gaboreau would do it if there was anything in it for him. If you'll take the advice of a friend, Mr. Everhard, you'll lay off that gang. They're bad. They're too clever to be caught. They're the only crooks I ever heard of that don't bungle. Brains back of them. Police can't touch 'em."

"The police are handicapped, Johnny. They play the game according to rules. They have to have evidence and warrants before they make a move. That is all right in a way, and is designed to save decent citizens from annoyance. But it also is a great advantage for the crooks. I have no such scruples. I don't play the game according to the rules of evidence and warrants. If I suspect a man I give him the chance to explain—that's all. I don't wait till I can *prove* something on him, as the police have to do. I think I'll pay a call at the Tremaine and ask Mr. Gaboreau a few questions."

And I did. I had scarcely stepped into the lobby before I saw the same man, or at least I supposed it the same man, that I had spoken with at the Oriel.

He was sitting alone in a leather chair watching the people. I walked up to him and stopped. He looked at me but gave not an inkling of recognition, and apparently expected me to pass on. But I did not.

"Monsieur Gaboreau?" I said, stressing the "Monsieur."

"Yes, monsieur," he answered with a glint in his eye and stood up.

He was a taller man than I, and I am not short. He was politely attentive, and searched my face with his dark eyes. His hat was on, and his thick, black beard closely trimmed, permitted me to see scarcely more than his nose and eyes. But I felt sure that he was the same man I had met a few nights before.

"What can I do for you, monsieur?" he asked.

We stared at each other for some moments. I never feel uncomfortable or rude when I take the time before speaking to look a man over carefully. Then I asked—

"You do not remember me?"

He appeared a little puzzled.

"Ah, yes—I seem to—but so many people—your face is familiar. Yes. Sometimes a name slips my memory—but a face never. I remember your face quite well. Now wait. Let me think—"

I let him think all that he pleased. No doubt he expected that I would hasten to tell him my name and the place where we had met, as people invariably do when they feel that they have been forgotten and wish to jog the memory of the one who has forgotten them.

My silence did not assist him in the least.

"My wretched memory," he said with a slight effort at a humorous tone, "is playing me false. Just a word, monsieur. Just one word and it will all come back to me."

I spoke not one word, but three. I said—

"Franklin De Mey."

The gentleman was an artist at self-control. But we were standing less than three feet apart and I could see his face too closely to miss the slightest muscular reaction of even his eyelids. Just for an instant only—the briefest of instants, if there can be such a thing—he showed the merest trace of surprise. But the flash of light in his dark eyes was suffi- cient to let me see that at last I had thrown the mysterious name of Franklin De Mey upon comprehending ears; the first pair of ears that my assiduous questing had discovered.

But he at once assumed, or tried to assume, the appear- ance of one who is not sure that he has heard correctly.

"Franklin Deming?" he asked. "Did you say that your name was Franklin Deming, monsieur?"

I took my time about denying that I had said anything of the kind.

"Franklin De Mey," I replied. "De M-e-y."

He hesitated. I was sure that he felt himself to be in rather a tight place, and he didn't know whether or not to acknowledge that the name meant anything to him. But discretion evidently seemed to him the wiser thing, and knowing that he could readily plead that his discretion had caused him to act strangely in case he found that I really did have a right to inquire about De Mey, he again pretended not to understand.

"Did you say, monsieur, that your name was Franklin De Mey?"

"No."

I said that one word and waited. He waited, too. So we stood and looked at each other for some time. Then he broke the silence and showed that his patience was also being strained.

"I do not understand, monsieur. You say your name is not Franklin De Mey. May I ask what it is?"

I avoided his question and explained:

"I asked about Franklin De Mey. Do you know him?"

"Oh, I beg your pardon, monsieur. I misunderstood. No. I do not know Monsieur De Mey."

He started to turn away, yet seemed curious as to why I had approached him.

"Jeannette Deering—do you know of her?"

His attitude changed from suavity to one of open irritation. He indicated by his manner that he thought it presumptuous of me to be asking direct questions of him. He answered shortly, as he started again to turn away:

"No. You have evidently made a mistake."

"Evidently," I retorted. "But it was because I thought your memory long enough to reach from here to the Oriel café!"

That remark at least struck a sensitive spot in his memory. He was assuredly not the gentleman with whom I had had the few words in the Oriel, but he had heard something of those words, though perhaps the name Jeannette Deering had not been among them.

"Who are you?" he asked quickly and pointedly.

I saw no reason for allowing him to believe that I knew he was not the fellow who had approached our table that night. Since the Gaboreaus—or whoever they were—were at such pains to merge four persons into one identity, I preferred to make him think that I believed he had been pretending not to recognize me.

When he asked who I was I gave him an answer definite enough and yet calculated to rub his sleek fur the wrong way. There was something remarkably like the cat about him, too, as there had been about the other fellow. And I hate cats. I said—

"I was the escort of the girl you approached in a mysterious fashion—and to whom you apologized."

I had to add the last. I could not forego the pleasure of letting him know that his brother black-beard had apologized.

But it was my turn to be puzzled when he suddenly pretended to have remembered me and to recognize me. He laughed easily, or what he wished me to think was easily, as though our first encounter had been something of a joke. But I too vividly remembered the parting stare he had given me—or that rather the other fellow had given me over his shoulder when leaving. He insisted that I should come up stairs with him to his room where he could talk it over. And I went.

No doubt he smiled a little when I so abruptly refused the courtesy of entering his room first, and insisted upon following him through the door. Any one who knows me knows that I never take chances. I am always very careful and cautious; and I particularly object to running the risk of having my head cracked from the rear with a billy. It is bad enough to be struck from the front; but I much prefer to have the attack come from that direction.

THE ROOM WAS comfortably furnished, as any room at the Tremaine would be; but there was little to indicate that its occupant was more than a transient. Table and chairs were in it; but the absence of a bed denoted that another room was also in use.

He asked me to excuse him for a minute, and I said certainly. He went into another room.

I did not sit down, but took the precaution to stand away from any one of the doors and to have my back to the wall. I am not like Yang Li: I can not tell if there is any one behind me unless I see him. That Chinaman, however, seems to have ocular faculties at the back of his head.

The man had hardly left the room before he returned; that is, the man who came into the room with me had hardly excused himself and gone through a door before another man who looked like his twin brother came in. The second one was evidently the fellow with whom I had had the encounter at the Oriel.

Which was the real Gaboreau I could not surmise. I could not even have proved that they were different men. The second seemed a trifle shorter, and there was an intangible difference between them. They were both sleek, suave, polite, cold—cunning fellows. I might never have known that there were two men if I had let the first one I met understand who I was instead of keeping him puzzled. He would no doubt then have hurried me up stairs and turned me over to his fellow black-beard and twin brother—I supposed that it was a twin brother—by the simple device of excusing himself and going through a door and permitting the other man to come in as though he were re-entering.

He took up the cue just where the other had dropped it. He spoke again of his tricky memory, and reproached himself very severely for having been, as he said, so dense when we first met. Would I kindly pardon him and explain just what it was that he could do for me? And he was pleased to see that I had come to him, for now we could talk matters over and reach an understanding. The affair at the Oriel had been purely a misunderstanding. He wished to apologize. He had made a mistake. If he had known where to locate me he would have tendered apologies long ago. And just what was it I wanted?

I came to the essential point.

"I want to ask just why you wanted that girl?"

His nimble brain and tongue worked smoothly.

"Why, monsieur, I just told you that it had all been a mistake. The lady was with you all evening. You know that. Unfortunately, I took Miss Deering for some one else—some one with whom I have important business. It is so important, monsieur, that I must be pardoned for not explaining it to you. But of course you would not be interested. And you must have thought me a great fool indeed—as Miss Deering was with you all evening."

Indeed, he was a capable man with his lips. And his very apologetic words were so arranged as to mock me. He knew that I knew that he knew that I knew Miss Deering had not been with me all evening, or anything of the kind. Yet he meant to score decisively a point by pretending to believe the girl had been with me all evening. I could not very well ask him who he thought "Miss Deering" was, since he had so neatly turned the tables on me. But there were several things I could say to him.

"Her name is not Jeannette Deering at all. In fact, she is a young woman who has been warned to look out for you, if your name is Gaboreau, as you said a few minutes ago. And she knew from whom she was running when she dropped into the chair at my table. Very strange, is it not, that you should actually be looking for some other woman and mistake her for one who really knew you and was afraid of you—mistake her for some one with whom you had business?"

He could not, he said, in the least understand how such a strange coincidence had been brought about. He disclaimed all possibility of knowing how his name could have brought terror to the girl, of whom he never had heard before. He was very troubled, exceedingly troubled, to think that he had caused her fright by following her; and he was intensely annoyed to think that he had made himself so disagreeable to me in the Oriel. There was nothing pained him so much as to be disagreeable.

His manner was wholly different from what I had expected it would be after he had sent me a challenge with his eyes at the Oriel. He was so pleasant, so politely humble that I was confident the gentleman had some kind of a plan up his sleeve with which he expected soon to show me what a stupid fellow I was to be crossing purposes with Gaboreau. He was apparently so sure of success that he could afford to be agreeable and simulate an apologetic attitude.

However, I interrupted him to say in just so many words that he was wasting time, and that he knew quite well that I would be a dunce to believe him, and moreover it did not please me to be thought a dunce.

"Oh, oh," he said cheerfully, not unpleasantly at all, "I have heard of you, Monsieur Everhard. It is said that you are a bold man and I may believe it."

"Not at all," I assured him. "I am anything but bold. I try to say what I mean when I wish to be understood. That is all. I am not skilful with words—"

"Ah, but with cards!" he interrupted laughingly.

"Cards, yes. It is my business, the same as yours seems to be words. Now, Gaboreau, you know something of Franklin De Mey; and I want to know a good deal about him."

"De Mey? Franklin De Mey?" He was pretending that the name was foreign to his ears. "I know nothing of him. Why do you ask?"

"One reason is that another peculiar coincidence has occurred. It is strange that you know nothing of De Mey or of Miss Dutton—otherwise Miss Deering. Yet both know of you. And De Mey, evidently being of very uncertain address, had his letters directed to the Tremaine Hotel. The letters were called for, but the hotel knows, or pretends to know nothing of De Mey. Yet this is your headquarters. A peculiar coincidence, is it not?"

"Very!" he answered emphatically and unruffled—actually smiling as though it was one of the strangest and most intriguing coincidences he had heard of.

I looked at him but I did not laugh or smile. Then after a pause, he asked again—

"Why did you speak of—of this Franklin De Mey?"

"It would, I see, be a waste of time to tell you. And if you know nothing of him, you can not possibly be interested. I thank you for your time and," I added slowly, "your courtesy."

His easy, pleasant manner did not for a second leave him. He acted much differently than when we had first parted.

His manner made me wonder; it was the manner of a man who has four aces up his sleeve.

"No doubt we shall meet again, Monsieur Everhard," he said smilingly. "It has indeed been a pleasure to—ah, *apologize* to you. Please call upon me any time you feel that I can be of service. And would you be so good as to convey to the young lady my regrets at having inadvertently annoyed her."

I said nothing. I stood for a full half-minute and looked at him and his eyes did not turn aside, nor did the smile leave his face. I knew that he thought he had me baffled. I knew that he thought I was in no sense his match; but I knew further that the greater part of his assurance was in the comfortable knowledge that he was not standing alone, that back of him lurked the carefully organized and watchful gangsters held to heel in the name of Gaboreau.

For the most part I play my hands alone. I work alone. But I also knew that should I call them there would come to help me men as strong and daring as any that he held to heel; and that they would come and stand with me, not because they were afraid of punishment if they failed or lustful for rewards if they won. No. They were men with whom I had broken bread in friendship.

Aye, and if a man would have real friends he must go to the wastrels of the earth. Property and comforts and good jobs make men conservative. They dare not take chances for fear of losing a home or a salary, a reputation or a soft chair by their hearth. I would like to have told him what I thought of those men, such as he, who moved in gangs. But I said nothing whatsoever. I merely turned to the door and started out.

"Please call again," he laughed after me. "Call on me any time I can be of any assistance."

I rather fancied that I would.

5

IT WAS ARRANGED that Mr. Guernsey should be introduced to a young man, whose name is of no importance, who would take him to the De Meyervelts. Johnny said that there had been some difficulty in getting a promise of the introduction because the young man had said the De Meyervelts were particular; but it was pointed out that he could pretend that Guernsey was a friend from Los Angeles, and the young man called up over the phone and got permission to bring his "friend."

I assured Guernsey that he must be careful not to win. I did not think it likely that he would win, for I was sure that Gaboreau had taken the necessary precautions against any player having too much luck. But I emphasized the statement to Guernsey that he must lose generously: I wanted to see if he was the sort of fellow who could lose graciously. There are very few who can.

I was pleased that he dismissed the matter with a snap of his finger.

"I'll play the limit and bet blind," he assured me.

"And if you do, you will probably win. Don't do it."

"That's a go, but what is it you want me to do there?"

I explained to him that it seemed significant to me that Franklin De Mey should have a name so closely resembling that of the De Meyervelts.

"It would be a strange coincidence," I said, "particularly as he seems to have some connection with Gaboreau, and also as it is pretty well established that the De Meyervelts employ—or rather Gaboreau employs them—to run a gambling palace for the 'four hundred.' You pretend that you are a stranger in the city and that Franklin De Mey's is one of the few names known to you. Inquire about him. You met him in Los Angeles, you know. It would be natural for you to ask about your 'friend,' to try to look him up, and all that.

"And for another thing, note carefully the Gaboreau that you chance to see there. He will probably be in evening clothes, so you won't be able to tell if his street dress has five buttons on the vest, three on the coat, his shoes four eyelets, that there are no ring marks or jewelry on his fingers, and that his tie is a jet black—as I noted on both the Gaboreaus that I met today. But you can tell whether or not his ears have large, slight or no lobes; whether or not at the left of his mouth when he smiles may be seen a canine tooth— only one of the Gaboreaus smiled at me—slightly darker than the others.

"Notice the furrows above his nose—such as appear on the forehead when the eyes are contracted. A gambler's forehead is always furrowed. It comes from scrutinizing closely the cards and roulette numbers. Those on the men's foreheads I met today were not deep. Notice the cuff links. See if they are initialed, as they probably will be, with an ornate 'G.' Notice whatever you can that might be distinctive. I am anxious to discover if either of the men I met today is the one that attends to De Meyervelt's tables. I fancy the same man is always on the job.

"Leave whenever you are ready and telephone my apartment. If you hear no voice answer after the receiver is removed, but simply three sharp blows as though something had hit the mouthpiece, deliver what message you have. Yang is a mute and cannot answer otherwise. But if you speak slowly he will catch every word. I may not be in when you call up."

Mr. Guernsey was rather unexcited over the prospect of his adventure; but he was eager for it. He said that he would do his best, so I let him think it was of extreme importance, but I did not hope that he would be able to find out much.

It was getting late in the afternoon then, and I had some other things to do; so I left him.

I was interested in 22 Stillwater Place, where one of the Gaboreaus was known to spend what was left of his nights after he had presumably finished with the De Meyervelt parties. I could not very well go prowling around there, asking questions of the deaf servants or peeking into windows; but I took a taxi and drove out to have a look at the house and grounds.

It was a large house, an old two-story house, but well built; and was surrounded by a larger yard than is common in the city. The grounds were not well kept up, and much shrubbery was growing rank, as though the place had come from the hands of flower lovers to those that cared little about them. To the rear stood a garage, and the driveway into it passed under an arbor.

I did not think there was much that I could learn if the police had failed to find out anything to their satisfaction; but it cost nothing but five cents for the use of the telephone to make a trial. After looking over the house and ground as well as I could from the street, I drove to a drug store and went to the telephone booth. I made sure that no telephone was listed under the name of Gaboreau, then called upon "Information" for the number of the telephone at 22 Stillwater Place. "Information" said there was no way that she could give it to me; and continued to be disappointing when I also inquired for the number of Antoine Gaboreau.

I knew, as anybody would have known, that a man of such activity as Antoine Gaboreau—or any of the Gaboreaus—would not cut himself off from communication even for a few hours each morning. It was not reasonable to suppose it.

There are many telephones in each city that are not listed in the books, and whose numbers will not be given out by the company upon request. I was confident that there was a telephone of this kind in 22 Stillwater Place.

Every complication has a solution. It is not always easy to find, and often one may not find it; but the solution exists just the same. I wanted the telephone number all the more when I found, or suspected, that the telephone was private and was no doubt used only by those close to the chief Gaboreau. There was really the possibility that one might learn something of importance by using the phone. Anyway, I wanted the number.

I have a peculiar faculty for thinking quickly. Sometimes I feel that there is a section of my brain which anticipates my needs and prepares ideas so that when I need them they are ready. I realized that there was only one feasible way for me to get hold of that number without having to stall around and bribe some telephone company employee. So I decided to go for Johnny Blix and make him take me to his friend the inspector.

I stay away from the police department because I try to do very little that is wrong, in which case they have no need of me; and because in the little affairs in which I interest myself from time to time I try to take care of all the details myself, so that I have no need of the police. My friend the police commissioner knows me only socially, and I have always made it a point to ask no favors of any kind of him. I am afraid that I might possibly make him curious.

But I knew that "Information" would treat with consideration an inquiry as to the phone number at 22 Stillwater Place if it came from a police inspector; yet I had no intention of letting the inspector make the request for me, or of letting him know that it was to be made at all. If he had overlooked the detail of finding out Gaboreau's phone number it was no doubt because he regarded it as a matter of no importance.

And Johnny Blix was mistaken if he thought that I never made use of him or his gratitude for the little service I had done him at one time and another. I soon had him into the taxi with me and was on the way to headquarters while I explained that he had to leave me alone in the inspector's office for a minute, because I did not want the inspector to know what place I was trying to locate.

I had never met this inspector before. Ostensibly I was brought to tell him of how I had mentioned to Johnny about seeing two Gaboreaus that afternoon at the Tremaine Hotel. Johnny, knowing of the inspector's interest, thought he would be glad to hear my story.

My tale was a little vague and indefinite. I told of having seen one black-beard go into a room and another—at least I thought it was another—come out. But I remarked that I would not be willing to swear that they were different men.

The inspector was plainly dissatisfied that my story was so vague. I did not blame him. The police are pestered with people who know little or nothing of what they try to make into a tale of importance. Of course, I did not relate to what extent I had spoken with the Gaboreaus, or why. He might not have been so lacking in interest if I had.

While I was talking, Johnny left the room and went into the hallway. Presently, as I had suggested to him, he poked his head into the door and with an air of mysterious importance and urgency asked the inspector to step out for a moment. And as the inspector was leaving, I asked if I might use his telephone. He said certainly, and thought no more of it.

I then called "Information" again and said:

"This is police headquarters. I want the telephone number of Antoine Gaboreau, 22 Stillwater Place. It is important and we are in a hurry."

After some delay, in which no doubt my call was verified as being from headquarters, and perhaps somebody in authority gave permission to disclose the information, she told me the number and rang it for me.

Almost at once an irascible, snappy, high-pitched voice—unmistakably that of an old man—demanded without preliminary to know what I wanted.

"Is this Gaboreau?" I asked.

"Yes. Who else did you think it was, you fool. What do you want?"

"Franklin De Mey is in trouble," I ventured.

"What's that? What's that? Who are you. De Mey"—
he spoke the name with a sneer—"—— fool. Crazy thing
anyway. Who are you?"

"He is in serious trouble," I answered.

"What the ——'s he done now? Lunatic!"

"I can't tell more than that," I said.

The fierce voice was suspicious. I perceived that instantly
by the suavity it tried to assume in getting me to say who
I was.

"I can tell you nothing more than that," I answered.

"Who are you? Who gave you this number?"

"Whom would you imagine gave it to me?" I asked.

"De Mey, as you call him, doesn't know it," he said testily.

Then I knew that there was such a person as De Mey
and that De Mey was not his real name. Perhaps that was
why it had been so hard for me to locate him.

"Who gave you this number?" he began, and went on
without allowing me to answer. And he had a short temper,
for at once he was speaking furiously. "Tell me that! By
—— you will tell me!"

He forgot all of his assumed suavity and demanded the
information in the manner of one who is accustomed to
have men tremble when he speaks. I never insult a man
except to his face, or I might have made an insolent reply.

The telephone call had given me little information; but at
that, more than I had really hoped to learn came from it. I
had felt sure that any one answering would think that I was
a friend, and so perhaps speak a bit indiscreetly to me. But
I was confident that I was talking to the *real* Gaboreau at
last. The black-bearded fellows might be suave and catlike;

but this man was avowedly tigerish. And I was sure that he was the real power behind the name of Gaboreau.

I knew it would be useless to try to get anything more from him, and I wanted to finish before the inspector returned. So I hung up, then called central again and gave instructions—in the potent name of police headquarters—that no information should be given out to Gaboreau as to where the telephone connection with him had been made from.

WHEN THE INSPECTOR returned he was plainly disgusted. I did not know what yarn Johnny had concocted to entertain him out in the hallway; but it had obviously not been satisfactory. The inspector was curt with me, too. He thanked me rather sardonically for having offered my information about the Gaboreaus at the Tremaine, but added that I did not seem to know much about police work if I thought anything so vague as I had brought him would be of value. I admitted that I knew very little about the police or their work, and I fancy that I did it with a trace of humbleness. At least I tried to appear humble.

Johnny was much perturbed. As we left the police station he explained that he had not had the trace of an idea as to what he would talk to the inspector about when he called him into the hallway; and for want of anything else as a subject he had begun to protest that his place was not paying him anything like proportionate with the rake-off that found its way into the inspector's pocket for the privilege of going unraided. Naturally that had peeved the inspector, both because it was an inopportune time and place to mention such things and because it was a protest with which he could not possibly find favor at any time or place.

Johnny felt badly that he had put himself out of grace with the inspector, who had really been a good friend, though well imbursed for his friendships. Some inspectors, Johnny informed me, even when well imbursed, did not make good friends.

I expressed the hope that something might turn up which would reinstate Johnny in the favor of the inspector; but Johnny was pessimistic.

"This Gaboreau's a hoodoo, Mr. Everhard. He's got me in Dutch with the inspector. He'll get you in bad, too. I don't like to interfere, and I ain't interfering. But I wish you'd call it off. Take a trip or something. You haven't a chance in the world. The cards are marked and every member of the gang has a hold-out up his sleeve. Better cash in and quit, Mr. Everhard. You ain't lost nothing yet. The secret of poker and life is to know when to quit."

"That's right," I said. "But this isn't the time to quit, Johnny. Nobody ever wins a pot if he doesn't stay for the showdown."

When I got back to the apartment Vivian was already rigged out in the red wig and in Jessie's clothes; and she posed before Jessie and me for our comment on her appearance. But she objected in playful tones, but none the less sincerely, against wearing the long, flaming, red gloves.

"I'll be arrested sure! It will be committing an atrocity."

I told her that she might carry them; and at once she poked them out of sight in her bag. She did it to tease, for she knew very well what I meant when I said she might carry them.

"No fair. You must have them in sight."

And she gingerly removed the gloves.

Jessie was extremely curious to know what it was all about and what did I expect would happen, and what would I do if "something" did happen. Vivian asked no questions. I believe she would have packed up and have gone blindfolded around the world if I had asked her to; and never a question would have been asked.

I was confident that none but De Mey himself would be able to tell that Vivian was not Jessie, and since he seemed to have an aversion to showing himself, I did not expect De Mey to put in an appearance. If he had not been able to appear on the street the night the girl who loved him had arrived in the city, I did not know of any reason to expect him on the street this evening.

I left the apartment first, walked a few blocks, took a taxi and drove back, then waited until Vivian came out and got into the taxi that had been called and kept waiting at the apartment-house entrance for her. I took that little precaution in the hope that it might not be discovered that I was accompanying her. I hardly expected that I would be able to deceive any one who might have been detailed to watch, but I thought it as well to try.

For the same reason, when we came within sight of the Oriel café, Vivian would get out of her taxi and walk along the street alone, and I would have the driver of mine move slowly, so that I could keep her in sight. I felt that she could very capably engage whoever she was to meet in conversation and probably find out something of interest to me, for I had told her everything connected with the affair, except that Mr. Guernsey was in the city.

When the Oriel came in sight, Vivian stopped and got out.

I told the driver to keep about a hundred feet behind her, and to stop when she stopped to talk to any one.

I was surprised to see there was considerable traffic on the street. There were several automobiles by the curbing, and some that passed up and down the street. Three machines were in front of the Oriel. It was as though the quiet little café had suddenly become fashionable.

I peered through the glass of the taxi and watched Vivian as well as I could. I saw her walk along swinging the red gloves conspicuously. I saw a man step from the curbing, lift his hat and speak to her.

She stopped and stepped to the edge of the curbing.

Then many things happened at once. I saw her suddenly jerked into the open door of a taxi that stood by the curbing. Its motor was running and it got under way at once. I shouted to my driver, but he had stopped and seemed to be taking an hour to get started again.

I started to jump out and run forward, but the instant I saw the other taxi was getting away, I knew that I could not catch it on foot and I shouted again to my driver to follow and overtake the taxi that was darting off. We started, and the next moment a heavy car rammed us. The collision was severe enough to put my taxi out of the running.

I jumped out and looked hurriedly around for another machine to chase the one that I caught a last glimpse of as it turned the corner.

I am not excitable, but I came very near being excited at that moment. To have Vivian seized and carried off under my eyes was something that I had not thought possible. I had not believed that any gang would be daring enough to do such a thing at that hour on that street. It was not only that it took a daring gang, but it took a large and capably organized gang.

Johnny Blix's repeated warning flashed across my mind: he had said I would need a royal flush up my sleeve to beat Gaboreau. Just then I wanted a fast machine. But a fast machine would have done no good, for the taxi had easily had time to turn three or four corners and be lost from pursuit. As much as anything, I was surprised that none of the pedestrians passing by had not seen the struggling woman being dragged into the taxi and had not protested. All the people in sight could not possibly have been arranged for by Gaboreau. But the whole affair had been carried off in a flash.

Now any one could have taken my money, could have taken what is more precious than that, my health, and I would have tried to find some sort of philosophical consolation. Money and life are all a part of the hazardous game. But Vivian—whoever touched her was sure to have whatever vengeance I could invoke launched at his head. That she had been seized for another woman meant something, but not much to me. It meant that the attack had not been directed against her. But that offered no consolation. She was gone, and had it been in my power, I would have blown that end of the city into the bay to have had her returned.

But for the moment I was very nearly helpless. My taxi had been rammed intentionally and hard. It was very cleverly done. I called out to first one and then to another machine, but no driver would take me.

At once a crowd gathered about the injured machine.

Gaboreau did not need to have arranged for the crowd. It always comes wherever there is the least commotion. It springs up in deserted streets, pours itself out of doorways and down stairs, up from cellars and from around the corners. It was the same stupid, gaping, wide-eyed crowd that gathers everywhere there is an accident—the vulture-eyed that swarm more rapidly to a smashed auto or an injured body than the hideous birds to carrion. Gaboreau may have counted on it, but he did not need to plan it. The crowd can always be depended on to rush forward and stare.

I STARTED TO push my way through the enclosing circle when a hand fell on my shoulder and a voice that I recognized spoke. It was a smooth, soft, velvet voice touched with a foreign accent.

I turned and faced the Gaboreau I had first met in the Oriel. He wore a motorist's coat and goggles, but I recognized him. He began graciously expressing regrets that our meeting had been in the nature of an accident.

Accident indeed! I listened, for there was nothing else to do, but my blood was hot with anger. I did not show it. I did not intend to let him know just how I felt. I had no intention of either warning him that he was on dangerous ground or of letting him gloat at my discomfiture.

He blamed my chauffeur for awkwardness, explaining that he was driving his own car himself and that he had tried to turn aside, but that the clumsy fellow at the wheel of my machine would not get out of the way.

But strangely enough, his car had not suffered. A great big heavy underslung thing of foreign make, it had driven its steel-capped radiator squarely against the front wheel of the taxi and wrenched the steering-gear so that it was helpless. No doubt the hood of his car had been designed originally for just such opportune collisions.

Gaboreau conducted himself with admirable finesse, though he must have known that I did not believe a word that he said. He spluttered amiably about the carelessness of my driver, and apologized for not having been able to avoid the collision. He talked and talked. Perhaps he was trying to hold me until all chances of my being able to pursue the taxi that had carried off Vivian were lost.

Of course, he said, such a meeting had been furthermost from his thoughts when we last parted some few hours before. That was how he dug at me; sarcastically cunningly, artistically.

But it was an ill time for such stage play. I said nothing to show that I did not believe it was an accident. I pretended to be entirely credulous and unsuspecting. I did not intend that he should get off so easily as he wished. I had an idea, too, that he was so taken with his own cleverness that he would tumble into a little design of my own.

It suited my purpose to appear vexed but agreeable. I seemed to have forgotten the unpleasantness of our previous meetings. I explained that I was in very much of a hurry; that an important engagement would be broken if I could not make quick time.

Then he sardonically proposed to take me himself, since he had unfortunately been the cause of my delay. He no doubt thought that would be the climax to his joke.

Perhaps he was a bit surprised when I accepted his offer. But he did not try to withdraw.

"It is very kind of you," I said, looking at my watch. "But I am in something of haste. I simply can not afford to be late."

"No trouble at all," he laughed. "It is a pleasure, monsieur. A real pleasure. I told you to call on me whenever I could be of service."

The inevitable policeman had arrived to take the numbers of the cars and our names. The injured taxi limped to the curbing to await a mechanic. The crowd thinned somewhat.

Gaboreau and I got into his big car. I was glad to see that he accepted no other passengers, for I caught the gesture with which he waved aside a man that came up as though expecting to be invited to get in, and who would, no doubt, have been introduced to me as a friend. But Gaboreau evidently thought himself a match, and more than a match for me. No doubt he had looked up my reputation and made inquiries; but the chances are that he had not believed all that he had heard.

Gaboreau started up the machine and asked me where I wanted to go. For a moment I pretended to be getting my bearings, and the delay permitted us to get a half block or more away from the Oriel. Then for an answer I swiftly withdrew a thirty-eight automatic from my pocket and pressed the muzzle against his side.

"Keep both hands on the wheel," I directed, "and drive just as I say."

"But, monsieur—"

"I shall do the talking. All of it. Don't speak unless you are asked to."

"But, my friend—"

"Another interruption like that and I am afraid something will happen to you. I am not in a very good humor just at present. And if you fail in the least to do as I say, if you make the slightest signal to any one, well—you will probably regret it. That is, if one has regrets after being consigned to the morgue."

He believed me, too. It was just as well that he did.

I was very insistent that he should not take either hand off the wheel. I could watch them there and I knew that as long as he kept them on the wheel that he was helpless, though I added a warning that if he had motor trouble of any kind or another accident that caused him to stop, I would consider it as an interruption and take the necessary precautions.

"And," I added, "you had better do a little silent praying that nothing goes wrong with your engine."

He understood perfectly.

I knew better than to demand that he follow the machine that had carried off Vivian, though I did not doubt that he knew exactly where it had gone; but I was sure that if I permitted him to drive anywhere he chose, on the pretense of following that taxi, that he would run me into some kind of a trap. As long as I could keep him away from his friends I had him at a disadvantage.

No doubt he thought that I did not know what to do with him, for I made him drive first down one street, then down another, and around and around corners. But I wished to make sure that we were not being followed, and if we were followed, I wished to shake off the shadowers. I did not think that we were being watched for it seemed likely that this Gaboreau was important enough to be considered able to take care of himself. Perhaps he would have been had I not got the drop as soon as I did. I meant to keep it, too; and I knew very well what I was up to. He would find out soon enough.

Allowing him to drive only as I directed, we went up and down the city until I saw no one was keeping us in sight, then we steered for the residence district.

Then I told him that he might talk as much as he pleased. And he seemed pleased to talk volubly, though I must say that he took the situation gracefully. He was almost witty at times, and protested amiably that this was no way to treat a friend. He evidently thought I was wholly at a loss to know what to do with him, and must have been quite sure that soon I would turn him loose and leave him free to exact what revenge he thought befitting my impudence.

My sense of humor was not sufficiently developed to appreciate witticisms while Vivian was in possible dangers; so I did not respond. I told him that he might talk, for I knew we were away from the place where he might be able to shout to friends, and I had hoped that he would be so angry that he would let slip something informative. But he was not apparently the least angry. My silence even failed to check his fluency. It was remarkable. I had never before been up against a man who could be so gracefully facetious while his life hung literally on a hair-trigger.

I can see how that easy, light, half cynical, and carefully Frenchified speech of his might have been disconcerting to any one whose nerves were loose. It made me wonder what he might have tucked up his sleeve. But I was not troubled over him. It takes more than a facile tongue to make me nervous when my finger rests on the trigger, and I knew perfectly well what was going to happen to him.

When we came to a spot quiet enough to suit my purpose I made him stop the machine.

"Stand up," I said.

He stood up.

"Put your arms above your head and keep them there."

He lifted his arms and I pressed the muzzle snugly against his stomach.

"Well prepared, aren't you?" I remarked as I took a gun from his hip pocket—where crude workmen always carry such things.

He was better prepared than I had fancied, though. I searched him, and did it thoroughly. I began with his hat-band and ended by making him remove his shoes. From his vest pocket I took a small, viciously effective revolver, one of the miniature kind that may be held in the palm of the hand. But he had not had a chance to get at it. From his belt I removed a dagger.

Perhaps he had a trace of the Southern Italian in him for all of his Frenchiness—he was dark enough to have had such ancestry, and if he had it, no doubt felt unarmed without a stiletto. Out of his coat pocket I took a small, oblong tube, built something like a compressed air gun. I had a suspicion as to what it was, and leveled it at his face.

"For God's sake don't!" he cried, forgetting to put the Frenchiness into his voice.

"What is it?" I asked.

He did not answer.

"Have to try it, then," I remarked, again pointing it at him.

He drew back until I thought he would tumble from the machine; then he gasped—

"Vitriol!"

I came near casting the thing aside as one would upon finding that he had a viper by the tail. But the vitriol gun had certain advantages. It was noiseless and effective. One could use it without attracting attention for blocks around. Instead of dropping it I held it leveled at his face.

"Don't move," I said quietly, soothingly. "There is no danger—at present. Perhaps none at all unless you become disagreeable. But I am glad to have this. It is noiseless. However, please remember that though I hold this in my right hand I am not putting all my trust in it. You might seize my hand and dodge the spray of vitriol, but my left hand is not far from a high-power automatic—with a hair-trigger. And I always carry guns cocked. Some people may think it dangerous—and it is for some people.

"This afternoon you were good enough to say that you had heard of me, and that I had the reputation for being something of a bold man. Perhaps that reputation isn't deserved, for I never take chances, as you can see. I prefer to take the drop.

"This afternoon you also expressed the hope of the pleasure of meeting me again. You are a most fortunate man to have your wishes so quickly fulfilled. And since you have heard of me, you know that I do two things besides playing cards. I keep my word and I shoot straight. And now I want to tell you something before I ask a question.

"You can probably bluff me out and pretend that you do not know, for you are a good actor, and I have at present no way of proving that you might dally with the truth.

But if I ever find out that you have lied to me you will very much regret it. I never make more direct threats than that, Monsieur Gaboreau. Now for the question: where is that girl?"

I threw the question at him and pressed the vitriol gun close into his face.

He shrank back, gasping:

"Oh, my God, don't! I don't know. Honestly. I don't know."

"Be careful."

"I don't know. Before God, I don't."

"It might be just as well to leave God's name out of this. Think again."

"I don't know. Take it away"—the vitriol gun was closer to his face, a handsome face of its kind, and he was anxious not to have it marred.

"Be careful," I cautioned him. "There is a bare chance that the old tiger of Stillwater Place may not be able to help you as much as you expect."

His eyes showed amazement.

"Oh, yes," I bluffed, "there are many things known about Gaboreau—or you Gaboreaus. For instance, there were two of you talking with me this afternoon at the Tremaine. But as I remarked, you may find it unpleasant if I discover that you are lying. I ask you where that girl was taken, and why?"

"I don't know. I haven't lied. We knew you were in that taxi—I was to stall it. That is all I know."

That was no place to hold a third-degree inquiry, so I continued the search. Out of his inside coat pockets I took papers and letters, and as these left his possession he seemed for the first time to realize that he was in a tight situation. His gay and facetious manner had left him and did not return. He looked gloomy, depressed.

When I was sure that everything transferable had been removed to my pockets, I told him to drive on and gave him directions that were not aimlessly made.

I was in more of a hurry than my leisurely search might indicate, but I have found that even in haste it is well to go slow and cover the ground well. Moreover, I am very chary about taking chances. There is a great difference between doing something along the lines of a carefully planned design and in rushing in blindly, expecting to plug through blindly, or to shoot one's way out. I usually know what I am about. I knew very well this time.

When I came to a spot that suited me, I made him leave the car standing at the curb and walk by my side. I made him walk and walk block after block until we came to my apartment. I had left the car at a distance because I did not want any of his friends to locate it near my place of residence and get suspicious that I might have something to do with the disappearance of this particular Gaboreau. No doubt I would quickly enough be suspected, for we had been seen driving off together, but that would not be nearly such incriminating evidence as if his car were discovered standing around the corner from my doorstep.

He was a very poor hostage to hold in exchange for Vivian, but he was better than nothing. So I told him when he stepped out of the car that we would walk for some distance. I also told him that he could, if he were desperate enough, call to any of the pedestrians we passed, or beg protection of a policeman if we chanced to meet one, but that I would not advise him to do any such thing.

I intimated that it might lead to sudden unpleasantness. He understood perfectly. He understood so perfectly that he kept his hands in the side pockets of his coat, as I suggested, pulled his hat over his eyes, and walked beside me all of the way without looking to the left or to the right. Perhaps it was just as well that he had heard something about me before; and no doubt he was beginning to believe much that he had heard.

I TOOK HIM into my room. Yang Li arose from the floor as we came in.

"Watch him," I said to the yellow-visaged, keen-eyed old fellow.

Yang made a quick movement and shot out his left hand as some men do to shoot their cuffs forward—a long, glittering blade was in his hand.

Gaboreau stared hard at the knife. No one spoke. No one moved. The Chinaman stood poised easily against the wall, his sharp, beady eyes on Gaboreau's face. Gaboreau looked nowhere but at the knife. He seemed fascinated. After a long time he glanced at Yang's face, then his eyes were drawn again to the fine shimmering ray of steel.

I spoke slow and distinctly and said:

"Once again I ask you to tell me where that girl is and why was she taken? Who did it?"

His nerves were badly wrenched. He trembled a little and his voice was not firm. But he was no coward. He said that he did not know, and I knew very well that he was lying.

"Denials are no good to me," I answered. "And you must see by this time that I don't care to hear them. If you can't tell me where the girl has been taken—well, you will be of no further use to me."

With that, I made a significant gesture toward the lean Chinaman, who stood with the blade slightly advanced, as though ready to lunge.

Nerves. It was a severe test for any man's. He must have known that Yang's arm would have shot out at the slightest word from me. One little thrust of that long, keen blade and Gaboreau would never more dream of vengeance on me! He understood that, too. And he must have understood that it was little I cared whether or not the arm did shoot out. But he protested ignorance; and he lied.

I knew he was lying, and I told him so. I told him quietly, unoffensively, for I do not abuse helpless men. I knew that he knew something of where the girl had been taken and why. He was a man of too much importance not to have known something of the game in which he had played a leading part that night in the Oriel and this night in the street by the Oriel. But not one word of information could I get. And I did not wonder that Gaboreau, the real Gaboreau, was a man of sinister power if he had such loyal fellows as this to work for him.

I thought of calling Gaboreau's attention to the fact that the girl he had tried to carry away was safely in my apartment. I could show her to him. But I did not do it. I felt that while he might be very much surprised, he would still have the same reasons for secrecy, if not in fact greater reasons. He might get it into his head that I was likely to be a match for even the Gaboreau gang, thus, apparently, to regain the girl with so little loss of time, when he had made I did not know what preparations to hold her; and that he would be less inclined to talk than ever.

He was silent now largely because he expected me to be swiftly dealt with by his friends. Convince him that I might possibly be a little more clever than his friends, since they, or at least some of them, had failed to hold the girl, and it would be much harder to make him talk. I intended, if other measures failed me, to hold another conversation with him, a more serious one, and I meant to make him talk.

I saw it would be a waste of time to question him further. But I made it plain that I had not believed a word he said, and that he would probably regret having tried to deceive me.

If he thought I was going to let him go with nothing but a threat, he was badly fooled. I had no intention of letting him go. I did not intend to let him go at all if I could help it, for there were already enough black-bearded Gaboreaus loose in the world to keep me busy for some hours. So I set about gagging and trussing him. And when he was tied so that he could not move, yet not severely bound, I laid him down by the wall and put a pillow under his head.

Then I spoke to Yang, and the Chinaman sank to the floor in the center of the room and fixed his eyes on the face of the bound man.

I had no further need to worry about the activity of this particular Gaboreau.

Jessie was in the next room.

When I went in I found her nervous from waiting and

imagining things, and she bounced at me with a storm of hysterical questions.

I told her something of what had happened and she was badly frightened and worried. She was good enough to say, and I liked her for it for she really seemed to mean it, that she wished she had gone instead of Vivian.

I wished it too, but I did not say so.

"If we could only find Franklin!" she wailed. "He would save her. But that terrible Gaboreau. Franklin said that no man could fight him."

"No?" I asked.

It was a theatrical thing to do, but she with her talk of Franklin and Gaboreau was exasperating. So I took her gently by the arm and I led her to the door. I threw it open, then pointed across the room where Gaboreau the mighty and dangerous—as she pictured him—lay bound and gagged like a fowl ready for the spit.

She almost shrieked her amazement, and one question stumbled over another—they left her tongue so fast.

"There is nothing to explain," I said. "This is merely a worthless hostage that fell into my hands after Vivian disappeared. As you see by his eyes, he is almost as amazed as yourself. Yes. He is wondering how on earth you got back here so quickly. He thinks that his good friends must have gone to sleep and let you slip through their fingers. Well, let him figure it out for himself."

Then I closed the door.

I went on to explain to her, however, that Gaboreau being there did not mean that she was by any means safe on the street.

"But you are safe here. Stay here. If you hear any suspicious noises, throw open the door and call Yang. You may not like him, and you may be afraid of him. But I know Yang well enough to be sure that he wouldn't let some one else meet a woman with whom he had an appointment because he was afraid to come out of his cellar."

For an instant she was shocked into silence, then she exclaimed in an angry, tearful voice:

"That's horrid of you! Compare Franklin to that Chinaman!"

"No. I am comparing Franklin to a cowardly Chinaman. Not to Yang Li."

With that I left her.

6

I LOOKED AT MY watch as I closed the door and shut out the indignant sobbing of the girl. I was sorry to have made her angry, but she with her talk of Franklin De Mey made me quite irritable.

It was after ten o'clock. I wished that I might have heard from Guernsey, but Yang said there had been no telephone call. I wanted to get some trace of Franklin De Mey—or whoever he was—above all things just at that moment; and Guernsey's visit to the De Meyervelt home was the only expectation that I had of doing so.

After I had gone down to the street, I even returned and questioned Gaboreau again, asking about De Mey. But as I expected he said nothing except that he did not know such a person or to whom I referred. I had no time to lose. I was sure, though, that once I got my hands on De Mey there would be no trouble in locating Vivian.

Since it suited Gaboreau to pretend ignorance, I thought I might as well search for other sources of information. Besides, I needed hostages.

I found a taxi and drove to the Tremaine Hotel.

I told my driver to wait for me, as I expected to bring back a sick friend.

I looked carefully through the lobby but saw nothing of the other Gaboreau. I went up to the clerk and asked:

"Have you seen Mr. Gaboreau around?"

"No sir. I think he is in his room. Just a minute and I'll find out for you."

"Never mind. Never mind," I said. "I expected to find him in the lobby as he isn't feeling well and I am to take him away. I'll go up to his room. Perhaps he is lying down."

"Shall I call the doctor?"

"It won't be necessary—I hope. I'll go up and see."

I bought an evening paper off the newsstand and went up to the room. A penny newspaper is a very effective instrument at times. I expected to make good use of it—at least get my money's worth.

I approached the door cautiously and listened. I heard footsteps crossing to and fro and a man whistling softly. He did not sound like a sick man. I would have to play the rôle of a poor physician. That would be easy enough since I had found out that he was alone.

I retreated several paces then came forward boldly so that my footsteps might be heard, and thumped loudly on the door.

Gaboreau, the other one, of course, opened it.

He looked at me coldly, appraisingly, no doubt wondering what on earth I was doing there again.

"Here," I said angrily, waving my penny newspaper in his face, "you are the cause of this! Look at it. Look here. Read this."

He was entitled to the opinion that I was crazy, but naturally he took the paper and held it in both hands, just as I expected he would, and began trying to see what was in the article I pointed out that could possibly have aroused my anger against him.

Both of his hands were out of his pockets and he was wholly off guard, so I was really taking no chances at all when I pushed an automatic into his face and told him to be quiet.

It may be that he had never heard of me; or it may be that he had a misconception of courage. He dropped the paper and made a grab for my gun, at the same time clawing at his coat pocket with the other hand. Likely enough he thought he had a lunatic to deal with.

I let him grab the gun which I held in my left hand. Then with the one in my right I hit him on the head, and he sank quietly to the floor.

I dragged him into the room and closed the door. No one had seen. It was a quiet hotel, and except for the anger in my voice, there had been no noise; and that was not much, for I am not a noisy person even when simulating anger. Anger may seem a queer ruse to throw a man off guard, but there are times when it is effective.

I hurriedly searched the rooms, but found nothing that seemed important. I hardly expected to find anything, for this being known as something of a headquarters for Gaboreau, it was not likely that anything of importance would be kept there, since it might fall into the hands of the police in case they found evidence elsewhere that made them willing to force a search.

From the unconscious man I removed a vitriol gun and a dagger, as well as some personal papers which I did not have opportunity to look at carefully.

I was anxious to get out. When I came to the Tremaine I had expected to bring this particular Gaboreau out with me. If I had found him in the lobby I would have tried to get him to take me to his room—where he would have been taken with sudden illness. I did not know how long he would remain unconscious, for though the blow had been anything but gentle he might begin to recover almost any minute.

But I felt reasonably safe in asking the clerk to send up a bell-boy at once to help me get Mr. Gaboreau to his car. Also I mentioned that Mr. Gaboreau was to be rushed away to where he could be given proper attention, and I again refused to consider the house doctor. Most assuredly I did not want him.

I put Gaboreau's hat on and had him sitting upright in a chair when the boy arrived. I wanted that hat to stay on, too. And I held him upright in the chair and talked to him as though he were sick, not unconscious.

"He may faint before we get him down," I said to the boy, extending a dollar, "but we can't wait for a stretcher."

Between us we practically carried him, but I doubt if the boy realized it. I drew Gaboreau's arm around my shoulder and so bore him that, while we walked slowly, it looked as though we were assisting a very drunk or sick man; and most of the weight was on me. I saw signs that he was beginning to come to, and as we started through the lobby I was much afraid that he would recover consciousness enough to make a protest before I had him safely inside the taxi.

Of course, a number of people gathered about to look and to comment and suggest and try to help. The clerk came from behind the counter and was very solicitous, but he remembered that I had mentioned before I went up that Mr. Gaboreau was not well.

I had much difficulty in keeping Gaboreau's hat on without seeming overly anxious to have it stay on. But I was anxious. Very much so. I didn't want any one to notice the large bump that I had raised. It might induce questions, suspicions, investigations and delay. There were enough questions anyway. Gaboreau was well known, as any man would be who lived in a hotel and had such a mysterious reputation as his own. I wondered if many or any people knew that there were two Gaboreaus, maybe more, living under the name of one. I wondered then and I have wondered since how the two of them managed so effectively to have a common identity. A wonderful organization, that Gaboreau gang.

At last Gaboreau was safely stowed inside the taxi, and for the benefit of those who had followed us out under the marquee I gave the chauffeur instructions to drive to the Hallowell Hospital.

But after we had gone a few blocks, I told the driver that my friend was feeling so much better that I thought I could take him home; and I gave another and entirely fictitious address.

Gaboreau was feeling better, too. He opened his eyes and looked hard at me, but he made no move. I knew he was trying to think, and was wondering what had happened to him and how he came to be there. Perhaps he expected to wake up in a minute and find himself comfortably in his own bed with nothing but the memory of a nightmare to trouble him.

I merely put the vitriol gun in front of his face and remarked—

"You are not feeling very well, so it would be best if you made no sound or move."

He understood. But I could see that he was much mystified as to what it was all about. Evidently he had a severe headache for his hand started up to his head, then he withdrew it quickly and looked at me apprehensively. I had said not to make a move.

"You may rub your head. I might have been more gentle, but you were inclined to be obstreperous. No, you don't need to talk—now."

After that his hand went repeatedly to the side of his head and he rubbed tenderly, speculatively, the large bump that stood out like a turkey egg.

IN TIME THE driver drew up at the address that I had given him. I do not know whose house it was and I did not care. The driver could show it to as many people as came inquiring for the place to which he had driven us for all that it mattered to me. I expected that somebody would be looking him up and making inquiries before morning, and it may be that the good people of the house were mystified and annoyed by strangers who came asking curious questions. I never took the trouble to find out.

I told the driver when he drew up at the curbing that my friend was feeling so much better that we would be able to make out all right without assistance, so he cheerfully drove off with a modest tip.

Then I explained to Gaboreau that we would have to walk for some blocks, as my apartment lay a half-mile away; and that while I would gladly have saved him the trouble if it had been convenient, still I did not think it was worth taking the chance of having that driver remember my apartment the next day in case there was inquiry as to who had taken Monsieur Gaboreau from his room at the Tremaine.

Gaboreau seemed to agree with me. That is, he made no objections. But in an injured tone he inquired as to what it was all about and what the devil I was up to.

I told him that the street was a poor place to talk over private matters, and holding the vitriol gun at the edge of my pocket so its moral force might not be lost on him, I conducted him to my apartment, past the sleepy boy on watch at the telephone switch, avoided the elevator and led him into the room where Yang Li solemnly kept watch over the bound body lying against the wall.

It was no doubt rather disquieting and astonishing for both Gaboreaus when they looked into each other's eyes, and each saw that the other was a prisoner. A fine to-do indeed when the king-pins of the Gaboreau gang should be herded into a room in a down-town apartment and not be allowed to move a muscle or speak a word without permission. They stared and stared at each other, and the unvoiced question was: how on earth were you caught?

"Now, Mr. Gaboreau," I said to the second one to be brought in, "if you will give me a little of your attention I may say something of interest."

He turned toward me, but glanced again and again at his double on the floor.

"Give me your whole attention, please. I like to look into the eyes of the party to whom I am speaking."

His eyes met mine.

"Something has happened this evening," I went on,

"which has called for this unusual procedure. You must not fail to understand that since I have taken the trouble to bring you here I am not willing to be put off with denials or pretension of ignorance. You must further realize that my man here—" I indicated the inscrutable Yang who stood with the sinister blade drooping in his hand—"has no scruples against drawing a drop or two of blood if the occasion seems to call for blood.

"Furthermore, you might as well understand that I know that you and your gagged double there are merely pawns in this little affair which has engaged my attention. No doubt both of you have felt from time to time that you were captains, or at least lieutenants. But you have been nothing more than orderlies carrying out orders—"here I was making something of a guess, but there was little risk in such a guess after my experience over the telephone that afternoon—"orders from the old man at 22 Stillwater Place."

I could see that he, too, was surprised at the familiarity with which I mentioned the old man of Stillwater Place. No doubt his identity was guarded with much secrecy.

"This evening a girl was seized and carried away from in front of the Oriel café. Where has she been taken?"

"I do not know," Gaboreau answered promptly and calmly.

"Think it over, think it over."

"I do not know," he repeated.

"Yang," I said significantly.

The Chinaman stepped forward noiselessly and swiftly as a shadow and gave the knife a twirl with his wrist.

"It would perhaps be better, Mr. Gaboreau," I said, "if

you were less speedy with your answers. I am not interested in what you don't know. Cudgel your memory a bit. And do not feel secure because you see your double, or brother, or whoever he is, lying comfortably there by the wall with a pillow under his head. Once more, Mr. Gaboreau, where was it arranged to have the girl taken this evening?"

He paused for a few seconds. Yang's knife was enough to make any one pause. Then he said—

"I do not know."

"No?"

"No."

"But you knew she was to be taken some place?"

"Yes."

"Ah, I see. We are getting on. And how did you learn that?"

"Felix told me."

"And just what did Felix tell you?"

He hesitated and glanced over his shoulder. I touched his arm significantly, but perhaps not until the eyes of the bound man on the floor had flashed a message asking him to deny all knowledge of the plan to carry off the girl.

Gaboreau faced me again, and said:

"Felix just mentioned that a girl was to be taken off this evening. I suppose that he referred to the same one you have in mind."

"You suppose it? Don't you know?"

"No—that is—"

"Don't fumble for words, Mr. Gaboreau. Speak promptly and distinctly, and if you again look at Felix there, I shall ask Yang to bring his knife closer to you. It is a sharp knife, Mr. Gaboreau, a very sharp knife."

"I can see that it is," he said.

"Make sure that you do not feel that it is. Now you started to say that Felix had been instructed or detailed to superintend the job, didn't you?"

Gaboreau appeared for a moment as though he intended to refuse to answer; but he changed his mind and thought it better to lie.

"No. Felix attends to his business and I know nothing of it."

"But you said that he mentioned a little job."

"Yes. He mentioned it. That's all."

I have hurt one or two men in my time, but I have never tortured one. That is something I can not bring myself to do. All of the men that I have hurt have either started the trouble or been dangerous. None of them have been unarmed. I might have been able to extort something from Gaboreau by putting him in pain, and again I might not. There are some men who will not yield. So I thought it better not to carry too far the pretense that Yang would use his knife, but merely allow Gaboreau to think that Yang *might* use it. I said:

"Very well, Yang. You need not wait for me to tell you—" I knew that Yang would wait for my signal, though—"but the next time Mr. Gaboreau lies or tries to evade a simple question, just prod his memory. Time is precious this evening, Mr. Gaboreau. I have none to waste. It may possibly be that you do not know where the girl has been taken. But you do know something of Franklin De Mey. Who is he?"

"I do not know any one by that name," he said quickly, too quickly.

"Did you ever hear of him?"

"Yes."

"Go on, go on. Don't stop when you are started on the right track. When and where did you hear of him?"

"You mentioned him this afternoon to Felix. I listened through the keyhole. I know nothing more than that."

"You mean that I mentioned him when you and I first met in the lobby before you took me up-stairs and turned me over to Felix. Isn't that what you meant?"

"Yes. But I never heard of him before."

"You don't intend to tell me about De Mey?"

"I know nothing to tell," he answered hurriedly as Yang gave the knife a flourish.

"I can't argue with you on that point. But there is another little point on which it will be more dangerous for you to pretend ignorance. I will see just how truthful you are. I know that one of you black-beards arrives every morning at Stillwater Place between three and six. Where does he come from?"

"I know nothing about it."

"At last you have put your foot into it. Did you ever hear of De Meyervelt? A name strangely resembling De Mey, is it not? Did you ever hear of that family?"

"Yes."

"Do you know that a man named Gaboreau runs a gambling layout in their house?"

He was reluctant to answer, but evidently saw that he was on dangerous ground, for I seemed to know much more about the De Meyervelts than about the De Meys.

"Yes," he admitted.

"Which one of you runs it?"

"Robert."

"So it is Robert," I said, as though Robert was well known to me. "And he goes to Stillwater Place?"

"Yes, sometimes. He is the manager for the De Meyervelt amusement room."

"Amusement room. Euphonious title for a crooked layout, isn't it. And when Robert doesn't go to Stillwater Place, who does?"

"Sometimes I, sometimes Felix and sometimes George—"

He caught himself too late. He had not intended to mention George.

"Ah yes, George. Now tell me about George. Yang, I expect Mr. Gaboreau will need to have a little prod on his memory before he is through talking about George."

I have always suspected that Chinaman had a sense of humor; and I came near not being able to suppress a smile when he bent forward menacingly, knife poised, peering hard into the face of Gaboreau as though ready to run him through at the first signs of reluctance to answer.

"Does George come to the Tremaine often?" I asked.

"No."

"Where may he be found?"

"He has no regular place."

"If you wanted to get in touch with him how would you go about it?" I asked.

Gaboreau hesitated, but his eyes settled on the point of Yang's knife and he said:

"He keeps in touch by telephone."

"With that at Stillwater Place?"

"No," Gaboreau said promptly, with every appearance of honesty, "there is no telephone there."

"No?"

"No."

Then I took a chance. I don't often take them, but it seemed a safe one because I had an idea that if George kept in touch with a telephone it was with none other than that at Stillwater Place.

I went to the telephone and called for the number of Stillwater Place—the number I had got through police headquarters.

Then I told Gaboreau to come and take the receiver.

"How on earth—" he began, unable to conceal surprise at my knowing it.

"Never mind that," I said speaking rapidly. "You find out where George can be located. And Yang will be beside you so that your first suspicious word into that mouthpiece will probably be your last."

I convinced him that I meant it, too. I did mean it.

"Charles speaking," he said. "Where am I? Tremaine of course. Yes, I went out. Felix? Oh, Felix—I don't know—" a long pause—"If George could relieve me. In an hour at the Crystal. All right—" another long pause—"I went out of the Tremaine to see—that is—I had to attend to that little matter you spoke of this afternoon. Yes sir. Yes sir, I will attend to that—" still another long pause.

I gently took the receiver from his hand and put it to my ear. The harsh, tigerish voice was snapping:

"Somebody keep that —— Everhard in sight. He may try to make trouble, and troublesome men—we must quiet them, you know—" he laughed in a fierce, cackling, satisfied way. "You'll attend to that will you?"

I clapped my hand over the mouthpiece and told Gaboreau to say "Yes" when I removed the hand.

He was slow to do it, and the irascible old fellow shouted back:

"What's the matter with you? Why don't you answer? Take all night! Answer me, you fool!"

I GENTLY HUNG up the receiver.

To try further to deceive the suspicious old tiger might lead to complications. But since he thought Charles had telephoned from the Tremaine, he would be trying to get the Tremaine connection again so as to continue his scolding.

"You can explain to your superior when you see him—again. He seems to be quite wrathy. Rather the usual thing with the old fellow. And since he has given instructions to you to have somebody watch me carefully, I think that I will see that you are watched.

"You asked to have George relieve you. What that means I don't know. But you will be good enough to explain and explain in detail. You have lied to me several times this evening, but I don't think you had better do it again. I am going to meet George. I want a letter from you—a note—something that will assure him that I am a friend and to be trusted. When I go out of this room I am going to tell Yang that if I do not return in two hours he will know your letter trapped me, and that he shall then cut your throat. Do you understand, Yang?"

Yang nodded his head profoundly.

"Now, Mr. Gaboreau, explain."

He went as far as to insist, perhaps truthfully, that George had not been called into the affair with Jessie at all, but had been attending to other work—though often all of them worked together.

He was ready to explain about George. But, he said none of the Gaboreaus were ever seen together, and that when one relieved the other it was usually done in a saloon. They kept the appointment to the second. One entered the front door and went toward the rear. The other entered the rear and went toward the front, so it appeared to any one who chanced to be standing by either door that the same man had come in and gone right out again by the same door.

I did not, and still do not understand fully why that arrangement was used. But I suppose there was a good reason. I have an idea that the two men, instead of passing each other in the saloon, usually went into a back room and had a confidential talk over the matter at hand. In that case there was reason enough to make sure that they did not enter by the same door or leave together.

"George is to meet you at the Crystal saloon at what time?" I asked.

"Twelve-thirty."

"It is almost that now. I am sorry, but I do not believe you will be able to keep the appointment. And now another question—one asked before: who is Franklin De Mey?"

"I don't know."

"Are you sure?"

"I am."

I looked hard at him. I could not understand the secrecy that enveloped De Mey. I believed that the man was lying. I did not tell him so in words, but in manner. That is, I made a slight movement with my hand and Yang's glittering blade almost touched Gaboreau's throat.

Gaboreau sprang backward, slightly raising both hands, palms outward, and a spasm of fear wrenched his face. The dazzling blade of Yang's played before his eyes.

"Tell me, quick. Who is Franklin De Mey?" I asked again.

"Stop that devil! Ugh—stop him! I don't know. But stop him—he'll kill me!" Gaboreau shouted hoarsely, his nerves broken down at last, and he shrank from the weazened, lithe Chinaman.

"Very well," I said, putting a hand on Yang and drawing him back. "But why don't you tell me. You have one more chance."

Gaboreau dropped his arms and leaned against the table.

"I can't tell you. I don't know. Gaboreau—the real Gaboreau—never tells us anything. We get orders and carry them out. We are orderlies, as you said. I know there is such a man as Franklin De Mey, but who he is or what he has done or where he is to be found, I do not know."

"And the girl—where has she been taken?"

"I don't know."

"Who took her?"

"I don't know. Felix was to prevent you from helping her. That is all I know. Gaboreau tells us nothing. We know nothing."

"You don't even know about Kingston?" I said, mentioning the millionaire who, so the inspector thought, Gaboreau had had murdered because he threatened to expose the gambling layout in the De Meyervelt home.

That question nearly paralyzed him. He stared at me in utter amazement. Then—either in astonishment or to throw me off guard—he asked in awed tones—

"Did Gaboreau do that?"

"Really," I said, concealing my ignorance under a bluff, "from the way you ask questions one would think that *you* had brought *me* here to find out things. I must remind you that it is the other way around. And," I went on, "you all take orders from the real Gaboreau at Stillwater Place?"

"Yes."

"Are you black-beards brothers?"

"Felix and I are. That is why we work together. We are twins. No one can hardly tell us apart. We can not work with Robert or George. The difference might be noticed."

"But they come to the Tremaine often?"

Again he seemed to be surprised that I knew so much about their movements. He admitted that they did, but always early in the morning when there were few people about.

"Now then," I said looking at my watch and noticing that I had no time to spare, "you will write a note to my dictation."

He wrote it. And when it was finished, I bound and gagged him, put a pillow under his head and placed him beside his brother on the floor.

I opened the door suddenly and found Jessie in a kimono hunched over where the keyhole had been.

She gasped and blushed and did not know what to say.

"Oh, Mr. Everhard," she began, "can't I help in some way? I would dearly love to. I feel that I ought. Really I do.

I didn't mean to listen, but I just couldn't help it. I am so excited. I do so want to learn about Franklin."

"I see."

"Is there anything I can do?" she asked hysterically.

"Yes. Go to bed and stay there."

She was not offended at my bruskness. She thought I was in justifiable anger at having found her at the keyhole. I did not care how many keyholes she was at. I wanted Vivian. Had it not been for this girl I would not have thrust Vivian into trouble. But I was not blaming the girl for that. It was no fault of hers. I was not blaming myself. I never blame myself. I try to do the best I can at the time and if I am beaten I figuratively shrug my shoulders and take the loss. But Vivian was a loss that I would not endure.

I meant that Antoine Gaboreau should humbly return my wife. I would take his black-beards as hostages until he would be left without captains, orderlies or whatever use to which he put them. I wanted to cut off his supports, and I intended to add George to my collection of black-beards.

So I hurried from the apartment and securing a taxi drove rapidly to the Crystal saloon.

ON THE SECOND the black-beard, George, appeared through the side door. He glanced about him, hesitated, stopped at the bar for a drink, and all the while looked around in a way that seemed to me to indicate restlessness.

I moved close to where he was standing and without a word slipped a folded piece of paper along the bar to the side of his glass.

He gave me a flashing, searching look. But I said nothing. I made no sign.

Then he picked up the paper and read what I had dictated:

The bearer will show you the way. Important.

CHARLES.

I had not said, "the bearer can be trusted," or that sort of thing. I expected him to think that I could be trusted or I would not have been given the note.

"Who are you?" he asked.

"I am not expected," I replied, "to either ask or to answer questions."

His was a thinner face than those of the other two I had met, a trifle thinner and more keen. He did not impress me as being catlike. There was something of the hawk about him. His nose was more prominent than theirs were. But he looked like the others, remarkably like them. But then I found afterward that these men had been selected because they did look alike and had been trained to cultivate the resemblance and the same mannerisms, so that it was very difficult to distinguish them; especially when they were not together.

"You are not to answer questions, eh?" he said dubiously, glaring at me.

"I am not," I repeated.

"How do I know," he said, dropping his voice, "that this is not a forgery?"

"You don't, I suppose, if you are not able to recognize the handwriting."

"Nothing of this kind has ever happened before," he

went on, tapping the note with a long forefinger while he looked hard into my face.

"I know nothing about that."

"You seem to be quite self-sufficient, my man," he said coldly.

"I can't see that that has anything to do with—" and I indicated the note—"It was given to me—and I delivered it. I said I would."

"Why couldn't he come himself?"

"It would perhaps be better to ask him when you meet again. I am not familiar with Charles's business."

"Have you worked with him?" George asked encouragingly.

"As you might surmise, we are not total strangers. And if you care to come with me," I added bluffing, "all right. If you don't—"

I left the sentence unfinished and turned slowly as though to leave. I tried my best not to appear to care in the least one way or the other whether he came. And of course, since he thought that was the case, he was ready to come.

It was easy to get him into my apartment-house, only I wondered what some close observer might think, if there had been any, who saw me come down alone and return each time with what appeared to be the same man. But I was confident that there were no observers keeping so strict a watch as to tell whether or not I had come in with three men that looked alike, though none left my rooms after being shown into them.

I did not say one word to George all of the way. I preferred not to try to assuage what suspicions he might have lest I make him the more suspicious in trying to reassure him. In other words, I was trying to outguess him, just as every poker player who has a degree of success must outguess a dozen times a night the man before him. I figured that if George was suspicious of me he might become more so if I tried to be affable. But if I appeared to be indifferent to what he thought, and not seem to care in the least whether he came with me, I reasoned that he would be sure that I was not acting like one who has a trap baited.

I have been led into and have barely escaped so many traps myself that I know the easiest way to disarm suspicion is not to be agreeable. It is all part of the great science called bluff upon which poker is founded. And if the college courses in psychology included a thorough grounding in the fine points of poker, I am of the opinion that the cherished sheepskin would more nearly approximate the value at which the annual freshet of graduates hold it.

When we came to the door of my apartment, I stepped forward as though to open it.

One hand was on the knob—when I turned and poked an automatic hard against his stomach.

"Not a sound or move from you," I said, throwing open the door.

He hesitated just the barest instant, then lifted his hands into the air.

"It is just as well," I remarked, "that you did not try to reach for the vitriol gun in your side coat pocket, or for the knife in your belt, or for the miniature gun in your vest pocket. Now just step inside."

He did so. I shut the door.

"You can see," I went on, "I am holding something of a

reception for Gaboreaus this evening. It might be called a get-together meeting."

He was seeing, too. He stared and stared at the two men on the floor, till I touched his arm and told him that he had better take notice of my friend, Yang Li. Then for the first time he seemed to notice the wicked knife that gleamed like a serpent's tongue in Yang's hand.

Before I started questioning Gaboreau No. 3 Yang called my attention to a message which he had painfully tried to make clear on a writing pad. Guernsey had telephoned that he was coming up to the apartment at once. Yang with difficulty managed to make clear that Guernsey had said much more, but that he did not understand it. He made signs that Guernsey had been excited. Yang could never understand why anybody should be excited at any time over anything.

Then Gaboreau No. 3 went through the process of being searched and of answering questions. He was keen-brained and no doubt lied from first to last, but he lied well. He told me nothing that I did not already know, and pretended ignorance of much that I did know. He claimed to have never heard of Franklin De Mey; but he had heard of the millionaire Kingston and seemed surprised when I suggested that the old man of Stillwater Place was responsible for the millionaire's murder.

These black-beards were such adroit liars and actors that I probably credited them with knowing more than they did. It is barely possible that no one of them did know just what affairs the old man at Stillwater Place did interest himself in.

When I had finished with Gaboreau No. 3, I gagged

and bound him and placed him beside his black-bearded brothers. Robert, the fourth and so far as I knew the last, would not be where I could get at him for some time. I could not very well break into the exclusive De Meyervelt home and carry him off. But I thought possibly I might arrange to attend to him later in the morning.

I knew very well that I was getting myself into the predicament of the man who caught a bull by the tail. As long as I held on to the Gaboreaus I was safe enough. But I could not keep them prisoners forever, and as soon as I turned them loose—the horns of the bull would be at me.

I did not see just how I was going to arrange it, but I knew that in some way I would have to make arrangement of one kind or another to keep them permanently out of my way—not for days or months, but for years. That was more easily hoped for than accomplished; but there is no problem without its solution. There is a way out of every difficulty, and I meant to keep on the alert and find the way to deal with my three desperate black-bearded gentle-men—as well as with the one that remained uncaught, and the tigerish old fellow also who had a lair in Stillwater Place.

AS YANG HAD said Guernsey was coming to my apartment, I thought it would be best for me to wait for him down-stairs, for no doubt Jessie was again at the keyhole and would likely remain there until she thought I was about to open the door. I was not yet of the opinion that it would be well for her to know he was in the city. She was still infatuated with that elusive De Mey, and until I discovered something about him I did not see how I could essay the rôle of Cupid and turn her eyes welcomingly toward Mr. Guernsey. I was much less interested in his love affair than when I had first concerned myself with it, for with Vivian's disappearance I had developed troubles of my own, but still I thought it well to serve him as best I could.

I went down-stairs to the unlighted reception-room, having first awakened the boy at the telephone switch and told him that if any one called, I would answer it from down there. I did not know but that Guernsey would telephone again.

I had not been seated long before I heard the buzzer and the boy called me. The call, however, was not from Guernsey. And as soon as I picked up the receiver the sound of the voice out of it gave me a thrill. It was the voice of the real Gaboreau.

"Everhard," he said, "your time's up. Tell me where Felix is or you'll be dead inside of an hour. You were seen to drive off with him tonight from in front of the Oriel café. He has not been seen since. What did you do with him?"

I shut one eye and looked at the ceiling while my brain hummed like a motor on a grade. I was not ready to have suspicion turned on me. It might prove embarrassing.

But as long as I had been seen only driving off with Felix I thought there was a chance to wiggle out of the situation. Yes, so long as I had not been seen driving off with the other two Gaboreaus I felt that my hour of life might be extended indefinitely; so I pretended to be the dupe. But first I acted as though I did not understand of what he was talking, and why he should be suspicious of me.

He was soon worked into an apoplectic rage. Then I made him think—or at least I tried to make him think—

that I had got into the car with Felix under the impression that Felix would pursue the taxi that had carried off a woman in whom I was interested. I explained also that though we had tried to locate the taxi, it had evaded us.

It was not easy to fool that clever old man, but I at least succeeded in mystifying him. He must have thought me the veriest of fools to have permitted Felix to get me into the car under the pretense of chasing that taxi. But I had been seen to get into the car. He knew that. I told him that after we lost sight of the taxi, Felix had brought me almost back to my apartment and then I had left the car.

I admit that I was using a lawyer's license with the truth; but then—one can't be squeamish when trying to hoodwink the devil. He hung up on me abruptly, so I did not know exactly what he thought.

But that telephone message made me rapidly decide upon a scheme I had been turning over and over in my mind just before he telephoned. So I wrote a note, called a messenger and sent it to Jerry Kelly. I disliked to get the reputable teamster out of bed in the wee hours of the morning on a lawless enterprise; but I needed a husky burglar.

GUERNSEY ARRIVED AT last. He was very excited. No doubt he had reason to be excited. He had got into the De Meyervelt home without difficulty, thanks to the companion Johnny Blix had picked out for him, and at once had been taken up-stairs to the gaming rooms.

These rooms were fitted out in gold-and-black lacquered furniture, and hung with heavy curtains of black velvet. A soft glow of yellow light from hidden bulbs fell from the ceiling. Thick Chinese rugs were on the floors; and soft-footed servants in livery passed continually back and forth serving liquors and cigarets.

Guernsey had arrived early, and only one of the roulette tables was running for the handful of people, mostly young men, who were already there and eager to play. There had been no introductions. As soon as he was inside his companion had left him and Guernsey did not see him again.

Guernsey looked about, but saw no one resembling Gaboreau. Then he sat down at the table. The people already playing seemed to take him for granted as one of themselves. Comments passed to and fro. More people came in and the wheel of another table was in motion.

Guernsey persisted in winning. He said that luck seemed to be infatuated with him. Once he made a desperate bet and won—then he let the money ride; and it rode on the red for seven times before it lost. His companions had advised him to pull it down. One young woman had begged with him not to tempt fortune after the fourth winning ride, and grew almost hysterical each spin after that. She talked so much and so loudly that attention was attracted to his daring play and people gathered around. The amount, when he did lose, was enormous, having doubled six times. But the blasé croupier had said there was no objections to a bet of any size whatever—and high stakes were the rule at De Meyervelt's.

Guernsey said that those who looked on were not justified in regarding him as a plunger, for he was sorely tempted to pull down after the bet had doubled three times and it became more difficult to let it ride each whirl thereafter.

The seventh turn of the wheel took the pile, and singing his monotonous formula, the croupier had reached out and gathered in the pyramid of chips.

Guernsey tried to take the loss calmly, and he said that he was sure he did take it calmly for every one around seemed to look at him admiringly, and some spoke of the nonchalance with which he had lost. Then a hand had clapped him heartily on the shoulder, and a voice that made him jump said:

"Some sport, my boy. Some sport. A regular plunger. Didn't know you had it in you!"

Guernsey looked up straight into the face of Franklin De Mey.

In his own words, Guernsey was too flabbergasted to say anything but a surprised—

"Hello!"

De Mey had added:

"Come to our wicked city to have a little fling, eh? Excuse me a minute. I have to see a fellow. Then I'll come right back and we'll have a chat over old times."

And Guernsey let him get away.

He had sat there like a chump for the next hour and a half impatiently waiting for De Mey to come back—and expecting him to come back. Guernsey was about as innocent as a babe of the way of this world's rascals.

After about an hour and a half he had walked around and made inquiries for De Mey, but no one seemed to know him. Yet, Guernsey said, De Mey had appeared perfectly at home as though entirely familiar with the place.

Along toward midnight the tall, black-bearded man whom he recognized as Gaboreau had appeared, passing suavely through the crowd, bowing and speaking on all sides of him. Then Guernsey had walked up and bluntly asked Gaboreau if he knew Franklin De Mey and where he could be located. That Gaboreau was, of course, the one known to me as Robert.

"He looked at me in the strangest way," Guernsey reported, "and hesitated. Then he answered coldly that he did not have the pleasure of knowing a Mr. De Mey. Then after the briefest pause he wanted to know why I had asked *him* about De Mey.

"I told him that I had known De Mey in Los Angeles, and mentioned how I had seen him a few minutes before. I also explained that De Mey was about the only person in the city that I did know, and that naturally I would like to get in touch with him.

"I think the old boy doubted me at that. But he acted a bit more civil. Only he couldn't remember any De Mey. He said however that he would inquire around. I waited quite a while, then he came up and said that he had made inquiries, but no one seemed to know my friend.

"It's the queerest thing I was ever up against, Mr. Everhard. What do you make of it?"

Instead of explaining what I thought, which would probably have caused me to offend Mr. Guernsey by letting him know that I considered him something of a bungler to have let De Mey get out of his sight, I asked Mr. Guernsey if he was ready to take a bigger chance than letting a bet ride seven times on the red? He promptly said that he would take any kind of a chance.

"It is both lawless and dangerous."

"I don't give a ——," he replied.

"It may get into your home town papers—if we fail."

"Let it get there. I'm on. Name it."

Then I told him how Vivian, while impersonating Jessie, had been thrown into a taxi that dashed away and left me stranded in the middle of the street.

He wanted to know at once why I had not given chase to the disappearing taxi; and I explained again that the one I was in had been designedly wrecked as the other flashed out of sight.

"I'd like to be at the wheel and follow those—" Mr. Guernsey's words became unprintable.

But he spoke with a note of fierceness in his voice that showed me that, for all of his thick-headedness, Mr. Guernsey was capable of making things lively for parties that might get in his way. And I remembered too, that I had heard by telegraph that he had been a racer in his day, and no doubt a reckless and skilful one. He had enough of the bulldog in his jaw to indicate the fellow of grit.

"I don't think there will be any racing," I said. "And I hope there will be no fighting, but I rather fancy we shall have some kind of trouble. I'd rather not have it though."

So I bundled Mr. Guernsey into a taxi and we drove off to keep my appointment with Jerry Kelly.

7

I **LEFT GUERNSEY IN** the machine and went into the saloon to find Jerry. He was sitting alone at a table toward the rear, sipping a glass of beer.

Jerry was a big, bulky fellow with an undershot jaw, steady eyes and a tread light as a panther walking over hot coals. He moved with an ease, an unhurried slowness, a deliberation that not only had something of grace in it—if "grace" may be applied to a bulky burglar—but also indicated the man who used his head. Most crooks are merely cunning. They have little of the quality called "brains," and that is why so many of them are easily caught and so few reform.

Jerry arose and put out a big, rough hand.

"Anything to sit down and talk over, Mr. Everhard?" he asked.

"Nothing, Jerry. I am sorry to drag you out like this, but—"

"Nobody's being dragged. I'm sure glad to do it. The little lady is sure glad to have me, too, Mr. Everhard. She said, 'Jerry, if Mr. Everhard wants you it means he's in trouble. And you get him out.'

"So I went out in the back-yard and spaded up my onion-bed and pulled out the kit of tools I had cached. She knew I had 'em, too. When I stowed 'em away she

155

objected. But I said, 'Bess, I hope I'll never have to use 'em again. But they're the best set that was ever made. I couldn't replace 'em for a thousand dollars, and I'm not going to give 'em to anybody.'

"She didn't like for me to keep 'em. But I explained that it would be good for my will power if I had 'em around. The little lady's strong on the will-power stuff. So we compromised on a burial out in the garden. Put 'em under the onions in case the police picked me up again on suspicion and started looking over the premises. I'm ready, Mr. Everhard. You said it was to be a 'job.' I haven't forgot how."

He asked no questions, but picked up a little brown satchel that was under the table, pulled his cap low over his eyes and waited for me.

"Jerry, I want to get into a house where I know people are in it and awake. I have an idea the house is rigged with alarms, too. I know the party inside is inclined to take all manner of precautions in other respects, so I wouldn't be surprised if he was provided with burglar-alarms. The servants are deaf—but he isn't."

"Easy money, just as long as there's no dogs in the house. I hate a white woolly poodle worse 'an all the mechanical devices ever invented. Burglar-alarms are kid's toys. Just so there's no poodle around. They yap their fool heads off and you can't shut 'em up."

"I don't know the first thing about this house except that it is surrounded by large grounds—comparatively large, with plenty of shade. But I am of the opinion that there will be all manner of electrical contrivances rigged up to the windows and doors."

"Don't let a little thing like that worry you, Mr. Everhard. I'm ready."

So I took him out to the taxi and introduced him to Mr. Guernsey.

We drove to within a few blocks of Stillwater Place, got out and sent the taxi on its way. Then I told Jerry the number of the house and placed matters entirely in his hands.

It was a pleasant night, not chilly, just comfortable with a light coat; but there was altogether too much moon for men who were not lying abed. I would have preferred a dark, a black night, as witnesses were not needed for the work I had at hand. But the moon was full and bright, and seemed like a huge bulb swung in the heavens.

We all walked together to within about a block of the house. Guernsey was so nervous he felt chilly and turned up his coat, and looked into the shadows like a timid boy expecting something to leap out at him. Not that he was afraid—he was nervous, unused to adventure.

About a block from the house Jerry told us to wait while he went forward and had a chance to look the place over. And he left us, slipping from shadow to shadow noiselessly as an Indian approaching a camp-fire from behind little clumps of sage.

Guernsey and I took a hiding-place behind the hedge fence in some good citizen's yard, who no doubt little thought to what nefarious use his ornamental hedge might be put. We stood together and said nothing; or crouched silently as a car whirred in the distance as though it might come along our street, and I listened alertly for the footsteps of any conscientious policeman who might be making the rounds of his beat. But the silence of night hung over the city, the silence of a city that had died. Guernsey could not be calm. The unaccustomed thrill of being abroad on an errand forbidden by the law was stimulating to his nerves, and he moved his feet about and drew out and peered at his watch every half-minute.

The wait was so long that I began to fear that Jerry had encountered a policeman. I wondered if the inspector might not still have men shadowing the house, though I had been informed that he had withdrawn his watchers.

Also, I began to ponder more deliberately the scheme of breaking into the house and encountering the old man, and to wonder if after all it were feasible. He would undoubtedly be an alert fellow. Perhaps he might still be up. I was forced to conclude that the plan was not what I would call feasible. But that made no difference. If one limits himself to doing only feasible things the chances are that he will not do much. And though I dislike to take chances, to rush in without the faintest idea of what I am to get into—still, if I have to do that sort of thing I try to arrange it so the other fellow will do most of the worrying.

The merest sound but a few feet from me made me turn swiftly. Jerry, having come up silently, was almost at my side.

"It's a pipe," he said softly. "Lights burning—somebody up, but that's all right. No dogs about the grounds and no signs of bones at the back porch or in the garbage-can. Went through it. Even the poodles get bones you know. So I don't think there's a thing that will yap. I looked the place over. Big garage in back. Locked—or was. Went in and had a look.

"Big machine there, and room for another. Been housing two machines. Located the kitchen of the house. It's the one room where nobody's likely to come. Light upstairs in the front of the house. But we'll go through the kitchen. I can't tell yet, but I think it's wired with alarms. They'll make us take a little more time, that's all. No trouble to beat burglar-alarms. Think all the burglars are going to starve just because electricians need work? Nothin' doin'.

"You and Mr. Guernsey go on first, walk past the house, then turn to your left and cut down through the alley and cut back to the house and wait for me. I'll stick around and follow to make sure no cop spots you and starts to follow. Wait for me by the left of the garage. It's dark there. Some kind of a vine there."

As Guernsey started off, Jerry caught him by the arm and hissed into his ear:

"You—don't make so much noise with your feet. Better take off your shoes after you get out of the alley. An' don't holler if you step on a tack. Keep still if it kills you."

Guernsey said nothing, and he tried to follow instructions. But about a half block later his curiosity made him ask questions. He was walking as though trying to step on egg-shells without breaking them—but he would have smashed hard-boiled eggs, at that—when he said in a stage whisper—

"Are we going to break into a house?"

"We are," I said, looking at him closely to see how he would take it.

"Lord!" he said impulsively.

"You may go back—if you wish."

"Not much! I haven't been so scared since I went into my first road race—and I like it."

Mr. Guernsey had wrongly diagnosed his feeling. There is a difference between being scared and being nervous. As far as being actually afraid was concerned, I was probably much more so than he. I am seldom nervous. But I was afraid my plan might be bungled in some detail; and a bungle—well, bridges are built to be crossed when one reaches them and to be burned afterward.

Mr. Guernsey could not help this nervousness. As we were sneaking down the alley, hugging the shadow of a board fence, something leaped from the ground before us and passed over the fence at one bound.

Guernsey jumped almost as high and said—

"My God!"

"If you were an Egyptian," I remarked, cynically, "your words might be appropriate. That was a cat—merely a cat—and a black one, too."

All cats look black at night—if they are in the shadows.

"Are you superstitious?" he asked in a thrilling whisper.

"Very," I said. "I believe it is bad luck when on a quiet and secret little enterprise for a man with a voice strong as your own to use it."

That silenced him.

AFTER A WAIT in the shadow by the garage, during which I stared at the faint light that could be seen coming from a side window on the second floor of the house and wondered how soon I would be using it to read the riddle of Gaboreau, Jerry came up. He came so quietly that he was almost beside us before either saw him.

"Now, Mr. Guernsey," he said, "you take off your shoes and move down through that arbor, work your way around the house and lay down behind the rose-bush just back of the front porch. You can watch the street. If you see anybody turn in, come back and tell us."

"I'm not going in with you?" Guernsey asked in disappointment.

"Not much." Then Jerry added, looking at me, "unless Mr. Everhard—"

"You're the strategist, Jerry," I whispered.

"You mean I'm the doctor?" he asked, doubtfully.

"That's it," I assured him.

"All right. Mr. Guernsey, if you're careful, you don't need to take them shoes off. But work your way up to the rose-bushes. We'll wait till you get settled. And for Heaven's sake, walk on your hands!"

"Some feet!" he added to me as we listened to the soft crunch of Guernsey's shoes on the gravel under the arbor.

When we were sure that Guernsey had had time to get settled into the place behind the rose-bushes, we carefully approached the house.

The hushed silence of the early morning hours made the slightest rustle of the leaves audible. It seemed to be a bad night for the work at hand. From time to time little night-noises would creak and crack, something would chirp, or a winged insect would sing its song at my ear—noises that would not be noticed unless one's nerves were tense.

Jerry bent over his satchel and reached in. I could hear the soft clink of metal that he unwrapped from oiled cloths as he selected the needed tools.

He stood up, and putting his lips against my ear, said in the slightest of whispers:

"This is something new. Ain't many on to the trick. Takes time, but watch."

I watched. There was so much light in the moon-filled sky that, though we stood in the shadows, my eyes became accustomed enough to what darkness there was by the kitchen window to see quite distinctly; and I could see him carefully oiling a small drill, which he wrapped with heavy flannel before he started to use it, and only the point remained uncovered.

He placed the point of the drill against the lower left-hand corner of the windowpane, and I could hear the dull, soft grind as the diamond-point bit into the glass.

It seemed to me at the time to make a great deal of noise, but he told me afterward that by actual test, since it was very important to him to know it, he could bore into glass and the boring would not be heard a hundred feet away even by one listening for it. I had been standing less than three feet.

The first hole made in the pane was not so large as a pin head. But then with infinite patience he set to work and drilled those small holes until he had made one hole large enough to poke a finger into.

"It will go fast from now on," he whispered carefully.

Then, holding his finger through the hole, and pressing with it from the inside against the glass to deaden the sound, he used a glass-cutter and cut a small piece no larger than a dime. He muffled the glass with a triple fold of flannel that deadened the snap, then broke off the piece outlined by the glass-cutter, and this piece was laid carefully on the ground so that there would not be the slight-est clink.

Taking piece by piece, he worked until he had made an opening large enough to poke his hand through; then he began cutting and removing larger pieces of glass, and at no time was there more of a sound than the soft snap with which he broke off the pieces that had been cut.

In less than an hour's time he had slightly more than half of the window out, and the rest came quickly.

But before venturing to climb through, he carefully repacked his tools and locked the satchel and handed it to me.

"Pass it in to me when I crawl through. Always keep 'em with me in case I have to make a break for it."

Then he climbed noiselessly through the window, paused, listening for a moment, and disappeared into the blackness within the house.

I waited for some time before his head again appeared at the window, and I stepped closer, while he whispered so low that his words could not have been heard at an arm's length:

"Unlocked the back-door for you. Had a burglar-proof catch on it. This window's wired, too! Guess we had the right hunch."

He said it with a note of glee, as the master craftsman speaks when he has circumvented the ingenuity of those who try to beat him.

I then handed the satchel in to him and, going carefully to the back-door, stepped into the dark kitchen. In a few minutes my eyes were accustomed to the darkness within the house, and I followed Jerry across the room.

Slowly he opened a door that led out of the kitchen. It might lead into a room where some one was sleeping. It might lead into a room where some one who had heard us, despite precautions, was waiting with an automatic shotgun. It might lead into any peril; that is the dreadful anxiety of passing through a door in a strange house. But presumably it opened into the dining-room. It did.

We stepped into that. Each step was taken with extreme caution, with breathless care. We did not walk. We merely placed one foot down, and then a few seconds later advanced the other, and all the while strained every nerve to listen.

Presently Jerry stopped. He turned and caught my arm.

I thought his ear, perhaps keener than mine, had heard some suspicious sound; and instantly I was on guard—an automatic in each hand, and my eyes peering forward to detect the outline of any one who happened to be in the room. But no one was to be seen. He indicated that we were to go back, but I shook my head. I was not ready to turn back.

But he insistently made signs; he did not dare even a noiseless whisper. They indicated that we were to go back into the kitchen and then return.

I followed him into the kitchen, where he whispered:

"I forgot Guernsey. Wait till I tell him if he hears anything suspicious while we are in the house that he is to throw gravel against the window. Then we'll know somebody is coming and have time to get out."

I did not think much of the suggestion one way or the other. I had given Guernsey no thought after he had disappeared into the rose-bushes. In the little affairs to which

I give my attention from time to time I am usually alone and never have to think of confederates. I have found it more convenient. There is less chance of bungling, and if there is any bungling one always knows who is to blame.

So far I have been able to take care of myself. Perhaps that is because, even when I am not the aggressive party, I try usually to have a surprise of some kind up my sleeve. True, the surprise is usually the two automatics that rest in my side coat pockets—but from there they speak unhesitatingly and with a degree of accuracy that is usually effective.

I was glad to have the opportunity to suggest to Jerry that he could go out and tell Guernsey and I would go on alone, that I preferred to do so, that both he and Guernsey could keep watch on the outside, and that if he thought it necessary to warn me of any one's approach, not to throw gravel, but bricks.

"Throw something that I won't have to stop and listen to hear," I told him.

Jerry was disappointed that I wished to go it alone; but he said that he guessed it would be all right.

As a last word he warned me not to walk up the stairs.

"Pull yourself up the banisters," he said. "One of the steps is probably wired to ring a bell when your foot touches it. That's part of the burglar-alarm system. There's wires all over the house. If we'd raised that window instead of taking out the glass we'd have had a patrol wagon down on us by this time."

"All right. I'll try the banisters. And I'll make out all O.K., Jerry."

"Probably will, but I'd like to help."

"You've helped—more than helped, you have made possible everything else I may do."

"If you want help, just call—we'll be ready," he said as he turned and went out of the back door.

I turned the other way and again went into the dining-room. The first door I opened off that led into the hallway, but I did not go out at once. I opened all the other doors and made sure of what would lay at my rear when I had passed on. It was slow work, done painfully cautiously—this poking about over the ground floor of the house; and I do not believe that I made more than the faintest of sounds.

WHEN I CAME again into the hall-way and looked at the curving banisters, I hesitated and thought it might be safer to use the stairs. But Jerry was an authority on the protective equipment used in houses that feared intruders. Yet to slide along up those banisters was a feat that required the greatest of care if it were to be done silently.

But I climbed on to the banisters and slowly, inch by inch, pulled myself up.

Before I reached the top I could see that the room where the light was burning was at the head of the stairs; had the door open, wide open, and the light was shining through.

I was afraid lest I had made some noise that attracted attention and that some watcher was waiting for me. But I had been as silent as a serpent. I determined to go on, and cautiously, barely moving, stopping to peer up and ready to fight my way forward if need be, I finally made my way to the top and gained the upper hallway.

Then standing back from the light thrown through the

open door, I could see the profile of a man who sat slumped in a deep swivel-chair before a broad desk.

A row of filing-cases lay on the desk; and about the room, on shelves, were other filing cases, much like the orderly records in an attorney's filing office. I wondered at the enormous amount of labor and material represented; and wondered also what it was all about.

The man Gaboreau, the real Gaboreau, was beardless, bald and old. His chin and nose almost touched, as is often noticed in the features of toothless, withered old men. But his chin was sharp, and his nose was long and sharp and beaked. He was bald as a vulture and had the beak of an eagle. There was more than cunning in his face; the broad forehead, the full-rounded skull, much too large for his frail body, showed plainly enough from where came the intellectual power that had baffled and defied the police and made the name Gaboreau one of sinister mystery.

I may have no liking for such as he; but I admire strong men whether or not they are wicked. It has been my fortune to come upon some of the strongest; and though I wish for what credit is mine, yet it must have been observed by those who know something of me that I have almost always caught them at a disadvantage.

The average fellows, even those with some ability, give me little trouble. Surely enough, they can strike in the dark; but they must be driven to do it, and told when and how and where, and likely as not be inspired with drink or drugs before they dare. Few crooks work alone. Most criminals work in gangs. And that gang is short lived that has no powerful head behind it.

Long ago I learned that, so when involved with crook or

gang, I ever reach out and up until I come to the saturnine
intellect that dominates the crooks and gangsters. There
is always such an intellect behind each criminal organization—sometimes a Napoleonic mind, but often enough,
fortunately for the peace of law and society, a mind of lesser
proportions that meets its Waterloo without even having
known Marengo.

But few men—none in just the same way—have ever
impressed me as that fierce old man who sat in the deep
chair with his head bent forward. I might have thought
that he was asleep but that now and then he lifted his hand
to the edge of the table and tapped noiselessly with his
lean, fragile fingers.

No doubt he felt secure, not only because he believed
he had effectively concealed his own identity behind the
mask of four black-beards, but with his house equipped
with alarms against intruders—especially needed alarms
because his servants were deaf. But it is in moments of
security that even countries as well as men are taken
unawares. What failures I have made—they have been
more numerous than I shall indicate—have almost always
been due to that form of security which underestimates the
quality of the man that must be beaten. Warned by such
failures, I have developed a hypersensitive caution. I may
sometimes put a butterfly on the rack to make sure that it
doesn't escape; but often enough the butterfly turns out to
be a powerful bird and the rack is none too strong for its
beating wings and powerful talons.

I wondered what sort of a rack I could put Gaboreau
on. Physically, he was a weakling. But the physical is not
the sum and measure of a man's strength. I could easily

have covered him with one gun or two, and warned him to make no move—even as I had warned and held three of his black-beards. That is sufficient to calm and suppress all but the odd man in a million. I needed nothing more than to see him to know that he was the odd man.

He might not laugh at me; but he was one of those rare men who know that none but a fool will shoot in a quiet neighborhood, where the very report of the gun will spread a terrific alarm. Many men in a tight place forget that, or else are not able to be sure that the man behind the gun is no fool. Gaboreau would be discriminating. He would, I could see, be wary and elusive as an eel, tricky as a monkey and dangerous as a tiger.

However, I believed that I would not fail to impress him with the opinion that I was in earnest; and that when I am in earnest it is well to be attentive. While I waited, studying just what to do or say, the telephone on his desk rang. In answering it he turned in his chair so that his back was toward the door.

I listened.

"HELLO—YES—YES," HE SAID waspishly. "It's time somebody got in touch with me. No. No. I haven't heard from Felix, Charles or George for two hours. Can't get any of them. Something's wrong. I want somebody to attend to that —— Everhard."

I stepped slowly, softly inside the door.

"What's that? What's that! Not the woman? What did that fool Felix take her for then? No wonder I can't locate him. The bungler! I won't have bunglers. Hear me. I won't."

A pause, during which Gaboreau listened.

"What kind of a muddle is this, anyway! You whelps! Yes, you too. What if he did know him by the name of De Mey in Los Angeles? You let him get away. You didn't find out who *he* was. How do you know his name was Guernsey? How do you know he ever was in Los Angeles? And that fool Frank—just because he killed Kingston is no reason I should keep him from the chair and let him play his —— fool tricks to impress some weak-minded girl. Oh, he's there now with you, is he? Feels foolish after his little bungle, does he? Ought to feel foolish—anybody that bungles. Let me talk to him. Let me talk to him, I said!"

I crouched low behind the back of his chair, so as to be out of sight in case Gaboreau glanced over his shoulder. But he was too interested in his telephone to let his eyes roam about the room. At once he began speaking with sarcasm to De Mey:

"So Everhard palmed the wrong girl off on you, did he? And you had your little theatrical for nothing! You're an idiot. Didn't I tell you when you went to California not to take that name. Didn't I? Didn't I tell you to take a real alias or keep your own? That —— Everhard is after you and I hope to God he gets you! He will, too. You idiot. You'd bungle if you tried to take a bone away from a blind pup.

"Somebody called over this wire—my private wire—this afternoon and said: 'Franklin De Mey is in trouble!' Who did it? Everhard, of course. You bring that girl here to have me kidnap her so you can frame up a fake rescue—then let her fall into his hands. You—you pretty, pampered, tin-horned piker, you half-baked swell, you society hang-er-on—you want to play the hero!

"What's that? What's that! Kingston? For me! You dirty

little liar. You know why you shot him. Don't say you did it for me! Don't say it! You did it for yourself and your precious uncle. I know he'd be ruined but for the rake-off I give him. I use his house—yes. He begged me to. You begged me to. You killed Kingston to save your graft—and I had to tell you how to do it. I covered your tracks. And now you—you want to marry an heiress and settle down. 'Oh, please, Monsieur Gaboreau, this means more to me than anything else you can do! Please let me engineer this all by myself. Just let me show you'—well, you've shown me!

"I was a fool, too. Everhard trapped you with those personals in the paper. You thought he didn't catch you, but he did. Don't you suppose he knew how you got his name and address! And you let him catch me, too. You —— fool. I told you not to take that name, De Mey, and then you have that girl write you at the Tremaine. Idiot. Stupid idiot. And when she came to the Oriel that night—you were standing across the street from the Oriel watching.

"Felix is a fool, too. Let Everhard bluff him out. And you and Felix sent a man in to watch him and follow him, and he chased that fellow off. Why didn't you watch him and follow him yourself? You were afraid. I'd give the whole pack of you for one Everhard. Who is he, anyway? How'd he get that name? Bogus name—how'd he get it?

Another pause.

"Gambler, oh, I know that. I know his reputation, too. He cleaned up the Bowers gang in San Francisco. I know that. But where did he come from? Who is he—not what is his name? Don't know? Of course not. You don't know anything. Of course you don't know why he's butting in.

He butts in because he wants to. Money has nothing to do with it. All men are not like you. Let me talk to Robert again—but don't you go away."

Again a pause, and Robert evidently took the receiver at the other end of the line.

"Robert, where in the devil is Felix and George and Charles? I've been waiting hours for you to call me. Because I'm a helpless old man you think you can ignore me. Think I'm slipping, eh? You do too. Shut up. I know you've been busy at De Meyervelts'. You're always busy when I want something. Everybody's busy then. Charles was supposed to come here tonight and help me with the records. Got George to relieve him about twelve. Then I couldn't get anybody at the Tremaine. Clerk said Charles was suddenly taken sick and removed to the hospital. Clerk's a fool. I don't know what's the matter. Frank has put a hoodoo on me—everything goes wrong since he brought that idiot of a girl here."

I realized that here was a cunning rather than a wise man; and something of a lunatic besides. Moreover, he was a cripple, helplessly shut off from the world with no outlet but the telephone for his fierce, restless mind. He could not help talking, could not help loosening vitriolic words calculated to make men wince. Naturally he did not expect to be overheard. But then, it is the unexpected that trips up the best of us. I chanced to overhear his cynical, gossipy remarks to both De Mey and the last of his uncaptured black-beards, and I understood perfectly all that had baffled me the moment before. His wire went on:

"George pulled off a good job? Of course it was. You'll get your share, don't worry. Don't worry, Robert. I'll see that your pennies are counted out for you. Oh, yes. I know you weren't thinking of that. You never are. None of you ever think of that. But my records mean more to *me* than money. You can't understand that, can you? No, you can't either. Money, money, money—that's all you judge a case by. And Frank De Meyervelt—too.

"Wants to marry for money and make his wife think he's a hero. Went to California to flirt and dropped the e-r-v-e-l-t because he thought it was too German-Jewish, and added an l-i-n because he thought Frank too plebeian. Oh, I know he said that wasn't the reason, but it was. I tell you it was! Don't I know him and his whole money-sucking family? All pretense. Stole the 'de' and stuck it on in front of their name—tried to hide their nationality. Ashamed of it. I tell you they are. Why do you argue with me? Shut up and let me talk a while. Umph. Haven't had a chance to say ten words.

"Now, Robert, what about this woman—the one you've got? The one Everhard stacked the deck with and slipped to Frank and Felix? Clever, that. I might have done it. What about her, I asked you? Why don't you answer me!

"She won't tell you who she is? She'd be a fool if she did. Laughed at Frank, eh? Then he told you and you went to see her? Oh yes, handsome Robert always goes to look at the ladies when he gets a chance.

"She is pretty, eh? Made fun of Frank and joked him about the red gloves he made her carry? Fine! Those red gloves were some more of Frank De Meyervelt's brainy engineering. Idiot! But I like that woman. Has a wedding-ring? Maybe she's Everhard's wife. Hardly? How the devil do you know he wouldn't! Not knowing what he would do has brought all this trouble.

"I don't know what he's done to Felix. Somebody's done something. He was last seen with Everhard. I had to call him up myself—couldn't get any of you busy, important men. He talked like he had done something with Felix because he very nearly made me think that he hadn't done anything. Yes, George and Charles are missing, too. Can't get anybody. How could I send somebody to watch him! Think I want every Tom, Dick and Harry to know who I am? What have I got you handsome fellows for? If I were to go about giving orders to your men I might as well have myself photographed and put in the papers.

"But what are you going to do with that woman, now that you have her? Frank wants me to help him again, eh? Idiot. You and Frank bring that woman here and let me talk to her. I'll make her say something. I like pretty women, too, you know—just as well as you. What's that? Well, come as soon as you can. I am tired of twiddling my thumbs and ringing numbers that don't answer. And be careful that Everhard don't steal that woman away from you before you get here."

He laughed as he said that and hung up abruptly. He took a deep breath and began rubbing his hands as though they were cold. Then as he turned in his chair he said meditatively to himself:

"I'd like to see that Everhard. He must be—"

I had been crouching behind the back of the chair, and as he turned on its swivel, I arose and stood erect before him. I said nothing. I made no movement. I merely stood with my arms folded and looked down into his sharp, little, gray eyes.

No doubt the quiet, uncanny manner of my appearance badly shook his nerves; but he held himself calm and slumped even deeper into his chair while he looked me up and down as an incredulous man of iron nerve might look at a ghost. He made no exclamation, no gesture; but he even bent forward and glanced at my feet, as though to reassure himself that I had not made a Mephistophelian appearance through a hole in the floor.

He breathed hard and rapidly, but otherwise he seemed calm; but obviously he was mystified, and wondering how it came that I had the suddenness of magic, and unheralded by the faintest footstep, appeared at his elbow.

His fierce eyes searched my face, took in every detail of my dress and again came back and met my own eyes. And I stared unwinkingly into his sharp, cunning features. He looked, and I knew him to be a high-tempered, irascible man; but he kept his poise. And at length when he spoke his voice had in it no note of fear, but rather a tone of petulant curiosity.

"Who are you?" he demanded.

"You expressed a wish to see Everhard. I came!"

8

IN THE SILENCE that followed, our eyes met and unwaveringly held. He twisted his withered lips tight and stared up at me with no trace of emotion, unless one may call his intense scrutiny an emotion. Perhaps it was. All the force of his powerful brain was concentrated in his small, deep, brilliant eyes that seemed trying to search into the hidden recesses of my soul for secrets of weakness, for the vulnerable, unguarded spots in my armor.

His was the face and the head of a fallen god; not a weak line amid all the traceries of age, yet the cabalism of the devil marked each feature. And be it remembered that the devil, for all his wickedness, perhaps because of it, is a brainy gentleman.

Minute after minute I stood over him and he sat, not so much with his face upturned as with upturned eyes, looking at me. We did not move. We did not speak. My arms were folded and my hands were empty. There are men to whom a show of violence is a confession of weakness. I knew him to be such a one. I knew that between him and me it was not a matter of blows, or threats or menace. Those things might come later; but in those moments we were taking the measure, each of the other.

How long I stood in silence I do not know. A clock was in the room, but I did not notice it. I did not then hear its ticking. It was no idle, abstract gaze that I focused on him; a wrestling bout with a heavier man than myself would have been less straining work, for as I stared into the bright light of his small, inscrutable eyes I was telling him who I was, what I had done and what I could do.

Not that I was consciously holding any such thought, or playing that rubbish game of mental-suggestion. But when two men who are not weaklings stand face to face they fight for dominance; and the clash of sword on buckler is oft no more decisive than the impact of eye on eye when two men stand silent and motionless.

At last he spoke. His lips barely moved, but the word was snapped out—

"Well?"

I said nothing. He had merely feinted to draw me on. To explain is to assume the defensive.

Again there was a protracted silence, then he repeated, more angrily—

"Well?"

But I did not answer.

His hand slipped forward toward the table. Whether it was done to grasp something, to press a button or test my nerves, I do not know. I stepped sidewise and interposed myself between him and the table. There was not much room for me to stand, and it brought me right up against his knees. But still I said nothing; merely stared down into his eyes.

"Who are you, anyway?" he snapped fiercely.

"Everhard."

He was incredulous, and his lips twisted into a sneer.

"What do you want?" he demanded.

What I had wanted when I came in had changed to something else. When I came I had been anxious to get through with him as quickly as possible and get away. But I had heard him tell his one uncaptured black-beard to bring Vivian to Stillwater Place; and I thought it better to wait for Vivian than to search for her.

I was no longer impatient to be through with him. I could play the waiting game with as much ease as himself, though he, too, no doubt, wished that I might stay until help of some kind came to him. I felt no need of the help for myself that was ensconced behind the rose-bushes down in the front yard; but I thought it likely that my reinforcements were more dependable than his own.

So I still said nothing. When one does not know precisely what to say it is better to remain silent and let the other fellow's imagination flounder about, than to start talking in the hope of making a lucky remark.

"I asked you what the devil you want!" he cried, hunching himself forward and placing his hands on the arms of the chair as though to lift himself up.

"You make your appeal in the name of the devil," I said enigmatically. "Is it advisable?"

I thought I might in turn test his nerves a bit further. If there was a strain of superstition in his blood I hoped to set it boiling.

"Are you the devil?" he demanded in a sharp, cynical tone.

"Are you such a stranger to him?" I asked, lowering my voice.

"What's that? What's that!"

"One of your long and varied experience should need no introduction to him."

He changed the subject abruptly by crying:

"How'd you get in here, anyway? Tell me! Tell me, I said!"

Unsmilingly I answered—

"I came—I came without touching a hand to your door or a foot to your stairs."

All that ingenuity could do he had done to keep stealthy intruders from entering without giving him warning; and he must have been sorely baffled in trying to guess how I made an entrance noiselessly. In fact, he blinked at me as though not quite sure that he was not after all imagining things.

"No," I said, "it is no dream."

"Oh, I know that," he snapped, as though ashamed that I had detected the thought that flashed across his mind. And at once he added in a chuckle:

"So you are the devil, are you? How do you do, Mr. Devil? Sit down. You make me nervous by standing. Sit down."

But behind his bantering there was more than jest. I was suspicious of him. I knew him capable of any villainy and any cunning, but he was so old, so thin, physically so weak that I felt as long as I kept him in the chair he would be helpless. I was not afraid of any alarm that he might give, for I knew a man who was well protected by servants would not go to such extreme in wiring his house with alarms. Servants, even deaf servants, might possibly prove troublesome, but I had little apprehension from that quarter at all.

"Sit down," he repeated, and waved an invitatory hand toward a chair at the end of the table.

But I did not take it. I had no intention of standing away from him.

"So you've come for your reckoning, Mr. Devil? All right, look at this"—and he swept his hand around the room, indicating the shelves of filing cases; but I did not take my eyes from his face—"there are your records! It's all there. I've saved your stenographers work. Why don't you sit down! Sit down. Take one of my record cases down and look through it. Why don't you take one down?"

"Perhaps, later."

"Some men collect money—like Indians did wampum. Money, bah! They call it power, Mr. Devil. But you and I know what power is! It is controlling other men. It is bending and breaking and taking from other men. It is crushing and racking and torturing—aye, it is taking their lives like putty between your fingers and making of it what shape you please!"

I began to see that the man was, as I might have suspected, close to a maniac. He was crazed by a love of crime. Almost every intense devotion to an idea is, so I have often thought, a form of insanity. The writer with his quill, the artist with his tube, the magnate with his money—all of it is that undeviating, fierce, mad lust for achievement that can not be suppressed by the will; that the writer, the artist, the magnate, does not want to suppress. But those forms only of intensity which harm society are called insane. If Gaboreau had sought to do good as he sought to do evil he might have got himself canonized, and yet been just as insane.

I understood him. He was the apotheosis of the criminal. He made of crime an art. With him it was a furious passion. He organized his men, planned, moved and struck, with the carefully developed precision of the chess-player. And as the chess-player counts his success not in money but in games won, in men baffled and defeated, and plays for the love of the playing, so Gaboreau played his ruthless game against the social group. Money was essential for hirelings; so money must be had. And he got it.

He made money one of the incentives for loyalty. There were other incentives. I eventually learned much about that fierce old fellow, and I found that no Maffian knife ever struck more readily in punishment than did his dagger when a gangster lagged or became distrusted. And those who took money from his purse were never again their own masters. Veritably, he took men's lives and molded them as putty between his fingers.

But I said nothing while he talked. My face, I am sure, showed no more than when a player across the green cloth dares me to call a bet. And he was puzzled. He had reasons for wanting me to move, to talk.

He succeeded in getting me to move, too.

I was so close to him that when he turned his swivel chair his knee struck me. He cried out in pain and clutched it.

But I did not at once step aside. I did not take my eyes off his face. Every boxer knows that as long as you watch a man's eyes the opponent can not make a gesture too quickly to have warning of it flashed from his eyes as though from a heliograph.

"Oh," he cried, as though in pain. Then swiftly he cursed me—"—— you! Can't you see my legs are withered—dried up from rheumatism! I can't walk. Here, if you must stand in front of me, let me turn this way."

He turned his chair slightly so that he faced the door, and I moved so that I was still close to, and before him.

"You haven't told me what you were doing here. What do you want? So you are Everhard, eh? The gambler. The hard man. Oh yes. Think you are a dangerous fellow, don't you? Supposing I was to cry for help—what would you do?"

He had been raising his voice so that the last words were uttered almost in a scream. It was a clever way to call for help—if that was his intention.

"Try it if you wish to learn," I said.

I did not know how many people were in the house, though I had heard from Johnny Blix what the police had said, and I wondered if the servants were really so deaf as not to hear his loud voice.

"I have tried it," he began, looking hard into my eyes.

Then he paused, and as he began to speak again he suddenly switched his eyes from my face and stared over my shoulder as though at some one behind me.

I came near taking my eyes off him. The impulse to look around was strong, unbelievably strong, though I was far from being sure there was not some one standing behind me. The ruse—if it was a ruse—was one with which I was perfectly familiar, having had occasion to use it at one time and another. It is almost invariably effective.

I slipped the two guns from my coat pocket, and leaning over, quickly pressed one against his body, while with the other cocked and pointed behind me, I turned my head.

I merely glanced backward. There was no one behind me.

I might have known there would not be, for had there

been any one, Gaboreau would have been far too wise and careful to have disclosed the presence by staring over my shoulder.

He was a daring and bold fellow, and there was much deviltry to come out of him, though he sat apparently helpless in his chair; and had I more than glanced to see what was to my rear, his ruse would have been successful—except that he would certainly have paid with his life for trying to blind me with the vitriol gun that he snatched from his pocket with one hand while with the other he tried to turn aside the automatic that was at his ribs.

But with the gun in my right hand, which I had put behind me when I turned my head, I struck his wrist sharply and the wicked little nickel-plated tube, which I knew was a vitriol gun, since I had removed three of them earlier in the evening from pockets of black-bearded gentlemen, fell to the floor.

It was a desperate incident and a close call for him as well as for myself. He came near to getting shot. But I did not want to shoot. I did not want to arouse the neighborhood. I wanted to wait until Vivian was brought right into the house. I knew that I could get her out.

GABOREAU WAS A man of surprises. His manner changed so completely toward me that I wondered what new evil he had ready. I expected him to be furious, for he had not only failed but had received a painful crack on the wrist. He had cried out when his knees were touched—but that was pure make-believe, used for the purpose of getting me to stand away from the table with my back toward the door so that he could try the ruse of staring past my head as though at some one behind me.

He did not even have rheumatism, but worse—paralysis. His legs were withered so that he could move only with the use of his arms. That condition explained entirely why he perforce kept himself in the background and employed others to do his work. He could not do anything himself but plan and devise contrivances and plots.

But he had no sooner failed with that ruse than he began something else; and he talked with a plausibility that, while it did not for a moment seduce me, yet had in it that heady flattery which will often imbalance the most careful of men.

"Everhard," he said in a matter-of-fact, straightforward tone as he looked at me, though still rubbing his wrist to ease the pain, "you've beaten me. I'm through. You win. I never thought that man lived who could do it. You wouldn't have done it either if I had handled the affair of that girl instead of letting that empty-headed, blatant fool of a Frank De Meyervelt 'engineer,' as he called it, his private theatricals. You tripped him up and caught on to me.

"You're a gambler. You've called me and I have nothing to show. My cards are on the table—but you don't even need to show your hand. You have brains. You have nerve. How you got on to me, how you got in here to me, I don't know. You don't need to tell me. You are the man I want. I hold no grudge. You can have anything on earth you want. I can get it. I can get anything from the Kaiser's crown to the prettiest woman this side of hell. That's where the pretty ones go when they die. I can get anything, Everhard, but brainy, nervy men. I want you.

"I've taken years training Charles and Felix and Robert and George—and they're bunglers. They can't think. I'd give the lot of them for you, Everhard. I mean it. They let me bully them and nag them—they know they are helpless without me. Give them a new pair of suspenders and they'd have to come to me to ask how to put them on. But I want you. If I had beaten you I wouldn't care a —— for you. That's straight. But you beat me. Name your price."

I expected to get Vivian without having to "name" her as a price. But I was playing for time, and also I was studying just how I could manipulate this fellow so as to get evidence that would put his black-beards behind the bars permanently. And I wanted to make no bargain with him—chiefly because I stick to my bargains and I did not expect that he would. But I asked, with what curiosity I could indicate in my voice:

"Just what is the nature of the work you would expect of me?"

"You and I work together and we'll do anything you want. You suggest it. I'll plan it. We'll make those fools carry it out. If anybody's caught—" he chuckled with glee—"they get hanged. Not me. Not you. Listen; Felix and Robert and Charles and George know that tomorrow I could send every one of them to the chair. That's why—" he chuckled again—"they're so faithful! That and the money they get out of me."

He paused, and I took the chance to remark that what he had just said did not appear entirely credible. I pointed out that some one of these men was alone with him every night, and that I failed to see why at some time or other they might not set fire to the house or hit him over the head if they desired to be free of him and his dangerous evidence.

"You know some one comes, do you?" he asked queerly, looking at me as though to see if I had made a lucky guess or spoke from certain knowledge. "And you sit here wait-ing for him? —— me, but you have nerve. A man after my own heart. And it's like you to think of that, too. Murder me and burn the house. You think of everything!

"It would be easy, too. I lied to you a while ago. I haven't rheumatism. I'm paralyzed. Helpless. But those whelps are afraid of me. They dare not raise a hand. See these record cases? They are mostly full. But I have other records too. They know I have. I make them out in detail every day, and at the end of the month I send four sets of records to four safe-deposit vaults. And Robert and Charles and Felix and George know it. I make sure that they know everything that is good for their souls!

"And they know that a friend of mine calls me up every day, but they don't know who he is. No. They would like to. And they know that when the day comes that I don't answer that friend the police will be notified by my friend of the evidence in the safe-deposit vaults. See? You are cunning and you guess the weak spot in my organization. But I am showing you that there is no weak spot. My friend is wise. I keep him well informed. He knows which man comes to me each night—and the next morning if I do not answer the telephone the police will be notified of the particular deposit vault in which the evidence against the man who was with me the night before is kept."

He told me that gleefully, proudly. It was interesting. I would have given much to know the name of that friend who was warder over the incriminating evidence against the black-beards. But I saw no way of getting it.

"Listen, Everhard," he went on. "Here is a book—" he started to open the drawer of his desk, but I stopped him.

"Not so fast, not so fast. I don't know that there is a book inside. Anybody who visits nightly with a desperate confederate that may wish to crack him over the head is likely to have more ruses than merely glancing past a man's shoulder or evidence in a safe-deposit vault that is not to be used until you are dead."

"Oh, you mistrust me!" he cried reproachfully. "Open the drawer yourself. In the left-hand corner you will find a book—it is marked 'Private.' I want you to see it. Look into it. Then you will understand me. You will know me better. Ah, then you will know why I am not afraid to be alone with cowards—a poor, helpless cripple, but not afraid of cowards."

I am a cautious person, a very cautious person indeed—but none too cautious for the good of my health. I dislike running the risk of being caught dozing, so there are times when I take elaborate precautions that probably seem ridiculous to more bold fellows who rush in—and are usually carried out on stretchers.

However, I was interested to see any book that Antoine Gaboreau would have as "Private." It could not be unimportant.

So I made sure that he was really paralyzed from the waist down and could not rise out of his chair unless some support was near for both his hands. Then I moved his chair back almost into the middle of the room so that he could not get his hands on anything. I searched his pockets carefully and found nothing dangerous. He endured it cheerfully. But his cheerfulness did not reassure me in the least. I very cautiously made sure that he could not trouble me during the time it would take to open the drawer and remove a book.

But I did not open the drawer by the knob. No. It might, for all I knew, have been charged with enough current to kill an elephant and have released the current when the drawer was pulled. I opened it by putting my fingers against the bottom of the drawer and pushing it out.

Nothing happened. I looked among some papers and clippings, noticed a pack of cards, and readily found what appeared to be an ordinary diary marked "Private."

I laid it on the desk.

"Sit there in the chair and read it. Go on, sit down."

There were only two chairs in the room; the one he was in and the other at the end of the table. I took hold of the back of the chair which he indicated and started to move it so that I might sit down closer to him. But it would not move. I gave it a quick pull, but its legs were fastened to the floor.

I pretended not to notice that. I let him think that I had merely changed my mind about sitting in it and said that "This will do," as I sat down on the edge of the table.

Why it was fastened to the floor I did not know. I did not see how anything was to be gained by investigating as long as I had no intention of using it. I was not curious, or at least that curious. I was suspicious of Gaboreau and expected all manner of villainy from him.

The chair appeared to be all right, but poisoned needles

can be concealed beneath leather bottoms. Also, trap-doors can be concealed beneath chairs that are stationary.

I don't think that he saw I had been made suspicious. I did not struggle with the chair to see how much force it would resist before being moved. I did not look at him accusingly or suspiciously. I merely half sat and half leaned against the corner of the table and glanced down at the diary and then at him.

"GO ON, READ the book. Open it. I want you to see," he said eagerly, watching me anxiously.

I looked long and hard at him before I touched the book. I was suspicious. There was, I felt, something wrong. I tried to make out what it was. I know there are times when I am overwary, ridiculously alert and untrusting. But there was a time when I was not. Commerce and intercourse with my fellow men have trained me in wariness as the jungle perils train the wily Malay to read a warning in a crushed twig.

"Go on," he insisted. "Then you will understand everything. Read the book."

I did not pick the book up. I let it lie. But reaching forward, I opened the cover. The first page was blank.

I started to turn it over and the page stuck slightly.

I raised my finger to my lips, as one naturally does when a page sticks, and wet it.

The page then turned. The other side was blank also. There was nothing to see. Not a mark.

I looked at him dubiously, wondering if it appealed to his sense of humor to offer blank pages as a diary record.

"Go on," he said excitedly. "Turn on—turn on. You'll find something."

I looked at him silently for some seconds. His face was bright with intensity. His eyes gleamed and he held the arms of his chair like a man struggling to keep calm. I stared hard into that fierce, sardonic face and I knew very well that I was being put to some kind of a test, through some ordeal, but I could not imagine what.

"Go on," he repeated. "It begins on the next page. I want you to see. Go on. Go on." He spoke excitedly in sharp staccato phrases.

I looked down at the blank page and started to turn it. It also stuck.

Again I raised my finger toward my lips—but stopped within three inches of my mouth.

On the end of the finger that had been dampened were a few specks of white powder. They had stuck to the moistened tip. A second later and I would have carried the poison to my mouth.

I dropped my hand to the table, took out a handkerchief with my other hand, wiped the finger carefully and then threw the handkerchief to the floor.

But I said nothing. I merely shoved the book, slowly, until it fell off the table, and all the while I stared at him. As the book fell to the floor he sank back wearily, muttering:

"—— you! —— you!" over and over.

But he did not take his eyes off me. Those eyes of his seemed lidless, unwinking, like the eyes of a serpent, peering steadily. Presently he said, speaking in the manner of one who is tired and has lost hope:

"You've beaten me. I'm not playing this time. I tried to catch you. But you beat me, Everhard. You beat me every time. If you'd moved your finger three inches more I'd have had you. An old trick, that. Two thousand years old. It was luck that saved you. You're lucky. Thank the devil for it. I'm beaten, Everhard. Sit down now and tell me what you want. I'm an old, withered, legless man. I've had to fight that way all my life. Sit down and I will tell you my story. Sit down."

"All right," I said, getting off the table. "I will sit down."

I took my time about moving and I watched him closely. But he continued to talk wearily, as though he were worn out and wished to have over whatever my business was with him—as though he had ceased to care what happened.

When he was like that I knew he was at his most danger-ous. So instead of sitting down at once, or instead of care-fully inspecting the chair, I lifted a heavy dictionary from its rack and without a word to him I carried it to the end of the table, and holding the book as high as I could above my head, I let it fall straight into the chair bottom so that it would hit with an impact certainly as great as the weight of a man sitting down.

Straight from the ceiling a bolt of lead dropped, hitting the book squarely with a dull, wicked thud. It would have crushed through the head of an ox.

At once I tumbled the lead weight and the book out of the chair to the floor and sat down.

I know that I did it with no appearance of excitement, for I felt none. I was sure no lead bolt would strike twice in the same place. And I knew that the chair was over no trap-door. I do not remember, but I do not think that I so much as glanced upward at the ceiling. I knew where the bolt came from, so there was no reason to gape upward. Nor did I inspect the chair to see by what apparently invis-ible mechanism the death-trap was controlled. The reason for its being fastened into place was explained, and that was what I had used the dictionary to find out.

Gaboreau's rôle of weariness had gone. He was through with acting, with his flattery, with his weariness. What other contraptions he might have around him I could not fancy. I could do nothing more than be cautious. I did not think there were many more, if any.

But I understood how that fiercely cunning mind, imprisoned in a withered cripple's body must have found exercise in planning and devising ingenious traps that he probably never expected to use, but which gave a certain stimulating pleasure to him by their creation, and a satisfaction in having them at hand where he could contemplate them. But then, he might really have been fearful that some day somebody would get to him and give him cause to wish for his contrivances.

He had become like a crazy man. In fact, I have not the slightest doubt that he was a maniac, physically helpless, but terrible in his diabolic mentality. He must have cursed me in many foreign tongues as well as in the one that I understand most readily. And too, I understand enough French to know that he used more than the native tongue of his ancestors, if it were not his own, to heap execrations upon my head. Fortunately, curses never killed anybody.

Instead of trying to quiet him, I added explosive to the flame. I was thinking of my three captive black-beards. I wanted evidence that would make them prefer to be in prison than to be at large busily engaged in thinking up ways and means of bothering me. If I could make Gaboreau angry at them he might give me the information I needed.

I knew that the black-beards who visited him nightly

must have been well aware of the danger of the chair. So I said—I wasn't telling the truth; I was far from the truth, but in the presence of a tiger one has little need for ethics—so I said, speaking easily in a matter-of-fact way:

"Felix told me about the chair—but evidently he didn't know about the diary. Or forgot it—"

If Gaboreau had had legs he would undoubtedly have leaped across the room at my throat. He squirmed about in the chair and beat his breast and head like a madman.

What I had said would have probably occurred to any man in my situation. I wanted to make Gaboreau suspicious of his captains. I wanted him to feel that they were traitors. I believed that they were sufficiently afraid of him to prefer prison to liberty with the chance of him striking at them. I by no means intended that he, too, should remain at liberty. Not much. But I hoped to keep Gaboreau and his black-beards separated so they could not possibly come to an explanation.

Explanations between them would leave me in the anxious seat. And as I have said, I guessed that Felix, and the others too, must have known of the chair. But the diary—that was hidden away. There was no need for Gaboreau to share its secret with any one; and possibly he had it in store against the day when some of his black-beards would no longer be useful to him.

Anyway, Gaboreau fell into my trap as a blind man falls over a precipice. The one horror and fear of his life seems to have been treachery from his captains. He was so helpless that loyalty on their part was the only legs his plans had to move about on. And naturally, as it was the most import-ant thing in the world to him, it was the one thing upon which his suspicions fastened without much encouragement. The man who sets pride before everything is always feeling that his "honor" has been offended; the jealous man is always quick to be suspicious of his wife; and Gaboreau, being fearful for the loyalty which his captains owed to him, needed nothing more than a little shove from me to plunge into the conviction that Felix, and the others too before I had finished with him, were traitors. He thought of evidence to prove it.

"You bought Felix!" he screamed at me. "Traitor!—" and another storm of unprintable abuse was upon me. "You hired him to carry off the wrong girl! You paid him to leave the Oriel that night! It was from him you got my telephone! Now I see—now I know—ah, he told you which of the steps was wired so that an alarm would ring! He gave you the key to my house! The traitor! Wretch—" and more abuse.

It was splendid from my point of view. But his imagination was getting much the best of him. I may be in what some people consider are comfortable circumstances, but I am hardly one fitted to bid against the loot that Gaboreau must have given his captains. Nor am I by inclination one to buy men. However, it did not seem the opportune time or place to explain all that to Gaboreau. He was going ahead and thinking up and believing evidence that had not suggested itself to me. But then, as he had said, I must have been born lucky.

"Oh, for that matter," I said easily, "why put all the blame on Felix. Not only Felix, but Charles and George as well were my guests this evening."

"You lie! You lie!"

He was convulsed with horror at the thought. He more than half believed me, but he was trying to convince himself that it was not so, that it could not be so.

"Indeed?" I answered. "In view of certain considerations they gave me little personal papers which may not interest you, but which will surely convince you that our relations have been intimate. You told me yourself that you were suspicious of them, and evidently you had good reason to be. As nearly as I can make out, they seemed rather dissatisfied because you never take them into your confidence. You simply give orders—and they are expected to carry them out. I gathered that they think the three of them together are competent to plan as well as you. They seem to think there is no longer need to serve a man who can not take any of the dangers—but gets all the profits!"

He listened to me fascinated by belief. He had himself given me practically all the information I had conveyed back to him as evidence of my familiarity with his blackbeards. He recognized it, not as his own information, but as information that agreed with his own suspicions. And when I had finished he cried:

"That is right! That is just like them! The traitors—cowards—miserable, —— thieves—" and other things more vicious that can not be repeated.

While he raved and raged, I took from my pocket the papers I had collected during the evening from the blackbeards, glanced through them to make sure that I was not handing away anything unread that might be important, then selected some papers that seemed to carry notations of instructions which he had given each of the men, and handed them to him.

FOR A TIME I thought he would faint from sheer weakness of rage. When he had read what I had given him there was no doubt in his mind that three of his most trusted men were traitors.

In the first place, he was in no condition to reason clearly and shrewdly. And in the next place, he no doubt thought it a physical impossibility—even if the idea of my having done so occurred to him—that I could have taken all three of his valiant, resourceful and tried captains as my prisoners. Into his crazy, yet powerful brain, the belief stuck like a poisoned arrow; his men had betrayed him.

He swore by the gods of heaven and the unnumbered demons below the earth that he would be revenged, that they should pay to the last drop of their blood for their treachery.

He ignored me completely. At least all bitterness, or feeling whatever toward me seemed to have left him—anyway for the time. A more important issue had been brought in.

He raised his hands above his head and swore vengeance. He pounded the arms of his chair and swore it. He cursed till I thought the man would surely drain the last bit of strength from his weak body. It was hideous.

I was for the time mystified that he, so helpless in body, had surrounded himself with deaf servants. He was a cripple, yet he did not use a wheel chair. He was unable to walk, yet no one appeared to assist him. I had more or less expected somebody to show up all the while I was in the room. And when they did I expected to take care of them. I am not what might be called an extremely nervous person. I knew that according to the police there was supposed to be a cook and a maid and an old man. The old man was evidently Gaboreau himself, whom the police detectives had seen before the window.

As I have said, how Gaboreau got about I could not imagine. Nor for all of his loud shouting were there any servants. I found out almost at once how he got about, and I found out afterward that his two servants were truly deaf, and that he wanted nobody around who could listen to his instructions and conversations over the phone, and he preferred to wait on himself as best he could by crawling about on the floor.

He suddenly scrambled out of his chair and like a monstrous crab started across the floor to me. He moved with surprising quickness, dragging his thin, lifeless legs like a man with his back broken—a pitiful object, yet fierce; maimed but venomous.

"They are mine!" he screamed at me, and I did not know of what he was talking. But I learned at once. "You've got all you want out of them. Traitors! They belong to me. I will settle with them! I will drink a glass of blood from each of their bodies!"

"You will not!" I said.

I almost shuddered at the horribleness of him and his words. It was frightfully repugnant.

"I will. You must give them to me or I will kill you. I will kill *you!*"

That is an excellent way to make me stubborn. I stood up and moved so as to bar his way. I did not know where he was going or what he was after, but he seemed determined to reach the table.

A wild light of cunning appeared in his eyes. He was crazy, crazy as a wounded cat; but his brain was not dull.

His hand shot up past me and began clawing toward the knob of the drawer. At least I thought he was reaching for the knob. But I reached down and enclosed his small, fragile hand in my fingers.

I had not carefully examined the contents of the drawer when I opened it to take out the poisoned diary and I had no intention of standing there and letting him find what he thought might be useful to him. He was too diabolically clever for the comfort of any man who had offended him, and I did not care for further experiments with his ingenuity.

He tugged at my hand, but I held fast. From the way he talked and the way he acted I was sure there was not a sane cell in his brain—a big brain, too; much too large for even a perfect body with no larger a frame than his.

"Take your hand away. Let go! Let go!" he screamed— and I removed my hand swiftly, not at his urgency or because of his strength, but because he had put his mouth against my hand as though to bite. He looked toothless and perhaps he was. But I did not hold my hand there to see. I felt then and I feel now that I would as soon be bitten by a viper. As I released his hand he again reached forward toward the knob. At least I thought it was toward the knob. But I struck his arm up.

"What do you want?" I asked.

He hesitated. For an instant I do not believe he knew what to say. No doubt he did some rapid thinking in that instant. He saw I had rebuffed and evaded him at every point, but he was as full of cunning as a cobra of poison. He knew I was a gambler; and he looked calculatingly into my face as he replied:

"I want the cards—they are in the drawer. Let me get them."

Again he reached toward the table, and again I pushed his hand away.

"What do you want them for?" I asked.

An inspiration seemed to come to him, for he shouted excitedly at me:

"We will play to see who wins!"

"Wins what?" I asked. I did not know of what he was talking, but he seemed to know perfectly.

"Let me have the cards. Open the drawer—open it."

"You move back a few inches and I will," I told him.

He seemed reluctant, but he moved back.

I opened the drawer and searched to make sure there was nothing in the shape of a weapon there. Then I tossed the cards to the floor beside him.

Before I knew what he was about he had snatched the drawer clear from the table so that it fell almost on top of him, and spilled everything. He quickly flopped the drawer over and put the cards on its bottom for a table.

I still stood between him and the table and watched him, wondering what he was up to. Perhaps he had suggested some kind of a card game to kill time until Robert and De Meyervelt could arrive with Vivian and help him make me prisoner. I, too, wanted to kill time, but I did not propose to do it merely as a pastime.

"What are we to play for?" I asked again.

"Sit down. Sit down and I will tell you, Everhard. It will be well worth your while. It will be the biggest stake you ever played for—and you are a gambler—a big gambler. I have heard of you. Sit down and I will tell you. Sit down."

He had urged me before to sit down—and have my head crushed with a bolt of lead. I wondered what deviltry was back of this solicitation.

"All right," I said, and again perched myself on the edge of the table.

"No, no. Here on the floor. In front of me—we will play. Sit down and I will explain."

He was a lunatic, undoubtedly. There was no reason that I could see why I should sit down on the floor and play cards with him. There was nothing to play for. I might have made the stakes his liberty against evidence enough to convict the black-beards I had in my apartment. But that would have been like playing coon-can with the devil himself to see whether I should have him at my heels or some of his imps. He would probably enough refuse to give me the evidence if I won, and it would be much easier and more sensible to strike an open bargain rather than fool around with a card game.

Those three black-beards were on my mind. I expected to get rid of them in some way that suited me. He had sworn vengeance against them, and no doubt if given the opportunity would make short work of his vengeance. If I were any judge of men, I knew that they would make it a part of their life's work to even up the score with me if they got liberty. But this fierce old lunatic considered them traitors and all he asked for was a chance to murder them.

But I could not countenance any such murder. If the black-beards had really been traitors it is possible that I might have shut my eyes and let him strike at them. Yet I did not intend to waste my time making their lives the stake of a game of poker. If he promised to let them off in case I won, I was satisfied that he would not keep the promise. Anyway, there was no reason to play. I did not know what he had in mind, but I told him there was no reason to play.

"But there is! There is!" he insisted. "Sit down and I will explain. Such stakes as were never played for in all the world—sit down!"

He was crazy.

I wanted evidence against the black-beards, but I did not dare let him suspect that I wanted it. It might lead him to think that after all my relations with them was not so agreeable as he believed. But it was nonsense for him to talk about playing for "such stakes as were never played for in all the world."

HE CONTINUED TO urge me to sit down even as he shuffled and shuffled the cards, and he did it with nimble fingers. No doubt he had found solitaire a comfort for him in his loneliness. He was at least thoroughly familiar with cards.

"I will tell you what I will do, Gaboreau," I said at length, determined to get the most I could out of the card game without having to depend on the so-called stakes for it. "Felix and Charles and George are waiting for me to return. They have some doubts as to whether or not I could get in here to you in spite of all the assistance they gave me. Now if you will write out a little note to them—something—anything—tell them you are going to cut their hearts out—anything, I don't care—so I can show them that I really reached you, well then if you give it to me, I will play a couple of hands with you."

There is something in human nature that urges men to make a threat, a violent threat when they are about to wreak vengeance. Why it is I can not understand. It is like the rattle of a snake before it leaps, the growl of a dog before it bites, the spit of a cat before it springs. Many men, most men, feel there is no satisfaction in killing an enemy without having warned that enemy. Perhaps they want the enemy to suffer from fear of being stricken down. I do not know.

I suggested some such violent threat to Gaboreau, expecting that he would write it for me. I did not intend to sit down and play unless he did. I did not know but that perhaps he would be glad to have them warned—but I did not know that he did not expect me to deliver it. He did not expect me to leave the room of my own free will. I did expect to. That was the chief difference between us.

With a written warning from Gaboreau I believed that I could so frighten those black-beards that they would be glad to seek the protective cloister of the prison to escape him, and that they would eagerly confess to enough real or imaginary crimes to get a long sentence. There would be something potent in a written death-warning that would be utterly lacking in word of mouth, particularly from my mouth.

"I will give it to you," he said readily—too readily, it seemed, and started scrambling toward the table. He was but a few feet from it, but I still stood between him and the table, and stopped him.

"Never mind," I said. "Here is my pen. I'll hand you a sheet of paper and you can write on that drawer."

I handed him a sheet of paper and my fountain-pen. He wrote fiercely:

FELIX, GEORGE, CHARLES:

You miserable wretches, before forty-eight hours I will cut your hearts out and stuff them down your throats.

GABOREAU.

It was a horrible threat, and from a crazy man. None other could be so fiendishly revolting. The writing of it seemed to give him satisfaction. He handed the sheet of paper to me, together with my pen, and I put both in my pocket.

"Now," he said, his eyes agleam with excitement, "we shall play. Sit down. Sit down. You promised. Sit down."

I had promised, it is true. I have told many lies in my time, but I have never broken a promise. Probably if I had known what he was up to I might have hesitated. I would have sat down, of course, but I would have been a little more particular.

All of the while I had been standing between him and the table. It was scarcely more than arm's length from him. But there was no other drawer, there was no weapon of any kind in sight, and he was a weakling as well as a cripple, so I did not see much reason to be afraid of sitting down across the drawer from him. Besides, that would leave his back to the door and I could watch it as well as him. Robert and De Meyervelt would certainly be coming soon, and though I did not expect them to get into the house without my knowing it, still I thought it just as well to have the door where I could see it. I squatted on the floor opposite him, and said—

"Very well, what shall we play for?"

He fidgeted about as though settling himself. I noticed, but did not pay any particular attention to the fact that in fidgeting he had squirmed a little nearer to the table. But he did not seem to have his mind on the table. I watched him for a while, ready to seize and drag him back if his hand reached toward it.

But he began again to shuffle the cards with adroit fingers and all the while chattered nonsense about what stakes we should play for. I decided that he was certainly trying to keep me there in the room until his friends came.

"What are we to play for?" I repeated.

His manner became a little more quiet. He went on shuffling the cards as he asked—

"What is the greatest thing in the world to you?"

"I don't know exactly. The same, I suppose, as it is to most men. My life."

"Yes. That is what we will play for. Your life."

He acted as though he really believed it. A fine state of affairs indeed when he, virtually a prisoner and helpless, could dictate such terms as though he were in control of my fate. He was a lunatic and there was no mistaking it. But there was nothing crazy about the way he could handle cards.

"Your life," he repeated, continuing to shuffle the cards.

"Indeed? That is interesting."

"I knew you would think so," he said quietly, and actually smiled.

"You seem to forget," I warned him coldly, slipping

my hands into my coat pockets, "that I have an automatic in either pocket, and if you know anything about me you know that I shoot straight."

"Yes, yes," he replied softly, continuing to smile. "I have heard. But you seem to forget, Monsieur Everhard, that I am Antoine Gaboreau. No man has ever beaten me. No man can. We shall play. If you win, you shall live. If you lose—"

He shrugged his shoulders. Also, he seemed to believe what he was saying. I said nothing. It was not worth answering. Then he went on, growing more excited, and said:

"It is true, Monsieur Everhard. It is true. I admire you. It may be that you do not believe me. But you are danger-ous. If you live you must live as my prisoner until I am ready to let you go. But let you go I will. I promise. I mean it. You would keep your word if you promised to let me live. I know it. I will keep mine. You think I have no honor because I have lied to you. But you shall learn. I am an old man, failure means more to me than death. I am ready to die when I can no longer beat men down.

"I must beat you. I have beaten you. You think I am crazy because I ask you to gamble for your life when you have two guns in your pocket and can take from me what you want without playing for it. You think you are strong and can overpower this poor old man with the twisted legs and pipe-stem wrists. But I have let you live, Everhard, because I was not ready to die.

"Look," he cried, at the same time extending his hand up to the leg of the table.

I looked apprehensively, but I saw nothing at first; then

I detected that his finger was touching an almost invisible button.

"If I press this, we go to hell together. This house is mined. Think I would keep all these records—" he indicated the filing cases with a gesture from his other hand— "and have no means of protecting them. Think I am a fool. You pulled my chair away from the table—that was not clever, because you did not know why you did it. That was luck. I tried you with the diary and with the chair. You are lucky. I had to get back to this table. I am back. This button controls a mine—and I control the button. Ha! Ha! Ha! Everhard, now do you see why we shall play?

"I admire you, Everhard. But if you move—we go together. You can't shoot quick enough to keep me from pressing the button, and we die together. You know I am not lying, don't you?

"See, I have my finger on this little button—see—I press down just so lightly—lightly—just so—and if you excite me I may forget myself and press harder, then— Ah, you don't squirm. You don't beg me to take my finger off. Your face is still calm—but your heart, is it not beating fast? A gambler's face—but you are afraid. You are afraid. No man could live and not be afraid. Why don't you cry out? An ounce more pressure, man, and you go to hell. Beg me to take my hand away! —— you, tremble! —— you, I will blow us both to—"

"All right. Go ahead," I said sharply.

I WANT NO one to think that I spoke in a spirit of bravado. No. I was quite sure that the house was mined and I was quite sure that he was crazy. Perhaps I was afraid.

Fear does not react upon me as it does upon some men. I am not excitable. But I realized with a good deal of apprehensiveness that if he continued to fumble with that button and try to frighten me he might press a bit harder than he intended. I told him to go ahead purely as a matter of a bluff. It was an easy bluff to make, because I knew that if he were ready to touch off a mine in the basement and put an end to himself as well as to me he would not be dallying around and talking about it.

I did not doubt for a moment, however, that he would hesitate between pressing that button and permitting himself to be taken prisoner. He had reasons for preferring death to failure. He was old and helpless, and if taken from that room, cut off from his associates, he would probably never again be able to get so clear of the law as to resume his criminal work. Death would be the easy way out.

But it was not a way that suited me—nor was it a way that he would choose readily. The situation was a sort of desperate draw. Neither had the upper hand, and either could carry the other to destruction, but both would have to go along. But if I had permitted him to think that I was terrified, then he would have had the upper hand. If I had been terrified—he hoped—then he would have been able to dictate almost any kind of terms. But I realized perfectly that he was no more eager to set off that mine than myself, though it did make me uncomfortable to have him fooling with the button.

He kept his finger on the button and was silent, while he looked at me.

"You are not afraid?" he asked at length and quietly.

"What has that to do with it?" I asked, taking pains to keep my voice as calm and even as I could.

He appeared not to understand.

"It is not a matter," I explained, "of which of us is the more afraid. We are both in the same boat, or more literally, both are sitting on the same bomb. One can't get off of it unless he permits the other to. And because you have your finger on that button you need not think that I am going to sit here with my hands in the air the same as if you had a gun at my head and wait for your friends to come. But if you feel that you are ready to cash in—go ahead, press the button."

Then he began again with his compliments. He spoke almost softly, persuadingly. I had come to know that he spoke that way when he had some special deviltry he wanted to try out. And I listened. But as I listened I twisted myself around slightly so that I could draw the gun from my right pocket without him seeing. I did not want to shoot, for the report would rouse the whole neighborhood. I wanted everything to be quiet and peaceable until Vivian came. But I knew very well that I could shoot and break his wrist, and that the chances were that I could do it before he pressed the button.

At that moment his wrist was the most vital spot in his body. If he were shot through the head or heart the convulsive death-throb might still force down his finger on that button. But if his wrist were broken, all muscular power would cease in his fingers. However, I did not want to shoot. It was almost sure to mean the escape of Robert and De Meyervelt with Vivian, for if they drove up and found a crowd about the house they would drive off again—and I would be left to explain to the police.

"Everhard," he was saying, "you are a brave man. The bravest man I ever met. Few men would have thought of that—that we are sitting, as you say, on the same bomb. And you are right, I don't want to kill you. I want you to work with me. I want to prove to you that I do admire you. I can make your fortune—give you anything. But I can't let you leave this house till Felix and George and Charles pay the price. You would warn them.

"The only reason I gave you that paper warning them was because I knew you would not leave this house. You have two guns in your pocket—and if I am not mistaken you have drawn one out of your pocket over there—but you can't shoot quick enough to keep my finger from coming down on this button. You hadn't thought of that, had you? We are still sitting on the same bomb."

As he talked I heard faintly the distant hum of a motor. It grew nearer and nearer. I was confident that Robert and De Meyervelt, with Vivian, were coming.

Desperate measures had to be taken, and soon. He was watchful and careful and trying to hold my attention until help should reach him. With my left hand I reached into my trousers pocket and drew out in my closed hand, so he could not see, a small bunch of keys.

"Now, Everhard," he went on, "I am an old man. I have lived a long time. I know men. I know you can be trusted. I am going to trust you, but you must trust me first. You must put your guns down here and let me have them. Then in a day or two when I have finished with those —— wretches, I will let you go. I hold no grudge against you. I want you to work with me, but you can go free—go your own way and we will call it off."

The car had arrived before the house. I heard something lightly strike the window—something like a few grains of sand—and I knew that the watchers below behind the rose-bushes were signaling to me.

There was no time to be lost. I could not wait for Robert and De Meyervelt to enter the house. Suddenly, and myself like a crazy man, I shouted at Gaboreau:

"Look at that button—look at it."

His finger was on the button and he kept it there. But he was amazed at my voice and manner. For a moment he hesitated, and then he did glance at the button as though to see of what I was talking. That took his eyes off me.

The instant he glanced away from me, my bunch of keys fell rattling at his side. That surprised him—for a moment took his mind entirely off his button—he glanced down to see what had fallen, and on that instant I shot.

His wrist was shattered. He could not have moved a feather with any finger of that hand. He screamed in pain and baffled fury.

Across the drawer I lunged at him and straight at his throat. Mine is a slim, soft hand to look at, but I can bend a quarter between the fingers of my left hand; and Gaboreau was as near to being strangled as he ever will be until the hemp goes around his neck.

With his free hand he struck out frantically, trying to reach the button, but no seconds were lost by his weak struggles. I got to my feet, and without releasing the hold I had on his neck, I dragged him across the room to the window. I could not risk letting go for an instant, and I smashed the window with the gun in my other hand, and shouted out:

"Kelly, Guernsey—get those fellows! Get them!"

A moment of silence. I could see the motor drawn up at the curb and a man standing beside it. Then a woman's voice called out—

"Don!"

It was Vivian.

9

WHEN I HEARD Vivian's voice call out to me from the shadows I raised the gun and fired at the man by the curbing. But my left hand was still at the throat of the Gaboreau whom I had jammed against the wall. But because I could not hold him up and because he could not stand, I had been forced to stoop, and he was still squirming. That was one of the things that made me miss.

Many things happened at once. The man at the curbing leaped into the machine. Two men sprang from behind the bushes by the porch and started forward. The fellow who sprang into the machine was at the wheel, and in the tonneau I could see two forms, one of them Vivian.

I flung the practically unconscious Gaboreau to the floor, and hastily beat the glass out of the window—but even as I leaped to the ground I heard the roar of the motor as the car started off.

It was a long jump and the ground was hard. I was badly jolted, and for two or three seconds I was rather dazed. It seemed minutes of torturous inaction as I scrambled to my feet.

Guernsey and Kelly, surprised and unprepared, had lost time in darting out from the bushes; but they did not lose time after the car started off. They thought more rapidly and clearly than I. As I got to my feet I heard some one cry—

"To the garage—quick!"

But my attention was fastened on the car that was getting under way from the front of the house. I raised the gun to shoot, then dropped it because I did not dare take the chance of shooting in the moonlight against a target where the head and shoulders of three forms were blurred, and one of those was Vivian.

The car was almost out of sight—I had run out to the curbing futilely watching it sweep away—when a miracle seemed to happen.

Out of the shadows back of the house and down the driveway leading to the street, rolled a big powerful roadster, chugging mightily, not a hundred feet from me. I ran forward. Guernsey was at the wheel and Kelly was astride the gasoline tank.

As I jumped into the car it leaped forward. But I became aware of lights flashing in the windows of the houses around about us and of the excited voices of people calling to and fro. The shots had evidently alarmed the neighborhood as well as warned the men who had come with Vivian.

"Kelly remembered this car," Guernsey shouted at my ear. "We'll give a chase they won't—" the remainder of the sentence was lost in the rush of wind and motor roar.

The ground seemed to spring from under the car and fall swiftly behind us. Far ahead of us, scarcely more than the red taillight of the fugitive car was visible.

I wondered at the time why the driver did not turn a corner and so have a better chance of shaking us off; but it was explained to me later that that machine would have had to slow down to make the turn safely and that we would have been almost on it before it could again get up speed. At least, that was Guernsey's interpretation. It may have been so. But mine is that Frank De Meyervelt, who drove, did not think of the advantage of turning a corner. And it was fortunate that he was no such driver as Guernsey.

A wild ride it was. The roar of our open muffler was deafening; and the speed that Guernsey tore out of those cylinders was something that very nearly makes me tremble to remember, though at the time I did not think of it. The road was clear and whole blocks of houses and trees seemed to sweep by in flashes as we sprang from one street light to another.

Once a figure appeared in the road and made an effort to flag us down. It was some lone policeman, evidently bent upon investigating the cause of such havoc with the speed law as the car before and our own were making. But he barely leaped out of the way in time to save himself, and the shot that he fired at our tire went wild. If he had hit that tire and caused us to stop I think he would have been regretful. I was in no mood to respect speed laws or policemen.

Straight ahead of us burned the red taillight. It seemed that for all of our furious speed we were not gaining, but distances at night are deceptive, and one can almost overtake a car in the moonlight without being aware that the distance has decreased.

Anyway, the car ahead was a powerful machine of foreign make. Guernsey screamed the name at me, but

I know little about cars and care nothing about their fine points. I did, however, know enough to wonder how much gasoline was in our tank and whether it would outlast that in the car ahead. But the one we were in was evidently kept for emergencies, for all that Guernsey had had to do was to jump in and press the starter.

Straining my eyes into the moonlight and watching intently, I soon realized that we were gaining. I could begin to make out more clearly the outline of the machine. Then De Meyervelt, either because he knew where he wanted to go, or because he had at last happened to think of the advantage of turning a corner, swept to one side and out of sight.

But he was too late to win by that maneuver. A few seconds later Guernsey took the same corner, and he took it on two wheels and with a skid that carried us across the street.

I was nearly catapulted from my seat. I did not understand why such an impetus seemed to concentrate at my shoulder and very nearly lift me bodily from the car. But I glanced over my shoulder. Kelly was gone.

Turning the corner had unseated him, and from his perch on the gasoline tank he had made a frantic grab for the first stable thing that came to hand, and that had been my shoulder. He came nearly taking me with him. But I was thankful that he had caught at me instead of at Guernsey. We might all have been spilled then.

I was apprehensive lest Kelly had broken his neck. But there was no time to stop. Who rides at the heels of the devil can not pause to give "first aid" to those who fall by the wayside.

We drove ahead. No glass was before the seats and the wind whipped our faces with a thousand lashes. From somewhere within the depths of that roaring hood Guernsey drew a new burst of speed, and he was crouched low over the wheel, steering ahead like a man who has fused his body with the cylinders and is driving the pistons by the beat of his own heart. I looked long and carefully at his face; it was a hard thick face and set with purpose. Some day a mighty sculptor will hew a man at the wheel, and it will look like Guernsey, for nothing else will so tensely and truly show the resolution and courage of those fierce centaurs that ride the rubber-shod engines.

The pace was rapidly leading us out of the city—in what direction or where I did not pay the slightest attention. I only knew that we had passed solid rows of houses and were pounding down the scattered rows of suburban homes.

But the fleeing red light was drawing nearer. It drew so near that we were close enough to be shot at over the tonneau. That was unpleasant and unexpected. I saw a burst of light and a second later heard the crack of the automatic. Another spurt of light and then the report. The man was firing carefully and taking time.

But instead of slowing down, Guernsey recklessly drove ahead straight into the line of fire. I could see the body of the car plainly in the moonlight, but I could not see any one in it. For one thing the roadster in which we rode was low, underslung, and we were nearer the ground. But there was no one sitting up in the tonneau. I wondered whether Vivian had been knocked unconscious, for I knew that as long as she was not helpless she would fight when I was near. The man riding behind with her was evidently crouching.

I hesitated to shoot. I raised the gun and thought to aim at a tire—but even for me, who am no less expert with a gun than with cards—that was no reasonable target. Besides, I was afraid that if I hit the tire the blowout might cause the car, going at such terrific speed, to skid and probably turn over. And Vivian was in it.

The man ahead fired again and again. He was crouched so low that he offered me no target. He shot deliberately. His aim was not only bad, which meant that he was evidently a poor marksman, but the jolting of the car did not permit him to take careful aim, and he did not know how to make allowances for the jars. But as it was, he came unpleasantly close, and twice the bullets rang against metal and I held my breath waiting to see if a vital spot in the engine had been touched.

I counted nine spurts and began to think that was all. But he must have taken another gun from the man at the wheel. Anyway, he opened fire again, this time more rapidly, as though frightened into haste.

The effect of the shooting on Guernsey was just opposite to what the marksman hoped for. When the second fusillade began Guernsey swore and stepped on the accelerator. I thought he had been running at full speed, but he knew the machine better than I, and he seemed determined to close in and come to grips. It was a make he said afterward, of which he knew every bone in its body, and that they never went so fast but that they could go a little faster. But it was reckless to rush closer while, less than a block away, we were being used as a target.

And being used as a target got on my nerves. I opened fire. I did not shoot at the tire. I shot at the middle of the righthand side of the tonneau, directly under the spot from which the spurts came. My first shot was answered. My second was not. The man in the tonneau had used but seven shells of his second gun. He had at least two more in reserve if he was in condition to use them.

We had come so close that I could have thrown a rock into the tonneau of the other car.

"Jump?" Guernsey yelled questioningly at me without taking his eyes from the road.

I bent to his ear and said—

"Yes."

Then I put both feet on the seat under me and crouched low, perilously swaying and rocking while with one hand I held on to the back. In the other I still held the gun. And I said a bit of prayer designed to keep us from having to turn a corner while I was in that position.

We were almost beside the other car, but it seemed that the gap would never be closed. I shouted at the man at the wheel to halt, but either he did not hear me or care to heed. Perhaps my voice was carried backward by the rush of wind. I could have shot, but that would have left his car to leap wildly to the side of the road.

Both machines were pulling at the highest notch of speed. But inch by inch, foot by foot, we crept alongside— up and up and up.

Guernsey was pulling in so closely to make my jump the easier that I was afraid he would bump the other machine. But he knew his work too well for me to try to advise him.

I crouched low in the seat and waited—waited until the tonneau was fairly beside me; then I leaped.

I barely caught the back. If any one had been on watch in the tonneau I could easily have been pushed off. There were two people in it. One was bound and the other was unconscious—dead. My second shot had taken Robert, the fourth black-beard, in the heart.

De Meyervelt was at the wheel and so intent on driving that he did not know what was going on behind him. I doubt if he knew Robert had been shot.

He knew the other car was creeping alongside, and with one hand on the wheel and his eyes on the road, he was trying to get something out of his pocket—a gun. De Meyervelt—or De Mey, for at last I had him—was afraid to look away from the road, and he was making a bad job both of driving and trying to shoot. The roar of both open mufflers, together with the wind sweeping away to the rear every sound I had made in scrambling into the tonneau, had prevented him from noticing how close I was.

The first he knew of my presence was when I poked the cold muzzle at the base of his ear and just behind his jaw-bone and, leaning over, told him to drop his gun and slow down.

"Slow down—but don't stop," I said.

He risked a glance behind him and very nearly slid from the road. But he saw enough to drop his gun and instantly put both hands on to the wheel. Then he slowed down.

Guernsey, from beside the machine, called to me. I told him to go back the way we had come and pick up Kelly.

"Take him to the hospital if you find him, and he is injured—then come to my apartment."

Guernsey never questioned and never hesitated. He turned around at once and started back.

"Take the next turn," I said to De Meyervelt, "and drive on till I tell you to turn again."

I wanted to shake off any police cyclists that might be on my trail, and then get my bearings.

VIVIAN, GAGGED, WITH her hands tied, and an ugly black welt on the side of her forehead, lay doubled up in the left-hand side of the tonneau.

No doubt it may have seemed heartless of me, but I made sure that the man on the floor of the tonneau was dead, and then searched the man at the wheel, before I gave attention to her.

I told De Meyervelt—a palpable coward—that if he wanted to get revenge by ditching the car to go ahead; but that he would not come out of the wreck alive. There was no danger of him attempting anything so courageous.

I slipped the gag from Vivian and even before I had cut the cords on her wrists, that irrepressible little woman put up her lips.

"Don, kiss me! It's been a horrible dream. I want to be awakened!"

Then I cut the cords, and she flung both arms around my neck.

"No, no," I said gently, removing one arm, "I have to watch that fellow yet a while."

"He needs watching, too," she said scornfully. "But this man"—indicating the body I had straightened out as well as I could, at the same time watchfully making sure that the man at the wheel did not reach back and crack me on the head—"was a gentleman."

I touched the bruised mark inquiringly on her forehead.

"Yes," she said, indicating De Meyervelt, "he did it!"

"I suppose you know that this is the handsome, gallant, courageous Franklin De Mey?" I asked, speaking loud enough for the ears in front of us.

"I know," she answered, with disgust.

"And the man who caught this car," I said, pointing backward in the direction Guernsey had taken, "is the old man, Mr. Guernsey—the real estate agent from Los Angeles—"

"Don, you don't mean it? How'd he get here?"

"I invited him some days ago. And he is a *man,* my dear. Each fellow to his own work. He would probably be awkward and crude in a poker game, but at that, I expect he would make a better showing than I at the wheel. Your chauffeur there slowed down at the corner—he should have taken corners when he first started to run—but Guernsey, he is one of the kind that doesn't slow down until the race is won."

"Oh, Don," she cried, "it has been awful—"

"I know. I know pretty much what has happened," I said, stroking her forehead, which she admitted was aching from the vicious blow, "but I think you had better save your story for the inspector and for the maiden who is being watched over by Yang. Other things are being watched over by Yang, too. And this—this young man on the front seat—well, I shall have something interesting to say to him before noon. It is almost sunrise now."

THERE IS NOT a great deal more to tell. A few little details needed to be attended to and I realized very reluctantly that I would have to call in the police. So when I had got my bearings and set De Meyervelt to driving us toward my apartment, I stopped at the first all-night drug store we came to. I did not care to leave De Meyervelt in Vivian's care, for it was very important to me that he be delivered to the inspector.

So I had Vivian telephone the inspector and ask him to have an ambulance, a detective, and to come himself as soon as he could to my apartment and wait in the office for me. I had Vivian tell him enough to interest him mightily without going into details; and she also suggested that it would be well for him to send somebody to Stillwater Place as soon as possible and apprehend an old man, paralyzed from the legs down, and to go to any extreme to do it.

The inspector did not take kindly to so many suggestions, particularly when full explanations were lacking. But he knew enough of Stillwater Place and of Gaboreau to be concerned, though he seemed from what Vivian said to have been quite peeved at being called from his warm bed at that early hour.

At the same time I had her telephone to Johnny Blix and ask him to come to the apartment as soon as he could. I owed it to Johnny to do what I could to reinstate him in the inspector's favor.

It was a longer drive back than I had expected, and took a good deal of time, for I would not let De Meyervelt speed. I did not think he had nerve enough to do anything desperate, but I did not want to give him a chance to ditch the car. A bold man in his position would not have hesitated a minute. He would have had as good a chance as I to escape; and all that a bold man ever asks for is an even break.

When we reached the apartment an impatient and suspicious inspector, the ambulance and a detective, were waiting.

The body of Robert was turned over to the ambulance, and I gave De Meyervelt into the keeping of the plain-clothes man, telling him it had been a long time since he had had so important a prisoner.

My situation was by no means comfortable. The inspector was suspicious of me and rudely insistent on an explanation as quick as I could make it. He even went so far as to put his hand on my shoulder and begin to tell me that I was under arrest.

I gently removed his hand and told him that the apartment-house office was no place to make a scene. I told it to him quietly, so that his pride would not be hurt before the detective who had taken charge of De Meyervelt; but I told it to him in such a way that he saw I was in earnest. I told him also that he would do well to suspend judgment for a few minutes and to allow me to do the explaining in my own way, and assured him that before I had finished he would be very glad.

I assured him also that it was only because he was a friend of Johnny Blix's and had treated me so courteously during the afternoon—he did not catch the sarcasm at all—that I had chosen him as the officer to whom I should turn over the murderer of millionaire Kingston, and that he would not have to share the reward money offered by the Kingston heirs with any one.

It was remarkable how surprised, interested and appeased he became at once. I am sure that he did not fully believe me, but he was ready to be convinced and really became quite patient.

I led the way up to my apartment and threw open the door. The inspector stepped in first and then shrank back, whipping out a gun. He thought he had been trapped, for Yang rose from the floor before him, and the long knife was held ready to strike.

"Merely a friend of mine, Inspector," I hastened to explain, "who has been detaining a few men I believe you will be glad to see."

"—— funny way of doing business," the inspector commented in surly, suspicious tones.

I agreed with him, and led the way into the room. He hesitated, then as though ashamed at the appearance of timidity, came through the door. I pointed to the three black-beards trussed and gagged and tidily corded by the wall.

The inspector swore from amazement; Vivian gave a little cry and looked at me inquiringly; but it was De Meyervelt whom I watched. He blinked as though struggling with a nightmare, then sort of crumpled in and dropped his jaw and shook about the knees. He had no doubt pegged all of his hopes on being released to those black-beards, who he expected to help him and who he probably thought were quite infallible.

For a few minutes there was something of a hubbub while the inspector, Vivian, the detective and even De Meyervelt asked questions. The noise of voices brought Jessie further than the keyhole, for she flung open the door and dashed embracingly toward Vivian; then seeing her Franklin De Mey, turned to him and was about to throw her arms around his neck.

But De Meyervelt, or De Mey as he had once called himself, looked rather depressed, and the detective interposed a forbidding hand when she approached.

"Just a minute, Miss Dutton," I said, assuming the rôle of stage manager and planning to make the situation as dramatic as possible for the benefit of both her and the inspector. "Vivian has something to tell, and please keep in mind that up to a certain point the adventures that she encountered were those intended for you. You will be interested, too, Inspector. And when my wife has finished I will have something of importance to add to her story."

Vivian caught and understood a sign from me, so she told for the inspector's benefit everything that had occurred from the time I met Jessie by chance in the Oriel, and of how she had that evening used a red wig to impersonate Jessie at an appointment, and had been thrown into a closed taxi and carried off.

"There were two men in that taxi with me. They abused me frightfully, jeering and swearing and doing their best to frighten me. I was frightened, too. One held his dirty hand over my mouth to keep me from screaming, and they made me think all kinds of fearful things.

"We drove fast, but not far, and the taxi stopped in a dark alleyway. I was carried out and taken down into some kind of a miserably dark cellar.

"They put me down and one of them pointed to an old cot with a box beside it on which was a loaf of bread and a pitcher of water, and he said that I would have to sleep on that for many nights before I again saw my beloved Franklin De Mey. I was kept there for some hours. I thought it was hours, anyway. I don't know just how long.

"The men stayed with me, and they talked most of the time about Franklin De Mey, and made out that they were terribly afraid of him, and that they were delighted with themselves at having outwitted him and carried off his sweetheart.

" 'My God, but I hope he doesn't track us here,' one of them exclaimed. Then the other said as though half frightened to death, 'He's been on our trail—what if he should come.'

"I was really frightened, but I began to see that all this had the marks of a rehearsal. The men were playing parts and parts that they didn't know any too well. Then suddenly one of the men struck me and the other tried to put his arms around me. I suppose I screamed. I was both frightened and angry, and I usually scream then.

"Anyway, just at that moment a tremendous pounding began on the door, and a voice called out: 'You ruffians! I've found you at last. Let me in here. Let go of that girl. You devils! I'll save you, Jessie.'

"And just as he said that, this fellow"—indicating De Meyervelt—"bounded through the door. He had a gun in his hand, but he did not shoot. He began knocking the two fellows around with one hand and kicked them and swore all manner of vengeance, but he let them dash out of the door.

"Then he turned to me and said, 'Oh, Jessie—my darling!' And he started to put his arms around me, and seemed to expect that I would hasten to embrace him. But

I laughed. I simply couldn't help it. The stage-play had been so amateurish. It wouldn't have fooled a country girl.

"Then he had a good look at me and saw that he had been fooled. My red wig was very nearly off, and I know that I showed on my face that I saw clearly through the scheme to make himself a hero. He began to swear in earnest at me, and to demand that I tell him how I got there and where Jessie Dutton was. I told him nothing— then he hit me"—and Vivian turned toward Jessie and touched the black bruise on her forehead.

"He tried to make me think that he thought I had been one of a gang that kidnaped Jessie, but I knew that he did not think anything of the kind. But I would not talk to him. He could not make me say one word. I wasn't afraid—not the least bit. I wanted to kill him, but he wasn't enough of a man to be talked to—even to be made fun of.

"When he saw that I would not tell him anything, he went to the door and called; and the same two fellows that he had pretended to defend me from came in. He abused them in earnest, and told them they were all kinds of fools and I don't know what all else. He forgot all about his pose as a rescuing hero, and ended up by having those same two men stay there and watch me while he went out.

"They looked pretty much ashamed of themselves, and one really tried to apologize by explaining that they had mistaken me for somebody else. I don't know what he thought that explained. They seemed to think that they were going to have something dreadful done to them for having failed to get the right girl, and they mentioned a 'Felix' over and over again, and seemed to wonder what Felix would say and do about it. I asked them why they didn't leave me and get away if they knew they were going to get away if they knew they were going to get into trouble, but they said that would not do any good, that Gaboreau could catch them no matter where they went. 'If we hid in China, he'd get us,' one of them said.

"They kept me in that cellar almost all night, then he—" again indicating De Meyervelt—"came back with a black-bearded man who I thought was the same one that had followed Jessie into the Oriel that evening when Don met her. But I soon saw from the way he talked that he wasn't the one—though he looked just like the man Jessie had described. He was surprised that the one called 'Felix' could not be found, and asked him—" again indicating De Meyervelt—"if he had tried such and such places and such and such other places.

"When he saw this mark on my forehead he asked me how I got it. I told him that he had better ask his friend. The black-bearded man was angry and told this fellow what he thought of him for striking a woman. But he—" again indicating De Meyervelt—"lied and said that he had not done it at all. I didn't say anything more. There was no use. Then they left me again, for a while, and when they returned they tied my hands and feet, put a gag in my mouth, and carried me out to an automobile. While we were on the way he took the gag out and tried to question me again, but I would not say anything. We drove and drove until we came to a house away out in the residence district.

"He—" again indicating De Meyervelt—"had just got out of the machine and the other man had started to untie my feet when we heard a shot in the house. The two men with me exclaimed something and stared at the house as though they didn't know what to do. Almost at once I heard a window being smashed, and looking up, I saw Don. He said something—I didn't catch it—but I called out to him.

"The black-bearded man said, 'Quick, get away from here,' put his hand over my mouth and then jammed the gag back, while the machine started off.

"He threw me down on the cushion and I could not see or do anything, but pretty soon I heard him swear and say, 'They're coming—got that roadster from the garage.' Then I was not frightened any more. I knew Don was coming. But I wondered who was with him, for I knew that he could not drive a car.

"In a little while the man crouched down in the tonneau and began shooting; then I was frightened again. But as long as he kept on shooting I knew that he hadn't stopped the machine in which Don was coming. He used all of his shells and asked him—" again indicating De Meyervelt— "for a clip. Then he began to shoot again. I heard a shot fired back. Then another, then the man gave a kind of a muffled cry like he was tired, and he fell off the seat down to the floor of the machine.

"The next thing was when I looked up, and though the machine had not slowed down the least bit, there was Don scrambling up over the back of the tonneau."

JOHNNY BLIX AND Guernsey had both come into the room while Vivian was talking.

"Just a minute," I said when the inspector started to question me. "I shall answer any and all questions gladly.

But first I want to explain that this man, Frank De Meyervelt, alias De Mey, is the murderer of Kingston. You know why he shot him. His uncle leased Kingston's house. The real Gaboreau planned it, and—"

De Meyervelt was gasping hoarsely and trying frantically to talk. He was yellow clear through, and was desperately trying to make the inspector believe that Gaboreau was entirely to blame, though he admitted that he killed the millionaire. But Gaboreau, he said, drove him to it.

It was a wretched spectacle—the half-crazed youth begging to be let go and promising to reform, when he was in the same breath pleading guilty to the foulest kind of a murder. The inspector was bewildered and elated. He was elated at having the murderer of Kingston, but so many Gaboreaus and such complications rather befuddled him for a few minutes.

I took him aside and said that details would be forthcoming in a few minutes, but I thought it well for him to call up his office and find out whether or not the real Gaboreau—the old man with the withered legs—had been caught. He went downstairs to use the office telephone so that the three black-beards still lying by the wall could not hear what was said.

I tapped Guernsey on the arm.

"She is waiting for you," I said, pointing to the girl, sobbing in Vivian's arms.

But he held back.

"Now come with me," I said, taking Guernsey firmly by the arm.

He still hesitated. He remembered too vividly how he had heard Jessie speak of him while he was playing eavesdropper, and he held back on pretense of telling me about Kelly. Kelly had fortunately not broken his neck; only a few ribs and a leg, and badly scratched his face and body. Guernsey found him by the curbing and carried him, protesting, off to the hospital. Kelly said he did not care anything for his little "bruises," and he was delighted that the other machine had been overhauled.

"When I tumbled off," he said to Guernsey, "I shouted for you not to stop. 'Go on,' I said. 'Go on. I'm all right.' And I thought maybe you heard me."

Jerry was well taken care of, and I saw to it that he got a better job than teamster when he was able to get about. But such is his sense of gratitude that he still thinks that *he* is indebted to *me*.

When Guernsey had finished telling about Kelly he had no more excuses for hanging back. I led him across the room, and said:

"Miss Dutton, here is a friend of yours. It was entirely due to his skill and courage that—"

I got no further. There was no need to go on. Guernsey was blushing like a schoolboy that had been kissed by the lady teacher, and Jessie looked up with surprise in her tear-filled eyes. Whether she had noticed before that he was in the room or not, I do not know. She looked at him and he looked at her, and then she was in his arms. I looked at Vivian and Vivian understood.

"Don Cupid," she whispered, taking hold of my arm.

When the inspector came back, he and I and Johnny went into the next room. I made Johnny a party at the conference because I wished to rather overemphasize the help he had given me, so that he would be reinstated in the inspector's good graces. And the inspector was the happiest and proudest man in the city when he left my apartment that morning. All the credit for all of the captures was his. He modestly tried to share honors with me, but I would not have it that way. Of course, my name had to be mentioned, but it was to be given out that I had worked under him.

The news he had brought back from over the telephone also added another dramatic feature to the situation. The house at 22 Stillwater Place, even while people and one or two policemen had gathered, having been attracted by the shooting, suddenly burst into flames. Before the fire department could get there, a terrific explosion occurred that seemed to lift the house from its foundations and scattered the burning timbers in all directions. Nothing had been seen of an old man with withered legs or of the two servants.

"He's done for," the inspector said with a kind of official finality.

"For my part," I added, "I have irrepressible doubts about that old tiger being burned up in that fire. I have the best reasons probably of any man in the world for hoping so, but I have seen too much of his cunning and resourcefulness to be very hopeful. But I am quite sure that there was evidence in that house that he wished to have destroyed before the police arrived. That accounts for the fire."

Then I told of my experience with him, and many times as I talked the inspector whistled in astonishment at such ingenuity and cunning as Gaboreau had displayed.

I explained in full the significance of the written warning I had secured and what I hoped to do with it. The inspector entered fully into my suggestions, and when we confronted Felix, Charles and George with the terrible threat Gaboreau had made against them they showed signs of agitation. They believed that the old man's vengeance was due to descend upon them because they had bungled into my trap, and Gaboreau would never forgive bungles.

They recognized the writing as his, and asked questions; but I evaded the questions and did not tell them how I came to have the threat. They knew it was authentic, they believed they understood fully why it had been made, and they did not know that there had been a fire at Stillwater Place and that Gaboreau was thought to have perished in it. They were ready to plead guilty to almost anything, and carefully encouraged by the inspector, all of them signed statements that meant at least ten years in prison.

Then they were hurried off to jail, to be kept *incommunicado* until they could be taken into court and sentenced.

As the inspector left he pressed my hand warmly and assured me that he was entirely at my disposal in the future.

"And I mean it," he added emphatically.

When he left it was well into the middle of the morning. I was tired but not sleepy. Only Yang remained in the room. Vivian had gone out, and Jessie and Guernsey had retired into the kitchen to find a cozy place where they would be entirely out of everybody's way.

"Well, Yang," I said, "I think you can slip that knife back up your sleeve and go to bed. This little affair seems to be pretty well over, and I think that tomorrow we shall begin packing for a little trip to South America or South

Africa. It doesn't make much difference which, and I expect that—"

The telephone rang. It gave a vicious, sharp jingle—another and another before I reached out and took it off the desk.

"Hello," I said.

Then a voice spoke and my fingers tightened on the receiver and my eyes narrowed as though I were looking straight into the face of him who was speaking.

"Everhard?" the voice that I knew well asked.

"Yes."

"This is Antoine Gaboreau. I will get you yet." He spoke like a man who has been greatly injured.

His voice was high and trembled slightly from the intensity of restraint. Then fury getting the better of him, he shrieked into the receiver—

"—— you, Everhard, I'll cut your heart out and jam it down your throat!"

Then he hung up abruptly. He had made what seemed to be his most terrible and solemn oath.

Yang still stood before me, immobile, enigmatic, sinister. I looked at him for some time and said nothing while I thought of Gaboreau. He was a man of immense cunning and power and vengeful as an Indian. He would be heard from again and soon.

"Yang," I said as quietly as I could. "You may go to bed now, but perhaps you had better not slip that knife back up your sleeve. And the trip I just spoke of will have to be postponed. These little affairs do not seem to have been so nearly settled as I thought."